YOUR MOTHER-IN-LAW LOVES YOU

An Afghan Girl's Story of Family,
Love, and Friendship

by

LILA SAQIB

ISBN: 978-1-7774335-0-5

Contact:
Email: lilasaqib@hotmail.com
Twitter and Instagram: @lilasaqib

Special thanks to Loverna Journey on Unsplash for the cover image.

To my niece, Mila, may the only obstacle to your dreams be the limits of your own imagination.

Table of Contents

CHAPTER ONE

∽

"Fate is like a strange, unpopular restaurant filled with odd little waiters who bring you things you never asked for and don't always like."

-Lemony Snicket

Does one moment truly have the potential to change the course of an entire life?

In each moment, we all have choices to make that will shape our future. This may lead one to spiral, thinking about all the possible options and the endless subsequent consequences of each potential action. But take comfort in the fact that those hypothetical scenarios, despite seeming as close as the reality we are currently experiencing, are as far off as anything could possibly be. "So close," you whisper. But so far, simply because that was not what was written. Even had it been on the tip of your tongue, it would not have come to pass, simply because it wasn't meant for you.

Dear reader, before continuing any further, know that this is not a story where the helplessly oppressed Muslim girl falls in love with the white boy and abandons her faith and values to be with him. Her parents aren't restrictive and opposed to her getting an education.

Although these are outdated tropes, it is nonetheless imperative that these facts are stated. If that was the type of story you were hoping to find, I regret to inform you that your search has been in vain. Although I am sure, there are a plethora of stories of the like for you to indulge in. However, this is a story of a girl who is fiercely devoted to her faith and her family. So, if that's what you're into, then I implore you to continue reading.

The main protagonist of this particular tale is a girl, a twenty-year-old girl, to be specific. Her name is Marzia Mahnaz Rashidi, and she lives with her brother Ameer, her sister Nabeela, and her parents Nafiza and Ali, in Vancouver, British Columbia. That's in Canada for those directionally challenged folks who don't know basic geography. Kidding. But anyway, I'm getting ahead of myself. To really get a feel for why Marzia is the way she is, we need to go back to her childhood…

When Marzia was six years old, she attended grade one alongside her best friend Reiyna Haddad, whose family had recently immigrated from Lebanon. It was her first Canadian winter, and Marzia was hell-bent on showing Reiyna the proverbial ropes. All along the school yard, there were patches of thin ice glazed over the dull grey pavement. Their goal was to get to one and slip and slide to their heart's content. But that wasn't so easily achieved. Teachers were strategically stationed all over, doubling as recess monitors. And they had one rule: Do. Not. Slide. On. The. Ice. But naturally, Marzia could not accept this. And so, the duo watched and waited until their eyes were elsewhere and the patches of ice were left unguarded. When the timing was right, and the coast was clear, they dashed towards the nearest ice as though it was a stream of water in the middle of the Sahara Desert. As soon as their neon boots made contact, they began slipping and sliding, as though in slow motion.

"I bet you can't do this!" Marzia said, attempting a spin. She stumbled and then landed on her feet.

"I can too!" Reiyna said back, nailing a spin and then landing on one foot.

Something you should know about Marzia is that she is competitive. Very competitive, almost to a fault. It's the reason why she was always one of the last ones standing when her class played dodgeball. And it's why Marzia, at that point, attempted to do a double spin. As soon as Marzia propelled herself into that second spin, she knew she had made a mistake. No sooner did she resolve to show up her friend than she felt herself losing her balance. But it wasn't her own zealousness. She caught someone from the corner of her eye, sticking their foot out, tripping her. She didn't get a good look at his face; all she remembered was a pair of cold brown eyes staring back at her with malice only accentuated by his bright red hat. Within seconds she was on the ground. Her face was warm. She was bleeding. Reiyna called for a teacher, and they rushed over with looks of horror that Marzia would never forget. But by the time they got there, the boy was already gone.

She'd never admit it, but she loved having the attention all on her that day. She was hauled into the nurse's office, and she got a pack of ice to put on her tender eye, a wound that would eventually leave a scar under her right eyebrow. Within the confines of those four grey walls, she swore to herself that she would never let herself be hurt like that again. Next time, she would be ready. And after that day, she had a scar under her eyebrow as a token of that private oath.

Marzia held true to that promise. At every turn in her life, she guarded herself, keeping almost everyone around her at arm's length. She refused to be vulnerable because what she realized was that to be vulnerable was to be weak. And weakness could lead to being hurt, not just physically, but emotionally too. She had a handful of friends, only half of which she would consider close ones, two of whom were her cousins, Ameena and Soraya. They were the same age and practically grew up together. Their antics would be enough to fill up a book of its own, but we'll get to that later.

Fast forward more than a decade. Marzia is now a third-year university student studying psychology. She gained comfort in understanding how the human mind works because, in her own words, if she understood how it worked, she could understand how to best it. Her grades were good, but not fantastic, but she didn't like talking about that. She claimed it was because she also worked part-time at an indoor playground. She liked working there, for the most part. She even eventually became desensitized to screaming children and learned not to think about how germ-infested every surface of that playground must be.

If you're wondering how long this exposition is going to go on, just hang on! I'm setting the scene, okay?

Our story begins one Saturday morning as Marzia was headed off to work. She was wearing her neon yellow uniform shirt, with her mustard-coloured fleece sweater. A combination that screamed: please put me out of my misery. But I digress.

"Here's your breakfast! And don't forget your lunch," her mother said, handing her a bagel in a Ziplock bag and a grocery bag filled with Tupperware containing palaow [1].

Marzia's mother always took such good care of her. She was sometimes a hard-headed and stubborn woman, but her heart was made of gold.

"Oh, and by the way, we're having a meymoni[2] tonight with guests coming from out of town, so come straight home after work!"

"Greaaaattttt," Marzia thought. *"I'll be spending the evening in my room then."*

But that's not what she said.

"Okay, I will," she said, swallowing a sigh.

---

[1] Palaow: A type of pilaf made in Afghanistan. It includes steamed rice with carrots, raisins and beef.

[2] Meymoni: A gathering, or party, usually held at someone's house.

You see, reader, a meymoni is not just a regular party. Most of the time, it was okay. You spent time with family, you laughed, and then they went home—done deal. But sometimes, there are those days where there are lots of people, some who you barely even know who come over to your house. You and your family serve them dutifully like the good hosts you are, but that doesn't stop them from going home and commenting on every aspect of the evening. Now, this may not seem so bad, but when you're an introvert, it's more or less like a nightmare. Don't get me wrong, Marzia was a very friendly person, to a fault, sometimes. But you just can't help it when your social battery runs out. Still, like the loyal daughter that she was, she did it for her parents without complaint. Besides, they had given up so much more the day they left Afghanistan to make a better life in Canada. Ahh, there it is, immigrant child guilt.

At work, Marzia clocked in like any typical shift. She nodded and shared pleasantries with her co-workers and manager as she made her way through the break room.

"Ew, it's Marzia!" one of her co-workers said teasingly. That was Davis. He was cute in an unconventional way; his ginger hair was always a mess and his glasses were perpetually askew. She had a feeling he liked her, but she would never go for it. He just wasn't really her type. But admittedly, she enjoyed the banter.

"Girl, where have you been?! You will not believe what I have to tell you!" Karissa, Marzia's work best friend, said. The thing is, your work best friend is different than your out-of-work best friend. Both are close, but one of them you're not paid to be around.

"Fill me in while I'm setting up for the 12:00 birthday!" Marzia said. The two of them made their way to one of the birthday rooms. Like many indoor playgrounds, and to Marzia's dismay, her workplace had rooms that people could book for birthdays. As the two of them laid out plates and napkins, Karissa went on about some wacky happenings at work the other day.

"...And she just walked away!" Karissa finished, her braids swishing as she talked.

"She's lucky I wasn't there!" Marzia replied, knowing full well that she hated confrontation and wouldn't have said a word.

The gremlins, also known as children, there for the birthday party started trickling in. No sooner had they had pizza than they were ready to scarf down some cake.

"I'll be back with the cake!" Marzia said to the birthday parents.

She headed to the back freezer where all the cakes were and took out a fresh vanilla one. She covered it with sprinkles and added candles as the finishing touch. After almost three years working there, she had it down pat. She pushed the backroom door open with her feet, gingerly holding the cake with both hands.

And then it happened.

No sooner had she exited the backroom did a guy who looked no older than herself collide with her. As though in slow motion, Marzia fell flat on her face, vanilla icing splattering everywhere.

"You've got a little something on your face," a voice said, motioning to her face. She had a glob of icing on her nose. He handed her a single napkin, and Marzia wasn't sure if he was mocking her or if it was a lazy attempt at helpful advice."You know it helps when you're looking in front of you."

Definitely mocking. She gave a sickly-sweet smile and walked away.

"You've got a little something on your face!" Marzia said mockingly to herself while trying to clean herself up in the staff washroom. "Smug little—"

"Admissions to birthday party host," Marzia almost jumped, realizing it was coming from the walkie-talkie still clipped to her jeans.

"Go ahead," she replied.

"Your next party is here," said the voice.

"On my way!" Marzia responded.

Pizza, cake, repeat.

Despite the slight bump at the start of her day, the rest of the afternoon wasn't nearly as eventful. The rest of the scheduled birthdays went pretty smoothly. She was good at engaging the kids and keeping their chaotic energy in check, but she'd never say that out loud though because she thought it sounded kind of braggy, you know?

As she pulled into her driveway after her shift, she saw a slew of unfamiliar cars already perched on the gravel like they belonged there.

They're already here, Marzia thought to herself in horror. "Okay, just say Salaam, and then you can go upstairs. Just say, Salaam[3]. That's all you have to do."

She put her keys in the door, her heart beating out of her chest.

Click

"There she is, khushuyet dostet dara,[4]" Marzia's mother exclaimed.

Marzia never understood that saying. Why did it mean that her non-existent mother-in-law loved her if she came home just as food is being served? But like many things, Marzia smiled and conceded that there were things that she would never understand. And she would have to be okay with that. She scanned her living room where she spent so many nights (and, let's be honest, days too) on the couch watching

---

[3] Salaam: Short version of Asalaam Alaikum; Islamic greeting meaning "peace be upon you"

[4] Khushuyet dostet dara: Dari for "your mother-in-law loves you", an Afghan saying when you enter the house just as food has been served meant to acknowledge the moment of happenstance and serendipity.

Netflix. There now sat many unfamiliar faces whom she had no intention of getting to know.

Just say Salaam.

Now, reader, this may seem very harsh, but Marzia was never the social type. Weddings and large gatherings of any kind were not her idea of fun. Even as a child, she always kept to the back of the classroom. She practically crawled under the tables when everyone was sitting on the carpet for story time. Sure, she could put on the guise of a charismatic girl who could make all the elders go "Chika bojuraat ast!⁵" But deep down, she knew that wasn't her.

As she walked into the living room, she kissed the women on their cheeks (something that could be a story on its own, like is it two kisses or three? Can the Afghan community please reach a consensus as to whether it's two kisses on the check or three? There's nothing more embarrassing than going in for a third kiss, and the other person is already pulling away). She put a hand to her heart as she greeted the men, one of whom had a goatee that could only be described as...geometric. She was almost scot-free when she turned to see a familiar face. It took her a second before realizing it was the same guy at work who had caused her cake fiasco.

What is HE doing here? she thought to herself.

---

⁵ Chika bojuraat ast: Dari phrase meaning "look how outgoing she is!"

This is fine. Everything is fine.

"Hi," Marzia mustered with a meager wave.

"Hi," he replied, giving a single nod.

Maybe he doesn't recognize me?

"Got all that icing off?" he smirked.

He recognized her, alright.

"Yeah, good as new," she said, smiling with only her mouth. "I'm sorry I didn't get your name?"

"Elias," he replied.

"Noted," was all Marzia said in response.

Noted? Who says that? Whatever. He was the weirdo who was at a children's attraction. And now that she thought about it, she hadn't seen him with any kids. Marzia resisted the urge to visibly facepalm and excused herself before she had the chance to make an absolute fool of herself yet again.

After freshening up, Marzia made her way downstairs, where she was confronted with another surprise face. Although, this one was a great deal more pleasant. It was none other than Mateen Heydari, the boy Marzia had been nothing short of obsessed with since she was about eight years old. To say she had a crush was an understatement. She was pulverized.

All of a sudden, she regretted not putting on eyeliner.

"Hey!" he said, with a beaming smile.

"Hey!" she returned, willing every muscle in her body not to turn into puree.

Cool as a cucumber.

CHAPTER TWO

"Come what come may, time and the hour run through the roughest day."

-William Shakespeare

By this point in the evening, everyone was having fruit, which, if you don't know, reader, signals that this soiree would be coming to an end shortly. The air was thick, filled with chatter and perfume. Everyone's cheeks began to flush.

"So, how's school going?" Marzia asked Mateen.

"Good. Exams are kicking my ass, but I'm surviving!" he replied with a laugh.

"More tea?" she asked.

"Sure, I'd love some!" Mateen said.

Marzia less than gracefully raced to the kitchen to fetch some refreshments for her not-really-beau. As she was waiting for the kettle to boil, she felt a presence behind her.

"You know he's not interested. Trust me. I can tell," Elias said, nonchalantly putting his plate in the sink.

"What?" she asked, trying not to sound alarmed. "I don't know what you mean."

"More tea?" he replied mockingly.

"What do you even know? I don't even know who you are," she replied, visibly flustered. She awkwardly darted her eyes and focused on a post-it note on the fridge.*Buy milk.*

"Whatever helps you sleep at night, short stack. I'm trying to do you a favour, really," he said.

"Short stack? Arrogant punk," she thought to herself, turning on her heel to go back into the living room.

"You're forgetting something!" he called after her, waving the tea kettle. Marzia quickly shuffled back to the kitchen and wordlessly snatched the kettle from his hand.

You may be wondering, dear reader, why Marzia was so enamoured with Mateen. Well, it began when she was five years old. Marzia met Mateen when they were both at the park with their mothers one day. He asked Marzia if he could build a sandcastle with her, and they had been friends ever since. Well, sort of. They were as thick as thieves for several years, but their friendship was weathered by the inevitable effects of time, as the story so often goes. Now, they shared pleasantries occasionally at meymonis, and that was about it. And so, they were not exactly strangers but they were undoubtedly far from friends. Though that didn't change how she felt about him. Although she wouldn't admit it, Marzia secretly longed for the day he would give more than a passing glance in her direction. She admittedly even still had the Baby Alive doll that Mateen had given her for her 5th birthday. She still kept it in her closet as a candle of remembrance for the friendship they once had. If you think this is melodramatic, dear reader, then you'd be right. But you'll get used to it.

But enough of this reminiscence, back to the present…

It should be noted that there is another character in play at this gathering, and that is Marzia's nemesis (yes, she actually refers to her as her nemesis, and no, it's not in an ironic way). Her name is Dalia Alimi. If you're Afghan, you're probably reading that thinking Dalia doesn't sound like a very Afghan name, right? Well, you would be right, dear reader.

Let me break it down for you; Dalia is only a quarter Afghan, a half breed if you will (her words, not mine). Her mother was Russian and met Dalia's father when he was in the army. Or so the story goes, anyway. But that is not why Marzia takes issue with her. The true reason why Dalia is her nemesis stems from childhood. Ever since they were kids, Dalia has always been the loud one, what the Afghans would call a Kalaankaar. Now, there is no exact word in the English language as far as I know that would perfectly encapsulate its meaning. The closest explanation would be a cross between a loud-mouth and a know-it-all. You see, anything Marzia did, Dalia had to do better and bigger. She took control of everything she laid her hands on, appointed herself the leader of every project she was a part of. When they were in high school together, they were both part of the Robotics team. Before the night of the big competition, Dalia gave Marzia the wrong address, so she was automatically disqualified for not showing up, and Dalia won the blue ribbon. So, to say they weren't fond of each other would be an understatement.

"Oh, let me help you with that, Khalajaan[6]!" Dalia said to Marzia's mom, taking the plate from her hand and bringing it to the kitchen.

Ughhhh. Show off.

Naturally, after dinner was the obligatory fruit serving marking the unofficial end of the get-together. After, everyone stood by the door to say their farewells for what seemed like at least half an hour. Probably longer. When all was said and done and the guests were on their way home, a sense of relief washed over Marzia.

This is what it is to be an introvert in an extroverted culture.

Quiet. Just...quiet.

---

[6] Khalajaan: Dari for "Aunt" or "Aunty" a respectful term for your maternal aunt or an older woman.

Marzia was washing the carnage of dishes left behind, drifting off into the land of daydreams. Marzia often did this when faced with a less-than-enjoyable task. It was one of the things she liked about herself; her ability to get away inside her mind, constructing a fortress in her head with a population of one. After cleaning up had concluded, Marzia retreated into her room, where she unsheathed the book she had been reading. It was a romance. Marzia was a sucker for romance. Even though she endlessly ranted to her favorite cousins Ameena and Soraya about how "love is a lie," secretly, she dreamed of the day her prince would sweep her off her feet. Some day... I mean, she'd even settle for a Duke or an Earl.

And just as the hero of her book was about to finally admit his feelings to the girl he loved, a Snapchat notification popped up on her phone from her group chat with her cousins Ameena and Soraya.

Soraya is typing...

Snapchat from Soraya

Soraya: Guys, I'm going to cry right now. I just dropped my iced cap on my carpeted floor.

Marzia: RIP man down (insert a slew of various emojis)

Ameena: A moment of silence for Soraya's lost iced cap loll

Ahh, I love these guys, was Marzia's last thought before she drifted off into the land of dreams.

And yes, Marzia really is that cheesy. Now as much as I'd like to go into detail on this very heartwarming moment, we must press on. That night, Marzia's dreams could be described only as the fruit of overindulging on copious amounts of hot Cheetos. Just when she was in the depths of her REM, she heard sounds, like an alarm almost? It was an alarm; it was the fire alarm. She woke up to the smell of smoke coming from downstairs. She thought about how she read so much about harrowing experiences happening to the heroes in her books, and she almost wished that some of their adventure would rub off on her own boring and uneventful life.

I guess it's true what they say, be careful what you wish for.

Remembering what she learned about fire safety all those years ago in elementary school, Marzia put on her hoodie and felt her bedroom doorknob. It was warm but not hot, which was a good sign.

She grabbed both her cats that were sleeping in her room and made her way down the stairs. She stuffed the felines in her oversized sweater. Who knew a hoodie would come in handy as a cat carrier? She felt the cats beginning to squirm, but she just held on tighter. She was not letting go, Jack. Stepping out in the hallway, she felt the air get thinner as she struggled for breath. Walking down the stairs, she felt her eyes begin to burn. Where was it coming from? The answer revealed itself when she saw the glow of red and orange flames dancing a show of lights on the walls of her once-beloved kitchen. But this was no time for nostalgia nor the time to think about everything she would be losing. She saw the rest of her family making their way out of the house and realized she was the last one out. Right before leaving, she took one final look at the home she grew up in, rapidly going up in flames. Once outside, she breathed a sigh of relief, taking in the gravity of the situation she was in and the potential perils she so narrowly escaped. She finally released her cats, and they instinctively scattered. Burning tears streamed down her face in between fits of coughing. At this point, she heard sirens blaring and lights flashing.

Most of the rest of that night was a blur for Marzia and her family. What was most important at the moment was that everyone was safe. But unbeknownst to Marzia, this night would change the course of her life, but not in the way that you might expect. Because this night was the catalyst for a string of events stretching across the next 12 months that not even Marzia could have predicted.

They say everything happens for a reason, and that statement couldn't be truer.

After being checked out by paramedics, Marzia and her family made their way to a local motel. Now, I'm sure if you're the child of immigrants, you can relate to what I'm about to explain next. Just like when they would go on road trips as a family, Marzia's parents drove around town trying to find the motel with the best price, and by best, I mean cheapest. To give you a rundown of what happened, Marzia's father would pull up to a motel, go inside and try to bargain down the price. After trying several different establishments, eventually, they would find a place to stay. Then, he would casually mention that he only said that two people would be staying there that night. And so, the rest of the family would sneak through some sketchy back entrance lugging all their belongings (and this time, their two cats as well). Now at first glance, this may have seemed like a silly cheap thing that her parents did. It was only as she grew older that Marzia realized that it was through scrounging and saving every penny that they were able to buy a house for Marzia and her siblings to live in and help pay for their education. It's yet another one of the nuanced intricacies of growing up that people say you'll understand when "you're older."

But such is the way of time, you never know what you should do when you need to know it.

CHAPTER THREE

"There are far better things ahead than any we leave behind."

-C.S. Lewis

That night Marzia dreamed vividly. Most of it was the typical running, but in slow motion scenes or the trying to scream but no sound came out type of deal. But one part stuck out to her even hours after being awake. She was walking down a long hallway, with nothing but dandelions at the end of the corridor. As she got closer to it, they began to wilt into wads of white fluff, and then the seed-bearing parachutes expanded and separated from the dried flower head and floated away. She turned to see an apparition of a beautiful red rose. She attempted to grasp it in her hands, and this time the flower didn't die when she held it. The specific shade of red was something oddly familiar yet utterly foreign at the same time. Like the smell of your mother's perfume mixed with the scent of cold air-conditioned leather couches at a distant relative's house. Later she'll realize why she felt this way, but for now, the image of the red rose imprinted into her brain for reasons she had no idea.

Marzia woke up to the sound of her mother on the phone. She could barely make out what she was saying in her sleepy haze, but three words woke her up instantly.

"Hazaar dafaah tashakur!"

A thousand times, thank you.

And just like that, she had a feeling something sinister was brewing. She just wasn't sure what it was just yet.

"What's going on?" she asked her. Marzia observed the room in the daylight. Think of one of those run-down motels you see in movies. This was worse. The curtains looked like they used to be white, but now were the colour of buttered popcorn.

"Oh, we'll be staying with a friend of your father's. I just got off the phone with his wife, and they're setting up rooms for us at their house. Don't worry, it's only temporary," Marzia's mother said.

Rooms? Plural? Damn, how big must their house be? Marzia thought to herself. But she figured that it was a hell of a lot better than all of them staying in a single hotel room for the foreseeable future. Whatever it was, she was all for it.

Or so she thought. Until she got there.

When pulling up to their house, Marzia's father's friend and his wife were already on their doorsteps, ready to greet them and ready for their arrival. They were young but still had deep lines on their face, a mark of the many years they had weathered on this earth. They looked familiar, like she had seen them somewhere, maybe at a party or a wedding? All of a sudden, Marzia got this sinking feeling in the pit of her stomach, though she couldn't place her finger on why.

"Salaam! Welcome to our house! Please consider it your home as well now!" the wife said. She was pretty and had webs of grey hair amongst her mostly dark chocolate strands. But there was a sadness in her eyes. She motioned them in, and Marzia and her family obliged. Their home was nothing short of a spectacle. They were greeted with high ceilings and marble flooring cooling their feet.

"Make yourself at home!" Marzia's father's friend said.

The first thing Marzia did was take a nice hot shower. It should be noted that the motel washroom was wanting for a certain je ne sais quoi— and basic cleanliness. After she finished showering, she was still exuding steam. She notices the adjoining room is left just a crack open. Oops. Was someone in there? Did they see anything? Marzia peeked through and saw that it was someone's room, but no one was there. Crisis averted. And yet, a creeping sense of curiosity pulsed through her. Against her better judgment she gingerly opened the door widely, revealing what looked like an angsty teenager's room. She tiptoed in as if hiding from unseen eyes. The bookshelf on the wall caught her attention. She ran her hands over the titles. Harry Potter, The Lord of The Rings...*He likes Fantasy,* she thought... and... Pride and

Prejudice? That last one took her by surprise. Her eyes darted to another title; Anne of Green Gables, the most surprising of them all. She opened up the book and flipped through to a random page. She remembered reading it for the very first time. She was twelve, and her parents had to practically pry the book from her during dinner. Warm feelings of nostalgia flowed through her.

Marzia was lost in thought when she heard the door open behind her. It was too late to hide.

"What the hell?" she heard a familiar voice say from behind her. In her panic, the book slipped from her hands and fell spine first to the floor.

"You! I-..." she stammered in bewildered surprise.

Standing before her was Elias, the arrogant snob that was at the meymoni at her house.

"It's bad enough you and your entire family are taking up our whole house, but do you have to pry into my personal belongings?" he snapped.

"I wasn't prying! I was...curious, okay? And I was just looking at your books. You don't have to be a prick about it!" she retorted, leaving the room in a huff.

"Hey!" he yelled after her.

"What?!" Marzia snapped, sticking her head back in the room.

"You might want to pick up after yourself instead of snooping through people's things!" he said, motioning towards her undergarments and dirty clothes laying on the washroom floor.

"I will!" she almost yelled.

"Good!"

"Great"

Marzia collected her clothes and then exited through the other door into the hallway to prevent Elias from seeing how red her cheeks had turned.

Dinner that night was nothing short of excruciatingly awkward. Picture the presentation you did in grade school where you fumbled your words and read off your cue cards the whole time because you did everything the night before, and then multiply that by ten.

"How's everyone settling in?" Elias' mother asked, breaking the silence.

"Amazing, thank you so much for your hospitality," Marzia replied. "You really embody the hadith[7] about treating guests with kindness." She made eye contact with Elias.

"Conveniently forgetting the part where it also says not to put undue hardship on your host," Elias muttered under his breath.

"What was that?" Marzia asked, even though she had heard what he said, her voice sickeningly sweet.

"Nothing," he replied, flashing a fake smile.

"You're studying psychology, yes?" Elias' father asked.

"Yes, I am, actually. Ever since I was in high school, I knew what I wanted to study," Marzia replied.

"My Elias is studying psychology too. Maybe you've seen him around campus?" Elias' dad said.

"We keep meeting," both Elias and Marzia said in unison.

"Marzia, look! A chinaaq![8]" Marzia's father said, pointing to the wishbone sticking out of her chicken.

---

[7] A Hadith: a collection of traditions containing sayings of the prophet Muhammad (Peace be upon him) which, with accounts of his daily practice (the Sunnah), constitutes the major source of guidance for Muslims apart from the Quran (Definition from Oxford Languages).

[8] Chinaaq: (meaning "wishbone") is a traditional game that starts with the breaking of a chicken's wishbone. Often, it starts during a meal with family and

"I think I'm a little too old for that Padarjaan,[9]" Marzia said with a half-hearted laugh.

"Oh, but it's so much fun! You should play with Elias Jan,[10]" Elias' mother said.

"I'm all for a little fun," Elias said, smirking.

"Of course," Marzia replied with all the graciousness she could muster up so as not to offend anyone. Especially Elias' mother, who had been so sweet to her.

The two each took one end of the wishbone without breaking eye contact as they stared daggers at each other. It snapped like Marzia's father's ankle did when he thought it was a good idea to ride her scooter when she was ten. But that's a story for another day.

After dinner concluded, Marzia helped clear the table and wash the dishes. Despite no one asking her to, she felt almost obligated to do so. I mean, what do you do when you feel like you're invading someone's personal space in their home? She felt like a complete alien

---

friends. A wager is usually made before or directly after the breaking of the wishbone. To win the game, they must get the other player to accept any object in his or her hand without that person saying "Mara Yaad Ast", translating to "I remember". Games can last anywhere from minutes to days. If one player forgets and accepts the object, the winner must say "Mara Yaad, Tura Faramoosh" which translates to "I remember, you forgot".

[9] Padarjaan: Translates to Father dear. An affectionate and respectful term for one's father.

[10] Jaan: An endearing term used after a name which means 'dear'.

in someone else's house. But unexpectedly, she found that she really got along with Elias' mother, who was, in fact, a sweet woman who, by some cruel twist of fate, had an absolute trash bag of a son. But make no mistake, dear reader, I am a completely impartial narrator.

"Thank you so much for helping. You really didn't have to!" she said.

"It's my pleasure. It's the least I can do in return for you guys opening up your home to us so graciously," Marzia replied.

"Oh, don't mention it! It's nice to have some women around! I'm used to being surrounded by men between my husband and my two sons," Elias' mother said with a laugh.

Marzia politely stifled a laugh.

"Maybe you'll be a good influence on them," Elias' mother said wistfully. "I worry about them sometimes."

"Yeah, maybe," Marzia repeated.

After the table was wiped down and the dishes were put away, Marzia plopped herself on the couch, scrolling through her phone. While scrolling through Instagram, her heart rate quickened when she sees Mateen Heydari's name pop up on her feed.

He must be online! Marzia thought to herself. Instantly she went to the camera feature and fiddled with different poses, the TV that she has no intention of watching in front of her. It was actually really cozy, their living room. It wasn't one of those show homes, it really looked like a place that had some history. Photos lined the wall, and a hand painted vase sat atop the coffee table.

Ahh, what a time to be alive, staging the perfect Instagram story. She was just about to post it when she felt someone looming over her shoulder.

"He's not going to look at it," Elias said snarkily.

"What are you talking about?"

"That guy from the meymoni. If you're resorting to Instagram on the off chance that he'll reply to your story, then you're dreaming," Elias replied matter of factly.

"You think you have it all figured out, don't you?" Marzia scoffed.

"That's because I do," he said. "You've been stalking his profile for about a good half an hour now. And yet, you haven't followed him yet. Not going to lie, a little creepy and desperate if you ask me."

"Yeah, well, no one asked you!" Marzia retorted.

"Oof, struck a nerve there, princess?"

"You must be a lot of fun at parties," Marzia said.

"You know, if you think about it, you should be thanking me. Look, I'm saving you a lot of wasted time. I'm sorry to tell you, but he's just not that into you."

"Oh, what do you know?" Marzia shot back.

"Not much. Just knowledge of the male brain," Elias shrugged. "Look, I'll prove it to you."

Before Marzia registered what was happening, Elias took her phone out of her hand and pulled up Mateen's profile.

"This is him, right?" he said, flashing the screen, dodging Marzia's hand, desperately trying to get it back.

"Stop! C'mon, it's not funny. Give it back!" Marzia pleaded.

"Annnnndddd send," he said, finally handing the phone back to Marzia.

"You didn't! What did you send?" Marzia demanded. "Really? 'Heyy' that's what you decided to send?"

"Look, at least you'll know. If he responds and can hold a decent conversation, then you can name your first-born son after me. If not, then all's well that ends well." He shrugged.

Marzia rolled her eyes. Then, her phone vibrated with a new notification.

"Oh my God. He replied. He replied, what the hell am I going to do? He actually replied!" Marzia said with panic in her voice.

"Leave it," Elias said.

"What!? Are you crazy?"

"Trust me. Reply in the morning. You'll seem less...pathetic," Elias said.

"Ouch. I'm going to ignore that last part," Marzia said, already halfway up the stairs.

Now here's the kicker, dear reader. She actually took his advice. Maybe she was crazy, or perhaps she really thought he had some insight into the male brain, but that night she took his words to heart.

CHAPTER FOUR

❧

"I have not failed. I've just found 10,000 ways that won't work."

- Thomas A. Edison

I wish I could say Marzia had a restful sleep. But she tossed and turned the entire night. She worried that she had squandered her chances with Mateen by making him wait too long. She oscillated between kicking herself for listening to Elias like an absolute idiot and telling herself that if he really liked her, it wouldn't make a difference. And to make matters worse, she got an email saying the marks for her most recent statistics test had just been posted online. Her heart began to race as she meticulously enters her credentials in to access the course website.

Loading...

49%

This is fine. Everything is fine. It's not like this is a required course, and I failed the very first exam, she thought to herself.

And in classic Marzia fashion, spiraling ensued. For the first 30 minutes, she sat in her bed, overthinking every choice she ever made in her entire life. Eventually, however, she decided to get ready for class because... education. She gingerly made her way down the hallway with her bright pink toothbrush in hand. To her dismay, Elias emerged from his room, still half asleep.

"What's up with your face?" was all he said to her.

"What do you mean what's wrong with my face? This is my face!" Marzia replied.

"There's stuff all over your eyes!" he said with mild bewilderment.

"That? It's Vaseline! It's supposed to make your eyelashes grow thicker!" she responded matter of factly.

In the washroom, she examined herself in the mirror. Her eyes were swollen with tiredness, and her lips were dry and flaky. Not to mention eye boogers galore. However, like the valiant optimist she was, Marzia persisted. Moisturizer, concealer, blush...she couldn't help but draw comparisons to the scene in Wizard of Oz where they gave Dorothy a whole makeover. Eventually, almost an hour later, Marzia felt she looked presentable enough and descended down the stairs of the house she would be calling home for the foreseeable future.

"Took you long enough," Elias' younger brother Bilal remarked.

Elias let out a snicker of approval.

"You guys better get going, or you'll be late!" Marzia's mom said, cutting up fruit. She handed them peanut butter sandwiches on their way out. Little things like that were one of the many reasons Marzia loved her mother without measure.

They got into Elias' white Mercedes, which still had that fresh new car smell.

Of course, he has a Mercedes, Marzia thought to herself, rolling her eyes internally.

"Look. Let's get something straight, okay? I am tolerating you because, for some unfathomable reason, my mother actually likes you. But we are not friends okay, you will not say hi to me on campus, and you will not tell anyone you're staying at my house. Got that?" Elias said.

"First of all, get over yourself. I wouldn't look your way on campus if I were dying of thirst and you were the last bottle of water on earth!"

"Weird analogy, but whatever. Also, you get over yourself. Your entire family is staying at my house for God knows how long, and you expect me to be okay with that?" Elias fired back.

"Well, that's one thing we have in common. Do you think that I like living under the same roof as you and seeing your smug face wherever I go? Not my ideal either!"

"No one's forcing you to stay Peaches!"

"And you don't have to be a self-absorbed ass, but here we are!"

It should be noted, dear reader, that the rest of the drive was spent in awkward silence. Neither of them turned on the radio which turned into something of a game of chicken where neither wanted to admit they were uncomfortable stewing in the deafening silence. This 20-minute drive felt like an absolute eternity. The way time felt like it was passing at that moment was like when you're done with a test early, and you have to wait for everyone else to finish before you can leave.

I am going to lose it in this house... Marzia quickly typed to the group chat with her cousins Ameena and Soraya.

Ameena: Throw the whole boy away!

Soraya: Am I going to have to beat someone's ass?

Marzia: I'll keep y'all updated!

Once they got to campus, Elias pulled into a student parking spot and turned off the ignition, which somehow, he managed to do angrily.

"Two-thirty. Be here, or I'm leaving without you," Elias said dryly.

"You have a good day too!" Marzia yelled after him sarcastically.

Marzia made her way to her lecture hall and quickly scanned the room for an open seat. Apparently, people actually decided to be studious this week and actually show up to class.

The audacity! Marzia thought to herself.

You see, despite Marzia perpetually pining for Mateen, she still imagined meeting someone in class. She fantasized about sitting next to a tall and handsome stranger. Marzia was an idealist, and she constantly conjured up outlandish scenarios in her brain that she knew there was a slim to no chance of ever actually happening. But admittedly, in Marzia's defence it makes living in your head a whole lot more fun.

As Marzia settled down in her seat, she resolved to pay the utmost attention to the professor. This was no ordinary class. This was statistics, and statistics required a whole other level of concentration. Marzia was fairly good at a number of things, but God, it seemed, had decided to keep her humble by making her chronically deficient in mathematics.

"Some of you didn't do so well on the last exam," her professor said, addressing the entire class. "But there is still time to improve. So, I suggest going over the textbook chapters and pay extra attention to the lecture slides."

"That last exam was so easy! How could anyone screw it up?" someone behind her whispered to their friends.

Reader, at that moment, Marzia wanted to punch that person in the throat. Several times.

After class, Marzia was making her way back to the school's parking lot where Elias' car was when she heard the insufferable voice that so often haunted her dreams.

"Marzia!? Is that you?"

Dalia. Freaking. Alimi. The bane of Marzia's existence.

"Oh, hi Dalia," Marzia said in the most normal voice she could muster.

"I'm just doing work at the non-profit I'm working on starting up. I'm the president and face of the entire operation," Dalia said, even though no one asked, with the self-important smirk that Marzia had come to know all too well.

"That's great, Dalia," Marzia replied, tone drier than the Sahara Desert.

"Yeah, I really want to do some good for the animal community. There are so many dogs and cats on the street. It's a real epidemic," Dalia said solemnly. "What have you been up to, Marzia?"

"I've been good. Work and class are keeping me busy," Marzia said. "Anyways, saving the world must be hard work, so I'll leave you to it."

"See ya around!" Dalia said. "Oh, before I go, here's a flyer for my organization. Hope you can spread the word!"

Dalia handed Marzia a flyer for whatever ego-boosting initiative she was working on that day and took a sip of her coffee. Her heels clicked behind her as she walked away.

Marzia began walking towards the parking lot, stuffing Dalia's flyer in the trash before leaving the building. She vehemently refused to be a part of whatever self-absorbed scheme Dalia had cooked up in her head to gratify her gargantuan-sized ego. Marzia had enough of that girl's antics in high school.

She spotted Elias and let out a wholehearted sigh as she got in the car.

"Hello to you too," Elias said.

"Believe it or not, I just had a conversation with someone I can't stand even more than you."

"I don't know if I should be flattered or offended."

Once they got home, Elias pulled up to the house but not into the driveway.

"And where are you off to?" Marzia asked inquisitively.

"Are you my mother?" he retorted.

Marzia just rolled her eyes and walked towards the house. Sometimes you just have to pick your battles. She entered the house and was greeted by the entire family watching Indiana Jones and The Last Crusade.

"Salaam!" Marzia said to everyone.

"Salaam, dear! Can you believe Elias' family haven't seen a single Indiana Jones film?" Marzia's mother asked.

"Speaking of my son, where is he?" Elias' mother inquired.

"He has very important errands to run," Marzia said with a laugh.

Marzia made her way up the stairs to her room. She collapsed onto the bed and whipped out her phone with lightning quickness. She figured she had given Mateen's message enough time to marinate and finally buckled down to curate an acceptable response.

"Hey, you're so cool. I think we should hang out and get to know each other because you're hella cute," she began to type out, not really expecting to send it...or so she thought.

Her thumbs betrayed her and instinctively sent the message she never meant for him to read. Marzia immediately used the "unsend" feature and prayed that he was nowhere near his phone at that particular moment. Like a tidal wave, embarrassment slowly consumed every ounce of her being like when you forget why you were worried or upset, and something triggers you. All of a sudden, the feelings flood back in, and you remember what it was that was bothering you.

Marzia: Guys… I did something! I accidentally sent a message he wasn't supposed to read…

Merely a few minutes later, the group chat lit up with responses.

Ameena: How does that happen?

Marzia: IDK MAN! I DIDN'T MEAN TO SEND IT I WAS JUST TRYING TO GET MYSELF WARMED UP

Soraya: Don't worry, if you unsent it maybe he won't get the notification!

Marzia: I hope he doesn't! I would never be able to face him if he did! Excuse me while I disappear and expunge any trace of my existence from social media!

Ameena: Unsend, unsend! Then reply with something else quick, so when he clicks the notification, that's the message he'll get!

Marzia: Smart, I'll do that now!

"Hey. How's it going?"

Marzia sent a screenshot to the group chat.

Soraya: And now we wait…

Now, reader, you may or may not have experienced such a situation in your life, but I am sure I do not have to explain further the depths of Marzia's bottomless embarrassment. It's the type of humiliation that makes you want to become very small and disappear into obscurity.

That night Marzia set up camp in the Hakimzadas' dining room. The lighting was dim, matching her somber demeanor. Even the oak table looked sad. She was determined to ace that next exam. Okay, ace is a strong word, but she vowed to do moderately better than she had on the last exam. She hoped, however foolishly, that she may yet salvage her grade and get the credit she needed to graduate on time. Wishful thinking? Probably. But Marzia was nothing if not optimistic.

"That's wrong," she heard an annoying noise from behind her. It was like when a fly buzzes right by your ear as if it knew just how to annoy the living daylights out of you.

"What? What do you mean?" Marzia said, mildly annoyed but ever so slightly curious.

"Your calculation for the standard deviation. It's wrong," Elias said matter of factly.

"Have at it, hotshot," Marzia replied, motioning to the sheet of paper in front of her.

Elias took the mechanical pencil. (Marzia only uses mechanical pencils for writing and refers to them as superior writing utensils). He scribbled on the sheet with a furrow of his brow.

"You're welcome," Elias said, handing her pencil back to her. He was about to walk away when Marzia broke the painfully awkward silence.

"Wait!" she said. "You...took statistics, right?"

"Yes, over the summer, actually," he replied.

"I see…"

"If you have something to say, you might as well just say it. I have a couple of greasy hot pockets with my name on them waiting for me," Elias said. He caught the look that Marzia gave him, somewhere between desperation and pleading.

"Oh, no. No way—" Elias protested.

"Hear me out!" Marzia said.

"If you think I'm going to tutor you just because you're, by some cruel twist of fate, living in my home for the next who knows how long, you're absolutely crazy!" Elias replied.

"I didn't want to have to do this, but if you don't help me, I'm going to kill myself," Marzia said.

It should be noted, dear reader, that Marzia was not serious at that moment. She just has a very dark and inappropriate sense of humour.

"Wow, you are so messed up!" Elias muttered, almost at a loss for words.

"The choice is yours," Marzia said.

And so, to his dismay, Elias tutored Marzia in statistics that evening.

CHAPTER FIVE

"I am a slow walker, but I never walk back."

- Abraham Lincoln

Marzia was never a particularly good student. In fact, until grade six, she was quite academically challenged, so to speak. A ne'er-do-well if you will. Report card day was always a dark mark on Marzia's school year. The big manilla envelopes sitting on the teacher's desk taunted her through every period of the day. Then, when they were finally distributed, she would wait a few seconds once she left the classroom doors before ripping it open and facing her fate. And that was only the half of it. The worst part was having to get one of her parents to sign it and bring it back to class the next day. As if that wasn't bad enough, the kids would continue comparing their grades for the next few days. Unlike in some TV shows, when Marzia was growing up, it was actually cool to be smart. In fact, sometimes, you would be teased if you didn't get good grades. Suffice it to say, it would take approximately a week to recover from report card day.

But, one day, that all changed. It was the first month of grade six, and she had just completed a math test which she knew she had completely bombed. After her teacher Mrs. Perkins had graded her test, she said something to Marzia that really stuck with her.

"You see those bean plants that we're growing for science class sitting on the windowsill?" she asked Marzia one day after class when all the other students had left for recess.

"Yep!" she said, unsure where Mrs. Perkins was going with this.

"They're like some of your classmates. They take, say, less than two months to grow," Mrs. Perkins continued. "But you see that cherry tree outside the window?"

Mrs. Perkins pointed to the beautiful cherry tree in full bloom outside the classroom window in the school courtyard.

"Yes?" Marzia said.

"That's like you," Mrs. Perkins replied. "They take years to bloom. But when they do...boy are they a force to be reckoned with."

Marzia didn't quite understand what her teacher meant at that moment, but what Mrs. Perkins was trying to tell her was to not be disheartened if things didn't come as easily to her as they did to the other kids.

"Marzia? Marzia!"

"Yeah?" Marzia replied.

"If you're not going to listen to me, I don't understand why I'm wasting my time here!" Elias declared.

"Wait, I'm sorry, okay, I just zoned out for a second!" Marzia pleaded. "If I fail statistics, I may not graduate! And if I don't graduate, then I won't find a job, and if I don't find a job, no one will marry me, and I'll become an old woman filled with regret waiting to die alone."

"God, you are so dramatic," Elias said. "And did you just quote Inception to me right now?"

"Maybe..." Marzia said back.

Elias wordlessly rolled his eyes.

Then all of a sudden, Marzia's phone lit up with a notification from Instagram. More specifically, a notification for a message from Mateen Heydari. Both Marzia and Elias' eyes flickered to the phone screen.

Mateen: Hey! I'm good. You?

Marzia's heart quickened, and her breaths became shallow as she read his words.

"What should I say now?? He wrote back!" she asked, turning the phone in his direction.

"I don't know. Whatever you want?" Elias shrugged. "Why are you asking me?"

"Because you're the one who claims to know so much about people," Marzia insisted.

"Say, 'I'm good. Studying with friends,'" Elias replied. "And wait for him to continue the conversation. If he doesn't, you end it there."

"Okay, I sent it!" Marzia said. "Hang on."

Marzia went upstairs and came back a few minutes later with what looked like an ordinary lamp.

"What exactly is that?" Elias asked inquisitively.

"This is my light therapy lamp. Studies show that exposure to daylight or some form of light can effectively treats seasonal affective disorder," Marzia responded.

"You're really something Peaches," Elias said with a laugh, rolling his eyes.

Marzia's phone lit up again, and a pang of excitement coursed through her body as she snatched it off the table.

"Nice. Being productive," Marzia read out loud. "What kind of response is that?! And no follow-up question?! That is NOT how you keep a conversation going!"

"Sorry to burst your bubble, but that's probably the point," Elias replied flatly.

Marzia scoffed.

"How do you know that he wants to end the conversation?"

"Simple," Elias said. "Because if he wanted to continue talking to you, he would have."

"What if he's just shy?" Marzia argued.

"Even if a guy is shy, he will make an effort if he's truly interested," Elias said dismissively. "Now finish these practice questions."

Marzia looked at the sheet of paper he had been scribbling on for the last 15 minutes as Elias then got up.

"Where are you going?" Marzia asked.

"Class dismissed," Elias said, yawning on his way up the stairs.

Marzia eyed the worksheet he cooked up for her and began working on the first question. After about an hour, Marzia's mother came in with a plate of watermelon.

"You haven't had any fruit today!" she proclaimed, placing the plate in front of Marzia.

"Thank you, Maudarjaan!" Marzia said, giving her mother a hug. She smelled like the wind from hanging the clothes out to dry in the backyard. Marzia always loved the way her mother smelled. Even being an adult, Marzia loved showing her family affection.

Marzia desperately tried to stay focused on the practice questions Elias had given her, but like the sirens in The Odyssey, her phone was calling to her, and she couldn't resist.

She decided to message Mateen back to keep the conversation going.

"Do you-" Marzia began to type and abruptly deleted the words.

Marzia: Yep! Really trying to get my stuff together this semester lol.

As a distraction, she immersed herself in her schoolwork. At least that way, it didn't seem like a complete waste of her time. After a solid 10 minutes of studying, she cracked again and checked her phone.

No new messages.

Out of curiosity, she clicked back to her conversation with Mateen to find one of the biggest taboos of the online age. He had read her message but didn't respond, also known as getting left on read. Now the rational side of Marzia told her that her message wasn't really a question that required a response, so there wasn't really much to say after that. But the other side of her was fuming that Mateen said nothing to revive the conversation.

And so, Marzia took to the group chat to dispel her woes.

Marzia: That moment when you get left on read.

Ameena: Ouch. Do I need to key someone's car?

Soraya: I felt that. Whatever. Forget him. It wasn't meant to be.

Marzia: I mean...what I said wasn't really a question or anything, but if he wanted to talk more, he would have responded, right?

Ameena: Definitely, if someone wants to talk to you, they will make it happen, no doubt about it.

Marzia: This sucks man. Why is it whenever I show the least bit of interest in someone, they immediately do whatever is in their power to distance themselves from me!

The conversation continued with much cathartic release, and many emojis were sent by the time Marzia was ready to turn in for the night.

Now, a lot of this may seem like an overreaction on Marzia's part. And to be honest, it just might be. But to get how she feels, you have to understand that Marzia is a very sensitive person when it comes to social interactions. The slightest comment could make her feel scorned and upset for the rest of the evening. And yes, she knows sometimes she is irrational. She's working on it, okay?

One of Marzia's earliest memories was of her very first crush, way before even Mateen. His name was Tariq, and they both went to the same Masjid for Quran classes (basically the Muslim version of Sunday School) when Marzia was eight years old. He was in another class with the other boys, but every time his parents would drop him off, Marzia would be mesmerized by his remarkable green eyes. It was actually the first thing she noticed about him.

Was that the only reason she liked him? Probably. But that's neither here nor there. Anyways, one day Marzia wanted to write him a note, telling him how she felt. Now don't ask me why she thought this was a good idea. Marzia still cringed every time she thought about the situation, even into adulthood. So anyways, Marzia worked up the nerve to write the most elaborate note known to man.

"I like you. Do you like me? (This is from Marzia BTW)" was what she wrote on that neon pink sticky note. Marzia had recently learned what the acronym BTW meant and never missed an opportunity to use it.

She carefully left it on the desk he always sat at and anxiously waited for a response. However, it should be noted that Marzia had hardly said a word to the boy the whole time she knew him. So why she believed he would reciprocate her very misguided feelings is an inexplicable mystery. The next time she went to class again, she saw a pink sticky note on her desk. Could it be? Marzia opened it up, heart pounding out of her chest with anticipation.

Five words were all it took to get the point across.

"No. You have a unibrow."

This was a particularly low blow for Marzia because when she went home to ask her mom if she could pluck her eyebrows, her answer was absolutely not.

You know, if I said that this story didn't still bother Marzia on some level, I would be lying. But eventually, Marzia got over Tariq, and he moved away, which solved that problem. After that, though, a part of her always felt inadequate. Then again, who didn't on some level or another feel that way at some point?

CHAPTER SIX

❧

"There are no secrets that time does not reveal."

-Jean Racine

When Marzia was young, her mother made her take the most putrid multivitamins you could ever imagine. Picture compost juice, but after it's been sitting out for a few days. In the summertime. That's how bad they tasted to Marzia. She wondered why she couldn't have some of the Flintstones vitamins that tasted like candy, like all the other kids did. One day she actually asked her mother why it was so important that she took them.

"They'll help you grow big and strong!" her mother told her.

"Then why do they taste so yucky?" Marzia questioned.

"Sometimes, what's best for us isn't always easy or fun. Sometimes you just have to do something because you know it will pay off in the future."

And that, dear reader, is something Marzia tried to remember when she was faced with something she found less than pleasurable. And it's what was in her mind the morning of her statistics exam.

Marzia was a nervous wreck. She felt a growing lump in her throat at the daunting thought of sitting in a lecture hall with a little under a hundred people. So, she did what she knew best. She studied and then studied some more. Although she took a plethora of breaks in between study sessions (more than she would like to admit), she felt somewhat prepared for her exam. As prepared as she'll ever be, she figured. Before long, it was time for Marzia to head to her impending doom.

As soon as Marzia entered the exam room, a sinking feeling of dread washed over her. The horror that was… her period.

This is fine. She was prepared. Nothing could stop her. Marzia very nonchalantly (read: immediately and very abruptly) wrapped her sweater around her waist.

Crisis averted.

Marzia took a seat next to a guy going through his cue cards.

He's kind of cute. And his glasses somehow make him even more attractive, she thought. *He kind of has that nerdy look that*— Focus, *Marzia! Look at the first question,* she thought, drawing her attention back to her blank test.

Bismillah.[11] *Don't know that one, I'll just skip to the next question for now.* Marzia flipped the page.

Okay, not that one either.

"Hey, do you have a pencil?" the cute guy beside her asked.

"Sure!" Marzia replied, instinctively giving him the one she was using.

Wait, was that my only pencil? Marzia thought, rifling through her pencil case. *CRAP. I have no other pencils. I could ask for it back. Maybe he'll laugh? No. That's weird. I can't do that, maybe the person beside me-*

"I'm sorry, do you have an extra pencil by any chance?" Marzia whispered to the girl to her left.

"This is just a reminder that there is no talking for the duration of the exam," one of the invigilators said loudly.

The girl beside her shook her head apologetically.

There was only one thing left to do. Marzia raised her hand gingerly. It took a couple minutes before one of the invigilators noticed

---

[11] Bismillah: Arabic for: in the name of Allah (an invocation used at the beginning of any task or event).

her, but before one of them could get to her, the professor made a B line right for Marzia.

"I, I don't have a pencil, Sir," Marzia said very quietly to the professor.

"I'm a little deaf in this ear. Please speak a little louder!" he replied.

"I don't have a pencil," she repeated.

"You came to a university examination without a pencil?" he asked with a look that was somewhere between pity and complete and utter disappointment.

"You see, I had one, but I must have-"

"Can anyone lend-" he looked to Marzia.

"Marzia," she replied.

"Can anyone lend Marzia here a pencil?" he said loudly.

The absolute Adonis sitting next to her gave her an odd look as she put her head down. A few rows down, a girl raised her hand, and the professor took a pencil from her and handed it to Marzia.

"Try to be a little more prepared next time, hm? This isn't high school."

Marzia resisted the powerful urge to profusely hit her head onto the table. However, when all was said and done, she felt reasonably confident about how she'd done on that exam. Would she ever become a statistician? Marzia would sooner declare that Dalia Alimi was her best and truest friend.

Before heading home, Marzia decided to meet for coffee with her friend Reiyna.

"I'm on my way now! Just got out of my exam! :)" She texted Reiyna.

She made her way to the nearest Tim Horton's and took a seat by the window, transfixed by her phone. Reiyna walked in and greeted her with a warm hug.

"You won't believe the day I've had Ray!" Marzia said in the most exasperated and Marzia-esque tone she could muster.

Because of how busy their schedules were, Reiyna and Marzia didn't get to see each other often. But when they did get together, it was as if no time had passed at all. And so, with the aid of numerous hand gestures, Marzia explained the story of the events that had transpired that afternoon in the exam hall.

"And you didn't realize that was your last pencil until you gave it to him?" Reiyna asked, wildly amused.

"He was just so damn gorgeous my brain must have malfunctioned!" Marzia replied, covering her face in shame.

"I swear, Mar, something like that would only happen to you!" Reiyna said, laughing uncontrollably.

Suddenly, Marzia's face went pale as she noticed who had just walked into the establishment. She was face to face with none other than the guy to whom she had given her pencil during the exam. The pencil that essentially started the whole fiasco in the first place.

"What's the matter?" Reiyna asked.

"You know that guy I gave my pencil to? He just walked in here," Marzia said.

"You're kidding!" Reiyna exclaimed. "He's looking right at us!"

"You're messing with me! This is neither the time nor place for that type of cruelty!" Marzia said, with a look of exaggerated sadness.

"No, I'm serious. He's walking right towards us!" Reiyna responded.

"I do not have the emotional capital for this right now!" Marzia exclaimed.

"Hey, you ran out so fast after the exam I didn't get the chance to give you back your pencil," the young Leo DiCaprio said to Marzia, handing her pencil back. The pencil that had caused her so much embarrassment.

"Thanks!" was all Marzia could muster.

"You have a really great pen there!" he said with a wink as he walked away.

"You too!" Marzia blurted out.

Really, Marzia? That's the witty response you decided to go with? 'You too'? That's it. I have to transfer schools, she thought.

Marzia thought her string of misfortune and embarrassment was over for the day. And it should be noted, dear reader, that she was sorely mistaken. When she got home, she found everyone having dinner in the dining room. Very Brady Bunch.

"Take a seat, Marzia Jaan. You must be so hungry after your exam!" Elias' mother said.

Marzia took a plate and began filling it with the various dishes spread across the table.

"How did the exam go?" Marzia's father asked.

"How badly did you bomb it?" her brother Ameer teased.

"The exam itself wasn't too bad, actually," Marzia replied.

"You know I've been reading some great poetry," Elias said abruptly and rather suspiciously. Marzia could have never predicted what he would say next.

"You know, back in Afghanistan, I used to be known for my poetry!" Marzia's father said. "Please share it with us!"

Elias cleared his throat rather ominously.

"I love you in the morning, with your piercing eyes as bright as day. I love you in the afternoon, with your heavenly smile that makes me unafraid. And last but not least, I love you at night. I only wish I could stay awake until dawn so as to not waste another minute without you. And like the stars shine and gleam, I'll love you forevermore, my dearest-"

Marzia recognized this piece all too well.

"I think we've heard enough!" she said, exasperated.

You see, dear reader, Marzia realized that Elias had somehow gotten a hold of a poem she wrote for Mateen over three years ago. He had memorized it in its entirety for the sole purpose of making her uncomfortable.

"That was actually very nice. Who was it written by?" Marzia's father asked.

Elias shot Marzia a devious smirk, with one eyebrow up as if to say, 'try me!'

"I think they're local, but you know what, I don't quite remember, actually!"

When dinner was over, it was Elias and Marzia's turn to clean up. And boy was Marzia itching to give him the tongue lashing of the century.

"What possessed you to go through my private property!?" Marzia whisper-yelled while collecting dirty plates.

"Next time, don't keep your crappy poems with your stats notes!" Elias said while wiping down the dining room table, laughing, and clearly amused by the situation.

"But what gets me is how you memorized the entire thing just to torment me!" Marzia continued. "If you had even a shred of human decency, you wouldn't have done all that just to humiliate me. I just wanted to say this to let you know that the bets are off, pal!"

"Is that supposed to scare me? Am I supposed to feel threatened right now, Peaches?"

"I'm not trying to scare you, Elias. I'm just saying that I won't placate you when you refuse to act like the adult that you are. What you pulled there was middle school level childishness, and I honestly have no idea what I did for you to be so combative!"

Elias scoffed.

"What?" Marzia asked.

"You forgot the part where your entire family took over my house," Elias replied, every word stinging sharply.

"At least I'm not a cynical loser," Marzia spat back.

Elias opened his mouth as though he were going to say something, but Marzia stormed off before he can. As she walked up the stairs her face burned with tears she refused to let out. Elias Hakimzada would. Not. See. Her. Cry. It seemed like an off-handed comment, but to Marzia, it struck a chord she never knew she had. It tapped into one of her deepest fears of being annoying, unwanted, and a burden. So, like anytime something pissed her off, Marzia turned to the group chat.

Marzia: This boy is the evilest person I have ever met...

And without missing a beat, the replies flooded in.

Soraya: Ughhhh what did he do this time?

Marzia: He said I was taking over his house. Can you believe the nerve?!

Ameena: What did you say back?!

Now, reader, it should be noted that at this point Marzia retells the story of her last interaction with Elias, however, with a few...embellishments. Now, I wouldn't go so far as to say she was lying because she truly did see it as a Passions-esque dramatic show-down. For those unfamiliar with the absolute cinematic masterpiece that is Passions, feel free to insert whatever soap-opera or teen drama suits you or is relevant when you're reading this. Riverdale, perhaps? Anyways, I'll spare you all the details of how she supposedly "made Elias cry like a little baby."

Marzia: ...and he hasn't been able to look me in the eyes since.

Ameena: You really know how to bring a story to life, Marzia.

CHAPTER SEVEN

∽

"Look back, and smile on perils past."

-*Walter Scott*

Do any of you have a sister? If you do, you know that it is a unique relationship in that they're an invaluable link to your past and one of the only things that you'll have left of your parents in the future. Or, maybe you haven't talked to them in years for whatever reason. If that is the case, dear reader, take this as a sign that some hatchets are best left buried. Once Marzia was little, her sister Nabeela made fun of her for wearing a black and white striped dress shirt. She told her she looked like an inmate. But, when they were on their way to school, and some girls were making fun of Marzia's outfit, she never forgot how quickly her sister came to her defence.

"Maybe you should do something about that unibrow before commenting on someone else's looks," Nabeela spat with her razor-sharp tongue. That day was a testament to what so many sisters have experienced and will experience until the end of time. Your sister can make fun of you, but she will go to bat for you just as hard if anyone does you harm.

One day Marzia was looking through her mother's closet for a vintage pair of shoes she had worn back when she was a teenager that her mother told her she still had somewhere. She finally found them; they were well-loved but still in great shape for how old they were. However, something was wedged on the box that she recognized as a photo album she had never seen before. It had a worn velvet cover in the deepest shade of maroon. And reader, you can probably guess what happens next, so I'll spare you the anticipation. You're welcome. Marzia gingerly opened the album, thumbing through the pages with her stomach on the hardwood floor. They were pictures from when her mother was in Afghanistan. One seemed to be her on the very first day of school in a forest green uniform. Another was her standing in a garden of flowers with a stylish pair of sunglasses. However, the very next picture she saw made her pause. It was a girl with similar features to her mother but a few years older.

Who is she? Marzia thought. As far as she knew, her mother had no sisters, and this girl looked like none of her other relatives. So, like any other nosy and chronically curious person, Marzia closed the book and made her way downstairs to confront her mother. She wordlessly placed the album onto the kitchen table where her mother was preparing lunch.

"Who's this?" she asked. As soon as her mother saw the photo Marzia was referring to, sadness flashed across her face. And at that moment, Marzia truly noticed how her beautiful mother had aged. Her hair was grey, and her face had lines like the faults in California. The brief look of sadness her mother displayed reminded Marzia of how much she had gone through. She rarely mentioned it, but Marzia's mother had gone through much hardship. Her mother was ill for most of her life, and her father was often on business trips for work, so she practically raised herself.

"Where did you find that?" she asked, trying to make her tone sound airy and nonchalant.

"In the closet when I was looking for the shoes."

And once again, Marzia's mother wore a solemn look on her face. As though there were about a thousand things she wanted to say in that moment, but she couldn't quite find the words to express them. She took a deep breath.

"I never told you this," her mother began. "But a long time ago, what seems like lifetimes ago now, I had a sister. But one day, she left for school and never came back. Her teachers said she never arrived at school that day. We kept looking for her, but eventually, we left Afghanistan, and I never saw her again. She was my best friend. Sometimes when I'm in the grocery store, I'll hear a laugh that sounds so similar to hers I run out of the aisle to see where it's coming from. But then, a wave of remembrance washes over me, and I remember she is gone."

"What was her name?" Marzia asked timidly.

"Her name was Sabahat."

"Do you know if she's alive?" Marzia asked.

"I often wonder that, but to be honest, I have no clue. And I have no way of finding out," Marzia's mother replied. She could hear the hurt in her voice. This was the first time Marzia had seen her mother so open and candid in the over two decades she has been alive. And at that moment, Marzia made a vow to herself, a personal goal if you will. She resolved to find out what happened to her long-lost aunt. Whether she was dead or alive, she was determined to find out what became of her. She had no idea at this point how she would do it, but by God, she was going to try.

With the conversation with her mother still weighing heavily on her, Marzia went upstairs to get ready to go to the mall with Soraya and Ameena. Regrettably, Marzia had to share a washroom with Elias, so she began to scroll through her phone, sitting on the top step of the staircase with her makeup bag beside her waiting for Elias to finish up. After quite some time, the washroom door swung open, and Elias emerged from his porcelain throne.

"You smell like sunscreen," Marzia remarked, noting the absence of his usually pungent Irish Spring deodorant.

"That's because I put on sunscreen Einstein," he fired back, surprisingly defensive.

"Why? It's cloudy out," Marzia asked, gesturing toward the grey sky visible from the skylight. And in a very un-Elias-like fashion, he seemed to not know what to say for a moment. Dare I say, at a loss for words?

"What is this, twenty questions?" he retorted.

"If we were playing twenty questions, I would have to be able to stand speaking to you for more than two minutes," Marzia replied snidely.

"You have a lot to say for someone staying in my house."

"Tell me something Elias, how does it feel knowing that your mother likes me more than you?" Marzia asked.

"I wouldn't know, but then again, she always had a soft spot for charity cases," Elias responded.

Marzia struggled to hide the look of hurt on her face, and Elias must have noticed this too because his expression softened just the slightest bit. Their eyes locked momentarily,

"At least I'm fun to be around," Marzia finally said, pushing past him and going into the washroom. But before she could close it, Elias put his hand on the door.

"What?" she snapped. Elias seemed startled by her reply. He furrowed his brow and seemed as though he's actually thinking about what he was going to say for once.

"Go easy on the bronzer," he said after a long pause.

"Are you my makeup artist?" Marzia shot back. Elias paused for a moment but chose not to say anything. He snorted and sauntered back to his room.

Before Marzia began getting ready, she made wudu[12], the cool water feeling particularly refreshing that day as she splashed it onto her face. Eying the time on her phone, she realized she was running late, as usual. With minutes to spare, she applied the last of her makeup. With one last look in the mirror, she blended her cheeks a little more with her hands. Before leaving, she rolled out her prayer mat and prayed dhuhr[13].

No matter how hectic her life got, Marzia always included prayer as part of her day. It brought her a sense of calm that gave her the courage to tackle each and every day. On her way to the mall, almost on cue, just as she pulled into the parking lot, she got a message from Ameena and Soraya saying they'd just arrived as well.

---

[12] Wudu: Ritual cleansing/ablution done before prayer.

[13] Dhuhr: The second prayer of the day, during the early afternoon.

After reuniting, iced coffees in hand, the first order of business was to get some new clothes. First stop: Urban Planet. All the clothes were so beautifully arranged that Marzia couldn't help but admire them. It was like Willy Wonka's factory but with pastel fabrics. Marzia palmed a floral blouse, eyeing its intricate design. Marzia was in an unusually good mood, she even found the mind-numbing pop music in the background uplifting.

"Not another floral top!" Soraya teased.

"You have two exactly like that!" Ameena chimed in.

"They're not exactly the same!" Marzia vehemently insisted. Then she fumbled the iced coffee in her hand and spilled it all over her shirt. Her white t-shirt. *This is fine.*

"How do you spill your iced coffee like that!" Soraya laughed.

"It was literally in your hand!" Ameena added. The trio broke into hysterical laughter. However, it was cut short when Soraya noticed someone from the corner of her eye.

"Is that Mateen Heydari?" Soraya said, eyes widening.

Marzia looked down at her shirt, then back up at Mateen. He was looking at a pair of jeans and hadn't seen them.

"Is this some kind of sick joke?" Marzia asked. "Let's slowly walk away and not draw attention to ourselves."

The three frantically tried to leave and almost made it to the exit when an alarm went off. At first, Marzia thought it was in her head, but then when everyone else turned to look at her, she knew it was real. And then it clicked. Her eyes darted to her hand, which was not empty but held the floral top she had been admiring earlier. In a fit of panic, she forgot she was holding it, and now it looked to everyone in the store like she was trying to make off with it. To make matters worse, she made excruciating eye contact with Mateen, who raised an eyebrow as if to silently ask what's going on. She shot back a pleading look as if to say, 'This isn't what it looks like.'

And it should be noted, dear reader, that at that moment, Marzia wished she could melt into the cold tiled floor.

"Ma'am, you need to pay for that," the security guard who had mysteriously manifested himself said sternly.

"I swear I wasn't stealing, I spilled coffee, and then I had to leave because I was trying to avoid someone and didn't even realize—"

"Sir, this is my...cousin, and she's a little on the slow side if you get what I mean," a voice behind her said. When Marzia spun around to see who it was, she found herself face to face with none other than Elias Hakimzada.

"We take shoplifting very seriously," the security guard said, with the store manager close in tow.

"Look, how about I take care of it, and we overlook this...misunderstanding," Elias said, handing the manager some cash.

"Next time, I hope your cousin is a little wiser," the security guard muttered.

Marzia, Elias, Soraya, and Ameena quickly exited the store without another word.

"But wait, I have to explain to Mateen that I wasn't—" Marzia protested.

"You're lucky they let us go. You can explain later!" Ameena said, dragging her away.

"What the hell was that?" Marzia said arms crossed, glaring at Elias.

"I believe the words you're looking for are 'thank you,'" Elias said smugly.

"I'll take care of it!" Marzia said mockingly.

"I'm sorry, maybe I'll go back and tell them that I made a mistake," Elias replied.

"No!" Marzia said quickly. "Wait, what were you doing here anyway?"

"I was meeting with my good friend Mateen," Elias said.

"Since when were you two all buddy-buddy?" Marzia placed her hands on her hips.

"It's almost like you give a damn," Elias replied.

"About him. He should know who he's dealing with."

"Now that's no way to talk to the guy who just saved your ass," he taunted.

"You know I wasn't stealing!" Marzia protested.

"Do I, though?" Elias replied.

"Whatever, see you at home, I guess!" Marzia relented.

Only slightly over the feeling of complete and utter humiliation, Marzia, Soraya and Ameena stopped by the ice cream stand and took inventory of Marzia's sheer unluckiness.

"That's it. I can never show my face at that mall ever again," Marzia lamented, shaking her head. "Or anywhere else for that matter."

"Maybe he didn't actually see you, and he was just looking at something behind you?" Soraya offered helpfully.

"He probably won't remember a week from now even if he did!" Ameena chimed in.

"Thanks, guys. But I think whatever sliver of a chance I had with Mateen Heydari has officially been ruined," Marzia said, taking a spoonful of cotton candy ice cream.

Despite the fluorescent lighting in the ice cream parlour, in Marzia's mind, things looked incredibly bleak. When she got home, she resolved to put the day's events out of her mind and focus her energy on finding her long-lost aunt. But there was only one problem, where would she even start? Was she even alive? All these questions and a myriad of others swirled through her brain, but Marzia decided she would begin her search on Facebook. First, she scrolled through several ancestry groups, but none of the members' names were Afghan. Then she found a group with just under 10,000 Afghans who had left Afghanistan around the year her parents did, so at least it was a start. She wrote a post asking if anyone recognized her aunt's name or had seen her at all after she went missing. After that, all there was left to do was wait.

CHAPTER EIGHT

❧

"If I get married, I want to be very married."

- Audrey Hepburn

Marzia always viewed marriage as something of a mystical beast. She obviously knew people got married, but it always amazed her how people could promise to be with someone for the rest of their lives. Through the good times and the bad, even through situations that they could have never had anticipated. They agreed blindly to take on together whatever life might throw at them, and that terrified her. Could someone truly love you that much? Did such selflessness really exist?

For the next little while, life went on for Marzia. She went to work, attended classes, and spent time with her friends and family. But she never gave up her search for her aunt. A few times, she thought she had found a photo on someone's Facebook that looked eerily similar, but alas, it was only a doppelganger. Despite all that, she was still constantly looking for her next lead. She wasn't exactly sure where this search would take her, but she felt it deep inside her that she had to see this through to the end, whatever the conclusion.

One particular Saturday morning, she made her way downstairs to have breakfast, typical of any weekend morning. But something felt different that morning. At the time, she couldn't quite put her finger on it, but it was something in the air. She greeted everyone like the respectful girl that she was and went to go get cereal.

"I mean, I know you've gotten comfortable here, but this is a little much, don't you think?" Elias said in his usual chipper cadence.

"Get to the point. It's too early for me to be decoding your riddles," Marzia replied.

"You've got toothpaste stains on your face; I mean, did you even look in a mirror before you came down?"

"I refuse to engage right now. Today is going to be a good day, and I'm not going to let you ruin it with your rudeness," Marzia said.

Though when Elias walked away, she took her phone out and opened up the camera. Lo and behold, he was right. There was toothpaste at the corner of her mouth. Determined to look unbothered, she strategically maneuvered herself to the sink and rinsed it off. There was no way she was going to let him know he got to her. Although it wouldn't hurt to look in the mirror before appearing in public. When she finally sat down at the table with her food, Marzia's father cleared his throat as though he was going to make an announcement.

"Today is actually a very important day," he said. "Your sister has a Khastgaar[14] , and the Hakimzadas have graciously allowed us to host them at their house."

"Wait, who?" Marzia said, unable to mask her curiosity.

"You know his brother, I believe, the Heydari family," He replied. "They'll be coming over this evening, actually."

At that moment, Marzia didn't know whether to scream or laugh at the sheer ridiculousness of it all. I mean, what were the chances that Mateen Heydari's brother would be interested in Nabeela after Marzia made a complete fool of herself in front of him at the mall. What kind of cruel twist of fate was that?

"You'll be able to make it, right, Marzia?" Elias said, feigning concern. "It would be downright criminal for you to miss it." Elias flashed a knowing smirk.

Now I know what you're thinking, 'Oh, I see what he did there!' Do not encourage him. Anyway, so at this point, if you're Afghan or frankly in any immigrant family for that matter, you know what's next. Impending guests means that the remainder of the time before they're

---

[14] Khastgaar: Dari word for a suitor. Often a young man will come over to a young woman's house to formally make their intentions for marriage proposal known, and she has the choice of either accepting or declining the offer.

set to come over is spent cleaning every inch of the house until you can eat off just about every surface.

Marzia was happy to help, of course. She wouldn't want Elias' mom to be burned out by a party someone else threw at her house. As per tradition, Marzia put on the flannel that she wore when it was time for a good old-fashioned deep clean. I'll spare you the unbelievably mundane details of Marzia scrubbing toilets, but just imagine a montage of her cleaning set to Rusted Root's hit song Send Me on My Way.

Marzia was so preoccupied with cleaning, in fact, that for a moment, she almost forgot what this all meant. Mateen Heydari would be coming over. To her house. Well, not exactly her house, but the sentiment was the same, nonetheless. Then it hit her how they would be seeing a lot more of each other if things went well tonight. After she finished cleaning, she raced to her room to clean up. She was unbelievably sweaty after spending the day mopping and vacuuming. She passed Elias on the staircase, and he ever so slightly chuckled to himself. This made Marzia stop dead in her tracks.

"What?" she asked flatly. "What is it?"

"Nothing, it's just...you try way too hard. It's pathetic." Elias laughed.

"You know what, I'm actually in a good mood today, so there is nothing a sad little man like you can say that can ruin it," Marzia replied.

"What, you're going to put on a little eyeliner, and he's going to fall in love with you or something? Is that the plan?" Elias sneered.

"He already knows my personality; I just want to show him I can look put together when I try," Marzia said.

This statement brought particular amusement to Elias. "You think Mateen knows you, Peaches? You actually think he knows you after a few conversations?" he asked.

"He knows me better than you do," she retorted.

"Oh?" he said, raising an eyebrow.

"What's my favourite food?" she asked, only half expecting him to answer.

"Burrito bowl," he responded matter-of-factly.

"Lucky guess. Favourite movie?"

"Two-way tie between the Harry Potter and Lord of The Rings franchises."

Marzia began to get slightly annoyed.

"Favourite colour?"

"Red."

"What am I allergic to?"

"Trick question. You aren't allergic to anything."

"I don't have time to play this game with you!" Marzia declared, storming past him.

"Skip the perfume! You already smell of desperation!" Elias called out after her.

Marzia resolved not to allow Elias to ruin her good mood. This was supposed to be a happy day. Her sister would probably get engaged, and if she got to see Mateen... Well, that would be a bonus. And where did Elias come off acting like he knew her or something? For all she knew, he had read her diary. She needed to do something to regain her centred calm again.

Marzia pulled out her prayer mat, raised her hands above her ears as though to swat the world away, and then began to pray. In times of stress and sadness, this simple thing grounded her and put things into perspective. It reminded her of what was truly important in life. For those few minutes, five times a day, she put the world behind her and prayed to the One who created her. She instantly felt more at peace. Now time for makeup. She decided to go for a soft, glam look. She didn't want to outshine her sister. Not that she thought she could, she always thought of herself as the plainer sister.

But nonetheless, after a base of concealer, powder, and mascara, she decided on some bronze eyeshadow, pencil eyeliner and topped it off with a muted taupe lip tint. And Voila, the look was complete. She then sauntered down the stairs to find that everyone was already there, including Mateen.

Okay, Marzia. Stay cool, calm, and collected, she told herself.

Mateen looked dashing and put together... And not in the trying too hard type of way, but in the effortless "I guess I'm gorgeous" kind of way. His hair swept across his face and the lavender dress shirt he was wearing brought out the green in his eyes. She could see the warmth in them, a stark contrast to Elias'. His were dark, almond-shaped, and almost always crinkled into a permanent scowl. And that was why she liked Mateen. He waved to her with a smile when she walked into the living room. After greeting Mateen's parents and brother, she sat down next to her mother. Most of the evening was a blur. The men discussed politics, and the women exchanged stories from back home. Marzia was staring off into space when her mother gently nudged her and brought her back to reality.

"Can you help me bring the tea?" her mother asked her.

Marzia nodded and made her way to the kitchen. She made sure to wait until the water was absolutely scalding. Anything less, and they might as well be drinking dishwater, as Marzia's mother loved to say. The entire kitchen was in disarray. Bowls, spoons, and various utensils littered the countertops. It was a perfect embodiment of her thoughts.

"Hey, can I use the washroom?" Mateen said, popping his head in the kitchen.

Marzia was startled by the sudden appearance of such a specimen. She missed the cup she was pouring into, and hot tea cascaded down her leg and onto her foot. She let out a muffled cry but was sure everyone in the house had heard her. To make things even more chaotic, she almost tripped over a furry mound, but with the grace of a gazelle she collected herself again.

"Asmaan beenak[15]!" her mother said, shaking her head. "Are you hurt?"

"I'm okay, no big deal! Just a little raw," Marzia muttered, trying not to draw any more attention to herself in this already mortifying situation.

"Oh dear, Elias, don't just stand there lurking. Can you get us some ice?" Elias' mother asked. Marzia didn't even notice that Elias had come in from the other room in all the commotion. Most likely only to revel in her misfortune, no doubt.

---

[15] Asmaan Beenak: Dari phrase meaning you have your nose to the sky, equivalent to being oblivious or having your head in the clouds.

"I can grab some!" Mateen said, opening up the freezer.

Elias rolled his eyes and disappeared into the dimly lit hallway back into the living room.

Marzia graciously thanked him for the ice and sat down at the kitchen table to tend to her foot. She couldn't help but think how chivalrous Mateen was. *That is how a guy ought to treat a woman,* she told herself. Admittedly, after a while, Marzia was milking the whole "maimed" foot excuse and lingered in the kitchen. She was scrolling through her phone when Elias' brother Bilal caught her eye. He was obviously texting someone while opening up the fridge with one hand.

"What's got you so preoccupied?" she asked him, raising an eyebrow.

Bilal looked like a deer in headlights.

"What are you, my mom?" he asked coldly.

As you can see, dear reader, it's almost as though they are all one big happy family.

As is customary, after meals at an Afghan get-together, fruit and desserts were served. This included Sheer Pira, a treat made with condensed milk that has the consistency of soft chocolate, and Firni, a specialty pudding. As everyone was enjoying the sweets, Marzia heard a ping from her phone, or specifically a vibration from her pocket. I mean, who actually had their sound on? Serial killers, that's who. Just kidding...maybe.

Like I was saying, Marzia got a notification from Facebook. Someone actually reached out to her about her aunt. Could this possibly be a lead? Marzia suddenly felt a rush of endorphins. She had wanted to try her luck online but hadn't thought anyone would reach out. She excused herself into the kitchen to not seem rude by texting on her phone in front of guests. Just as she opened up the message, Mateen came out of the washroom and noticed her standing there.

"Hey, what are you doing here all alone?" he asked inquisitively.

"It's a long story!" she replied with a laugh. "But I think I found my long-lost aunt!"

"Oh my God, that's amazing! What does it say?" he said, eyes widening. He looked like he genuinely cared. "Sorry, that's probably personal. You don't have to share if you don't want to!"

"No, no! I'd love to share it with someone!" she said. "The message says: Hi Marzia, I saw your post on the Facebook page, and I think my mom might be your aunt. Do you mind sending a picture?"

"What are you going to say?" Mateen asked, almost bewildered.

"I don't know! I think I'll ask her where in Afghanistan her mom is from!" Marzia replied, furiously typing away at her phone, clicking send with the fury of a thousand tween girls who just found out One Direction just broke up.

"Oh." Marzia's face fell. "She's said she's from Kabul. My mother's family is from Mazaar. It's not them."

Mateen had a look of sadness in his eyes that showed the deep empathy he felt at that moment. He knew what this meant to her, and it hurt him to know there was nothing he could do to help.

"I'm sorry," he replied. "But you've only just begun your search. There's still time. Don't lose hope, okay?"

"You're right. I'm not throwing in the towel just yet," she said with a weak smile.

After everyone said their goodbyes (which for Afghans lasted at least an hour), Marzia felt happy and relieved. Her social battery was just about out of commission. The best part of her day was going to the washroom and taking her makeup off. There was something satisfying about seeing the black mascara running down the drain revealing her somewhat sparse eyelashes. She walked out of the washroom and ran into her sister.

"Looks like you'll be seeing a lot more of Mateen!" she said with a wink, nudging her arm.

"You're getting engaged?!" Marzia said, engulfing her sister in a big bear hug. She was too happy for her sister to feign bashfulness over her comment about Mateen. Her sister walked off, and Marzia was left with a melancholic feeling in her gut, wondering when it would be her turn. But she waved this momentary pang of sadness away. She resolved to only focus on the good tonight. Just then, she heard the muffled voices of her parents coming from downstairs.

"Most of it is gone," her father said solemnly.

"And the insurance isn't any help," her mother added.

Marzia realized they were talking about something she had compartmentalized and pushed aside since it happened. She found herself listening at the top of the staircase like a little child. Then all of a sudden, she felt a shadow behind her.

"You're so creepy!" she said, making eye contact with Elias standing behind her.

"Says the girl eavesdropping!" he retorted.

She realized she had already taken her makeup off and suddenly felt perplexingly self-conscious.

"Why are you eavesdropping anyways?" Elias questioned. He then caught some of the conversation going on downstairs and realized the context."Well, hopefully, if your sister marries Mateen's brother, they'll take all of you with them."

"Believe me, there is nothing I want more than to no longer be under the same roof as you," Marzia said.

"How long are you guys planning on staying anyways? Can't you guys go to a hotel or something?" Elias jeered.

Marzia always knew Elias was unhappy with the current living arrangements, and she wasn't thrilled either. But his particularly harsh tone took her by surprise. Then suddenly, a thought occurred to her.

"Oh my God," she said. "You're jealous of Mateen."

"Oh, please," he said dismissively. "You're delusional!"

"No, I think I'm exactly right. You're jealous of him because he's everything you're not. He's kind, polite, and you're just bitter."

"That's not wh-" Elias began before giving up and storming off in an exasperated huff.

CHAPTER NINE

～

"Enjoy the little things, for one day you may look back and realize they were the big things."

- *Robert Brault*

All year long, there is something that Marzia looks forward to. She marks down the days, puts reminders on her calendar, she even plans her outfit months in advance. You may think, dear reader, that it might be her birthday, but you would be mistaken. No, the event she looks forward to is her town's annual fall fair. The entire thing is something out of a movie. She loves the leaves, the warm buttered popcorn, the crisp autumn air, and of course, the pumpkin pies.

Like every other year, she was going with Ameena and Soraya. She began the day by settling on what to wear. She decided on a mustard cardigan with dark blue jeans and a red scarf.

"What a beautiful day!" Marzia said melodiously as she waltzed into the kitchen for breakfast, where everyone else was already seated at the table.

"Do you have your wallet and anything you need for the fair?" her mother asked.

"Yep!"

"Do you have money?" her father asked.

"Yes, I have money." Marzia laughed.

"Bring me back a stuffed animal!" Nabeela said.

"And candy corn for me!" her brother Ameer added.

Marzia noticed Elias' insufferable silence as he continued eating his omelette. But today wasn't about him. Today was Fair Day. Nothing could get her down today.

She got in the car and turned up the radio, tuning to the station that played nonstop stand-up comedy. When she got to the fairgrounds, she saw her cousins already waiting. They exchanged the usual pleasantries and then made their way inside. It was more magical than she ever imagined. She took in all the sights and smells. She saw all the rides she wanted them to go on and couldn't decide what to do first. The smell of fresh corn danced into her nostrils like a symphony of smells. They decided to first go through the maze. Ameena and Marzia noticed Soraya texting on her phone. And since they were beside her, they wondered who it could be.

"Who are you talking to?" Marzia asked inquisitively.

"Okay, it's a long story…" Soraya said hesitantly. "But all I know is that he is Afghan, and he's on Reddit."

"WHAT!?" Marzia and Ameena blurted out in unison.

"Okay, you have to tell us everything!" Marzia said.

"There's really nothing else to say!" Soraya shrugged. "We mostly talk in the chatroom, but he's really nice and super funny…"

"And you have no idea who he is?" Ameena asked.

"Well, not exactly…"

For a moment, the trio forgot that they were in the middle of a maze and were suddenly hit with a dead end.

"Back that way!" Marzia pointed. "So, are you going to meet him?"

"Well, not unless it's in public. I'm not stupid. Maybe a Starbucks," Soraya said. "But we haven't even gotten there, so don't get too excited, guys!"

"I can't believe this one's been holding out on us!" Marzia said, nudging Ameena.

"And I thought we were family," Ameena said, dramatically shaking her head.

Eventually, the trio made it to the end of the maze without even breaking a sweat.

"That wasn't even hard!" Soraya sulked.

"Maybe because it's meant for kids." Marzia laughed.

After the maze, the girls decided on the Ferris wheel. While in line, Soraya noticed a familiar figure in the distance.

"Oh. My. God. Do not look, but you will never believe who is here!" Soraya said through gritted teeth. And as if on cue, both Ameena and Marzia spun their heads around.

"I said don't look!" Soraya cooed.

Just to their left, Mateen had a handful of cotton candy and was wandering rather aimlessly.

"Oh no, we have to hide, quick!" Marzia said, with a sense of urgency in her voice.

"I thought you guys were cool?" Ameena asked quizzically.

"I am not mentally prepared for this type of interaction right now!" Marzia said, throwing her hands up in exasperation. And with impeccable timing, it was their turn next on the Ferris wheel.

"And not a moment too soon!" Marzia said, relieved.

Just then, Marzia spotted someone trying to flag her down. Was it Mateen? A Bird? A plane? No. It was Elias. What on God's green earth could he possibly want? Whatever it was, it could wait. The three of them climbed into their seat, and the Ferris Wheel started to move again.

"Why aren't you just honest about your feelings for him?" Soraya asked as they reached the top of the Ferris Wheel.

"Huh? Why would I tell E-" Marzia snapped out of her daze.

"Oh, come on, we know you're interested in Mateen!" Soraya playfully shoved her.

"Maybe he'll tell his parents!" Ameena added.

"Okay, look, guys, as much as I'm obsessed with him, I don't think we're going to get married or anything!" Marzia said defensively.

"Woah, woah, woah, what's with the one-eighty?" Soraya asked. "I thought that's what you wanted eventually? You guys tell your parents, and then you get married. Boom. Nothing more to it."

"First off, he's just nice, so I don't even know if he sees me in that way!" Marzia shook her head dismissively.

"You know, if you saw even half of what we see in you, you would have a little more faith in yourself," Ameena said, with a tinge of sadness in her voice.

"To quote Jay-Z and Mr. Hudson, I'm hoping for the best but expecting the worst!" Marzia laughed.

As the girls hopped off the rotating apparatus, Marzia noticed that Elias was still waiting there. What a mood killer.

"I called you," was all he greeted her with. "See, the point of a phone is to pick it up when people try to get a hold of you."

"Sorry, it was in my purse." Marzia shrugged, pulling her phone out, and was greeted with missed call after missed call. "Didn't know you were that obsessed with me."

"Don't flatter yourself, Peaches. I'm not here for you." He sneered. "I need to know if you've seen Bilal."

"No, I haven't. Why, what's wrong?" Marzia asked.

"He didn't come home from school today," Elias said, a look of worry washing over him, his dark eyes ever so slightly glistening. If she hadn't known any better, she would have thought he was about to cry. But Elias Hakimzada did not cry. He didn't feel. And yet...

"Have you tried calling him?" Marzia asked.

"No. I didn't. I just sent a bunch of smoke signals!" Elias spat. "Of course, I've tried calling him!"

"You know what, this isn't my problem," Marzia said. "I came here to have fun, not be berated by you!"

Marzia began to walk away.

"Wait," he said. "Look, I'm sorry, okay. Can you just please help me find him?"

A look of genuine worry flooded his eyes.

"How do you even know he's here?" Marzia asked skeptically.

"It's a long story, but I think he's here somewhere."

Marzia closed her eyes and took a very long exasperated breath.

"Fine," she said. "Hey, Soraya and Ameena, can you grab a picnic table? In the central area, so if he walks by, we can easily spot him."

"Sure!" Ameena said.

"I've been craving some corn on the cob, and that's right by the food trucks!" Soraya said.

"It's on me," Marzia said, handing them a bill. Then she and Elias set out on their search to find Bilal.

"Okay, you're going to have to tell me what's really going on here," Marzia said, finally.

"If I knew I wouldn't be asking for your help, now would I?" he barked back at her.

"Do your parents even know?" Marzia asked.

"No. They're not home. And I prefer to keep it that way, which is why we need to find him."

The next hour was spent searching practically every inch of the Fairground. They checked the house of mirrors, the petting zoo, and even the haunted house. No sign of Bilal anywhere. One person she did spot, however, was Mateen Heydari.

"Let's, uh, check over there!" Marzia pointed in the opposite direction.

"But we just-" Elias began. He followed her eyes and understood the source of her sudden shift in mood.

"What, are you avoiding him now?" he commented.

"No, I just- It's just not a good time for that right now," Marzia said, attempting to sound nonchalant. She couldn't really explain her sudden anxiety around Mateen. Maybe she thought if she never talked to him, she wouldn't have an opportunity to make an absolute fool of herself.

Her thoughts were interrupted by Elias abruptly slathering sunscreen on his arms and face.

"Why are you wearing sunscreen? It's cloudy?" Marzia asked, which took Elias by surprise.

"We'll see who's laughing when you get melanoma," he said, twisting the corners of his mouth into what could be loosely described as a... smile? Before Marzia could think too deeply into it, her phone rang,

"Hello?" she answered. "Okay, we're on our way!"

"What? What is it?" Elias asked, his voice cracking.

"They found him!" Marzia exclaimed. They both breathe a sigh of relief...

"Where the hell was he?" Elias asked.

"His phone died. He forgot to tell you he was going to be here," Marzia replied.

"I can't believe that kid," Elias huffed.

"He's by the food trucks with Soraya and Ameena. We should meet up with them. It's probably going to rain soon."

"Right."

They were making their way through the winding booths and hoards of people when they were suddenly approached by someone doing caricature drawings.

"A souvenir for the lovely couple?" the balding man said, with the slightest hit of a French accent.

"Oh, we're not!-" Marzia said quickly, the vaguest feeling of panic trickling into her chest.

"We don't -" Elias stammered. "She honestly repulses me!" Elias couldn't keep from laughing.

"A simple no would have sufficed," Marzia said as they walked away from the booth.

"It was insulting, really, if I'm honest," Elias said, "To imply I would ever be in a relationship with you, it's just ridiculous."

"Please, don't act as if you're some kind of catch!" Marzia shot back.

"Like you're any different! You're pining over a guy who doesn't even want you! There. I said it. Mateen. Newsflash, Peaches! He. Does. Not. Want. You. He's not going to see you as anything other than an annoying acquaintance, and he sure as hell is not going to marry you!"

"What the hell do you know?" Marzia retorted.

"I know that it's pathetic going after someone who won't even give you the time of day!" Elias sneered.

"You're lying!" Marzia said, half as a response to him and half trying to convince herself. She could feel her face begin to burn. But she willed herself not to cry. She'd be damned if she let Elias Hakimzada see her cry.

"You're totally jealous." She laughed. "You can't stand that people like him more than you. You can't stand that whenever he's around, you're not the centre of attention."

"For me to be jealous, he'd have to have something I want. And he has nothing I could ever want," he said.

"I don't know why the hell you even asked for my help today!" Marzia said, storming off. She'd had just about enough of his belligerent disrespectfulness. She set out to find her cousins, but before that, she turned back and threw the stuffed porcupine that she won at one of the booths squarely at Elias' face.

"What the hell, Marzia?" Elias exclaimed.

She flinched for a second.

"Oh, I'm sorry, I'm just so pathetic I can't even aim right!" she yelled back at him while continuing to walk away. Marzia got back to Ameena and Soraya and found them sitting at a table with Bilal eating corn on the cob.

"Hey, you found us!" Soraya said, with a mouthful of corn.

"Yeah, let's go to the petting zoo. Right now." Marzia said, "Bilal, always a pleasure, but I'm afraid we have to go. Oh, and your brother's coming, so don't go anywhere!"

Marzia motioned to her cousins, and they say their goodbyes before making an abrupt exit.

"Woah, what happened? Is everything okay?" Ameena asks.

"It's- I don't even know where to start. He's just- He's an ass. Let's leave it at that." Marzia said.

"You know it's healthy to talk about your feelings," Soraya said.

"Feelings?" Marzia scoffed. "The only thing I'm feeling right now is contempt."

The three of them made their way to the barn, where the overwhelming smell of farm animals radiated out.

"Like, I don't get it. He doesn't have to be rude all the time. Isn't it exhausting?" Marzia said, grabbing a cup full of food pellets.

"Who, Elias?" Ameena asked.

"Yes, Elias. Have you guys been paying attention to a single word I've been saying?" Marzia asked, exasperated.

"Yes. We have. It's all you talk about. Elias this, Elias that," Soraya snapped. "But yet you keep putting yourself in these situations where you have to be close to him. I'm starting to think you actually like the attention!"

"What? You think I like being insulted by him?" Marzia demanded, aggressively holding out her hand to feed the baby goats. "You know what? I'm not dealing with this right now!"

Marzia dropped the cup of food pellets, which attracted a swarm of baby goats, and walked out of the barn. She didn't know where she was going or what she was going to do, but she knew she had to clear her head before either of them said something that they would swiftly regret. She had what could only be described as tunnel vision. Her eyes blurred as she tried to find somewhere to sit down. Off in the corner, she saw a wooded area away from the fairground, so she made her way deeper and deeper into the thick foliage until she reached an opening. She was greeted by a small pond and a serene stillness, away from the clamorous sounds of the fair. This would do. The sound of her phone going off startled Marzia. She thought it was Ameena and Soraya calling to see where she had gone, but it was only her prayer notification. That's what she should do. That would give her some clarity. She looked around over her shoulder to check if the coast was clear, raised her hands, and began to pray. It was nice praying in nature. Living in a suburb, and frequently commuting to the city, she rarely got to experience this level of tranquility. She already felt calmer.

"It's nice here, isn't it?" she heard a voice from across the pond call out. She squinted to get a better look, and she saw none other than Mateen Heydari. She was slightly taken aback. Okay, that was an understatement. She was shaken to her core. Her words failed her. What was he even doing here?

"Fancy seeing you here!" she replied, in a comically exaggerated southern accent.

"Well, not really. I live here!" he said, gesturing towards a building behind him somewhat hidden by a group of willow trees. Was that always there? It was…huge? A mid-century modern house with large windows in a secluded area where the main character would definitely get murdered during a horror movie.

"I did know you were…" Marzia trailed off.

"Rich? I like to think we're comfortable," Mateen laughed.

"That's exactly what rich people say!" Marzia teased.

"What are you doing out here?" he asked.

"I needed some air!" Marzia responded plainly after a slight hesitation.

"Well, you came to the right place; this is my favourite place to think," Mateen said.

"It's beautiful here. I can't believe this is your backyard!" Marzia said in complete astonishment.

"It's alright." Matten laughed."You get used to it!"

Mateen must have noticed the peculiar look that flashed on Marzia's face.

"I'm kidding! I'm very blessed, Alhamdullilah[16]!" he added with a laugh.

"Oh! Don't worry, I never thought you were a snob!" Marzia said quickly. "I mean not that you act snobby I-"

"It's okay!" Mateen said, reassuring her.

Just as Marzia opened her mouth to speak, her phone rang, sending a jolt of adrenaline up her spine.

"They're waiting for me," Marzia said apologetically, "But it was nice seeing you!"

"Likewise!"

Now, it might have been a trick of the light, or maybe even just plain wishful thinking, but Marzia could have sworn she saw him wink. But alas, duty called, and she knew it was about time to meet up with Soraya and Ameena. For as long as she could remember, they had never been mad at each other for more than a day, and she wasn't about to let that change. Looking at it objectively, Marzia realized she had been a tad childish. Okay, maybe very childish. But what else are cousins for other than to push each other's buttons every once in a while?

---

[16] Alhamdulillah: Arabic phrase meaning 'Praise be to God' used to express gratitude.

Marzia made her way past the foliage and back to the main Fairground, and in the distance, she could see Soraya and Ameena standing there with heads craned, presumably looking for her. When she finally got to them, the three of them stood in silence for a few seconds.

"I'm sorry!" all three said in unison.

"Let's just forget what happened earlier!" Marzia said.

"Never happened!" Ameena agreed.

"Already forgotten!" Soraya said.

The rest of the day turned out to be just as uneventful as the first half was chaotic and tumultuous. Marzia got home at a reasonable hour after saying goodbye to Ameena and Soraya. Although there were a few rough patches today, Marzia actually had a good time. Of course, that in part had to do with her impromptu conversation with Mateen. Her heart was practically beating out of her chest, but she was proud of herself for keeping her cool. If she hadn't known any better, she would have thought herself to be downright indifferent.

Mateen Heydari was everything a guy ought to be. I mean, she practically trespassed onto his yard (though through no fault of her own), and he was nothing but kind and courteous. He didn't insult or ridicule her, and he didn't make her feel self-conscious.

But Marzia was still seething over Elias' offensiveness. Just when she thought she saw some genuine emotion from him, she was reminded that he was nothing more than the disrespectful nuisance she knew him to be. Marzia trudged up the intricate staircase of the Hakimzada residence after a long day. Turning the corner of the upstairs hallway, she all but collided with Elias, who was just getting out of the washroom.

He opened his lips to say something, but no words came out. For a moment, Marzia stood in bewildered amusement, wondering what obscenity he would spout next. But he didn't. He pushed past her and disappeared into his man cave. Marzia didn't know what she expected him to say, but she was somehow disappointed. She had more important things to worry about, though. So, she refused to exert any more energy thinking about someone as insignificant as Elias Hakimzada.

CHAPTER TEN

◞

"There is nothing permanent except change."

- Heraclitus

For as long as Marzia could remember, she had hated parties. She couldn't tell if it was because of her social anxiety or the façade of social niceties that went along with them. That was just the way she was, for better or for worse. Her earliest memory was of a wedding, but the particulars of who or when were lost to her. However, what she did remember was falling asleep under one of the tables, the long satin tablecloths shading her like a cocoon, the bass of the music pulsing through her body, slowly lulling her to sleep. When she finally awoke from her slumber, she saw that the sun was coming up. They had quite literally partied the entire night away while she slept.

But today wasn't like the other parties. Today she couldn't get out of it even if she wanted to. Today was her sister's engagement party. Marzia woke up at the crack of dawn, and by the crack of dawn, I mean 9 o'clock in the morning. She was not a morning person, as you have probably gathered, dear reader.

So, Marzia made her way downstairs to the only thing that made her feel alive in the morning, caffeine. The rich smell of Arabica beans danced into her nostrils as she descended the staircase. Although Marzia was exhausted, she did not forget her manners. She greeted everyone with a pleasant hello. She would never dream of being rude, even when sleep deprived. She made brief eye contact with Elias, but she kept her expression neutral as she moved towards the steaming pot of java. She poured herself a cup and then opened the fridge to grab the bag of milk. She poured the milk into the dark roast coffee and watched as it slowly brightens in colour. It reminded her of how the sky changes after a particularly severe thunderstorm.

"Do you want some coffee with that milk?" Elias muttered.

"Do you want some personality with that snark?" Marzia fired back. "I happen to like my coffee this way, thank you very much. And I know you like to criticize literally everything I do, but can you please ease up just for today?"

"Is this you begging?" Elias taunted, low enough that he was out of earshot of everyone else.

"This is me appealing to the decent human being that I know is deep down there somewhere to not make this day any more stressful than it has to be." Marzia sighed.

"You know what? For you, Peaches, I'll be a ball of sunshine and sprinkles today!" Elias said.

"Really?" Marzia asked in skeptical optimism.

"Of course not!" Elias sneered, laughing uncontrollably. "What am I, the Dalai Llama?"

"I expected nothing less from you." Marzia rolled her eyes. She already had enough on her plate without having to worry about Elias being a loose cannon. But he wouldn't be low enough to ruin Nabeela's engagement party just to spite her, would he? She hoped not. In any case, she had party favours to assemble. Hundreds of decorative paper boxes that she had to stuff with various sweets were calling her name. Thankfully, she was almost done, but she just had a few more to put the finishing touches on before they were finally perfect. She was curling the bow on the final box when a peculiar sensation began to develop in the pit of her stomach. She couldn't tell if it was the tacos she ate last night or just nerves. Nonetheless, she decided to brush the feeling off. Just then, the familiar buzz of her phone alerted her to a message, and her heart fluttered when she read the name.

Mateen: How's everything going over there? Everyone ready for tonight? :)

Marzia cautiously considered how to respond.

Marzia: Great! Everyone is getting ready! :)

Mateen: Can't wait to see you guys!

Marzia: Me either!

Did Mateen say he can't wait to see her? I mean, he said 'you guys', but that includes her too, right? To stop herself from ruminating over their brief conversation, Marzia decided to start with her makeup in the washroom. But something was still making her feel uneasy, and it was killing her to not know the source of her discomfort. She unzipped her makeup bag and stared into the washroom mirror. She applied her foundation and solidified it with a dusting of pressed powder.

"You know you're going to get wrinkles if you keep frowning like that," Elias said, leaning on the doorframe, appearing out of thin air.

"I told you, Elias, not today," Marzia said. "I promise, any other day, you can say whatever the hell you want to me, but today, I can't deal with your crap!"

"What are you even stressing yourself out over? Everything is done already," Elias pointed out.

As Marzia went to apply her mascara she smeared it onto her cheek. That was the proverbial straw that broke the camel's back. Marzia threw the mascara onto the washroom floor with an irritated scream. It must have been pretty loud because a look of genuine concern flashed across Elias' face.

"Look what you made me do, you're like a fly buzzing around my ear that I can never get a single moment of peace from!" Marzia said, raising her voice.

"It's just mascara, chill!"

"It's...it's not just mascara, it's everything!" Marzia blurted out. "Everything is changing!"

Elias' expression softened ever so slightly. "Look, I know your sister getting engaged must be tough on you. I know you guys are close."

"I never said that-"

"It doesn't take a genius to know that you hate change."

"Don't act like you know me!" Marzia spat, almost on the verge of tears. She swore she would never cry in front of him. "You're not even my friend, you're nothing you're- you're less than nothing!"

"Because I'm a sad, angry, pathetic little man who's going to die alone, right?" Elias said an octave quieter. "Look, I know you're going through something right now, or whatever, so I'm going to walk away before you say something you'll regret and overthink for the next month and a half."

"Elias, wait." Marzia sighed. "I'm...sorry, okay? I say a lot of things."

"Hey, I'd be a hypocrite if I couldn't take as much as I give." Elias shrugged, handing her the rogue mascara from the ground.

"I don't even know what to wear," Marzia said, mostly to herself. This, admittedly, was one of Marzia's faults. She was a chronic procrastinator. She assumed she would figure out what to do later, but she found herself with a closet full of clothes but not a single dress she wanted to wear when later finally arrived.

"Let me see what you have." Elias sighed.

"What makes you think I'd take fashion advice from you?" Marzia scoffed.

"In case you haven't noticed, Peaches, I'm a guy. And don't pretend you aren't flustered over what to wear because you know Mateen is going to be there."

Without even bothering to protest his completely true statement as she returned with an array of dresses of various colours and fabrics.

"I was thinking this one," she said, gingerly picking up a teal chiffon dress, which had an ombre bodice.

Elias unconsciously scrunched up his nose.

"Fine. What would you have me wear then?" Marzia threw her arms up in exasperation.

Elias examined the different dresses until he pulled out a taupe-coloured mermaid-style gown.

"This?" Marzia said, puzzled. "Why?"

"It matches your olive undertone," Elias said nonchalantly.

Marzia peered at him quizzically.

"I had meningitis one winter, so I watched a lot of Project Runway with my mom, okay? So I know a thing or two," he replied defensively,"And you look...beautiful. It suits you,"

Marzia pauses for a moment, questioning whether she heard correctly. She struggled to find the right response. She began feeling uncomfortable, like the walls were about to close in. Just then, she heard her phone ring, catching her off guard. It was her cousin, Soraya. Elias took this opportunity to make himself scarce.

"Hey? Yep! 237 Blue Spruce Lane, that's the address of the venue! Okay, see you there, bye!" Marzia said into her phone.

After momentarily being distracted by YouTube videos and the mobile game she had been obsessed with as of late, Marzia began to apply a soft brown eyeshadow on the back of her lids. Soon she felt a presence behind her, and she turned around to see Elias standing there once again. Without a word, he just held up two different ties. One was a forest green, while the other was mocha.

"That one." Marzia pointed at the mocha-coloured tie with her makeup brush.

Elias raised an eyebrow inquisitively.

"Just trust me, okay?" Marzia sighed.

After everyone was primped and preened, they all piled into their vehicles and made their way to the venue. It was an exquisite locale; it had pillars, French doors, the works. But as soon as they arrived, Marzia knew something was amiss. She noticed several people with name tags and business suits walk past her into the venue. She was slightly confused but didn't think much of it. It was only when they got into the main hall where they were having their event when they realized they had walked into some business conference.

All at once, an uncomfortable number of eyes turned to look at them. Some looked confused, while others seemed vaguely amused. However, they all looked at them, wondering why they were so overdressed. At first, Marzia thought they were in the wrong hall, but she double-checked and tripled-checked the reservation, confirming they were in the right place. She knew what she had to do. She went to the banquet hall's office area with nothing but her bedazzled purse and an iced coffee in her hand.

"What are you going to do?" Mateen said, trailing behind. He and his parents had met them in the parking lot, both parties fashionably late, of course.

"I'm going to figure out why a Wolf of Wall Street convention is going on in what's supposed to be our engagement hall!" Marzia said, looking determined.

"Hi there, I think there's been a mistake, and I really need to talk to like a manager or someone, anyone really, who can help me out here. My sister's engagement party is today, and we're supposed to have that hall over there but there's a whole business conference going on in it!" Marzia long-windedly said to the receptionist sitting at the front desk.

"Last name, please," the receptionist said in a bored monotone.

"Rashidi."

Marzia held her breath as the receptionist tapped loudly onto her PC that must have been from around 1998.

"Nothing here," the receptionist replied.

"Nothing here?" Marzia repeated, bewildered.

"Nothing came up," she shrugged.

"I mean, we have the email confirmation right here. Today is my sister's engagement," Marzia reasoned, flashing her phone screen with the correspondence pulled up.

"Sorry, there must have been a mix-up. We're all booked up."

"Yes, by us!" Marzia replied, getting progressively more agitated by the minute.

"There's nothing in the system, so there's nothing more I can do; you'll have to talk to someone else to get a refund."

"So you're telling me that on the day of my sister's engagement party, that even though I just showed you a booking confirmation that we paid for, there's nothing more you can do?" Marzia demanded.

The lady just shrugged.

"What's your name?" Marzia asked.

"Stefania," she answered.

"Stefania," she repeated. "You seem like a really nice girl, and I know that you don't want to be the reason my sister is devastated on the day of her engagement party. So, I'm just going to ask who I have to speak to in order to get this unfortunate mistake on your end all sorted out."

To both Marzia and Mateen's surprise, she picked up the phone on her desk and punched some numbers into it.

"James, you better get down here. I have something that's going to need your full attention," she said into the receiver.

Marzia beamed a triumphant smile. She could be quite persuasive given the right circumstances. She got a discount on the hall for their troubles, and they were moved into the bigger room within the venue. But they weren't in the clear just yet. They still had to get everything set up in the new space. So, you can imagine the chaos of more than ten people hanging up decorations and laying out tablecloths like their lives depended on it.

When all was said and done and the party began, everyone breathed a sigh of relief. Marzia's sister was still getting ready, so she had no idea about the absolute madness that preceded her entrance into the hall. Marzia loved her sister, so she was happy to have done it.

Once everyone began to trickle in, Marzia felt her social anxiety bubbling up. She made her way to the coffee station and poured herself another cup, although that would probably only make it worse.

"Isn't that your third cup today?" Elias said with an accusatory tone.

"And what about it?" Marzia snapped, whipping her head around to face him.

"Hey, is everything okay?" Mateen asked, walking up with his own empty cup.

"Prince freaking charming always here to save the day," Elias mumbled, disappearing into the crowd of people standing by the Hor D'Oeuvres.

"What's up with him?" Mateen asked, confused.

"Nothing, he's just moody," Marzia said dismissively.

There were a few moments of silence that, to Marzia, felt like an eternity.

Say something, say anything. Say something witty.

"Finally made it all happen, eh?" Mateen finally said, easing the tension.

"Yeah, thank God it's almost over, right?" Marzia laughed.

Mateen gave her a confused look but smiled politely. Marzia realized that was probably was one of those thoughts she should have kept to herself. She always managed to say something awkward and embarrassing. Why couldn't she ever think of something clever to say when he was around?

When it was time to eat, Marzia and her family were amongst the last ones to grab a plate. After she finally got her food, she found a seat next to Soraya and Ameena at her cousins' table. She felt her mouth water just thinking about the food. She practically inhaled the first few bites, then heard a voice buzzing by her ear like an annoying fly.

"Mateen's mom is looking at you," she heard a voice from behind her say. Elias was sitting with his own cousins in the seat directly behind hers. He barely even turned his head as he made the comment.

"What? No. Stop lying. You're being mean, Elias," Marzia said, barely above a whisper, her back still facing him.

"I'm not lying. See for yourself," Elias said, with a gesture of his chin. Marzia followed his eyes. It really did look like his mom was looking at her, but what for? Was she talking about her? Was she just looking at something behind her?

"I said look, not turn your whole body!" he grumbled.

"What do you mean? I was being discreet!" Marzia challenged.

"If by discreet you mean completely obvious, then yeah," Elias fired back.

"Well, look at the bright side. If I get married, then I'll be out of your hair for good," Marzia said.

"Please, like Mateen would be able to last living with *you.*" He sneered.

"Well, I'm kind, considerate, I'd say he'd last a while."

Elias tried to stifle a laugh. "You snore, you forget to screw the cap back on the toothpaste, and you sing in the damn shower. And by the way, Broadway's not giving you a call anytime soon, Peaches!" Elias said.

"I do *not* snore. That was one ti- okay maybe twice, and my voice is decent okay?" Marzia rebutted. "And while we're at it, you always leave the empty milk jugs in the fridge, you never say please or thank you, and by the way, being mean isn't a personality trait!"

Marzia turned to Soraya and Ameena.

"I'm getting dessert!" she grumbled. Her cousins followed in tow.

Soraya was texting away on her glossy white iPhone.

"Is that mystery man? Do you think it could be someone here?" Marzia asked.

"Maybe he's that guy right there!" Ameena pointed to a handsome young man scrolling through his phone.

"Okay, I've been meaning to say this, but I think I know who it is..." Soraya trailed off.

"And?" Marzia prodded.

"I think it's... Elias," Soraya blurted out.

"What?" Marzia laughed.

"What do you mean 'what'?" Soraya asked.

"I just mean...it's a little unrealistic, no?" Marzia replied.

"What, you don't think he could like me?" Soraya said, folding her arms.

"I don't think that's what she meant I-" Ameena began, trying to ease the tension.

"Well, what makes you think it's him? What I think is that he's not even in the same league as you," Marzia suggested with curiosity.

"What I know is that my mystery guy lives in this area, he has one brother, and he's Afghan, and he said both his parents' first initial of their names. It all matches up! It's like he wants me to know it's him." Soraya said thoughtfully. "Look. I just got a text right now!"

Marzia shifted her gaze to where Elias was standing at the other end of the room, introspectively looking at his phone. Logically, there was a possibility that it could be him. But the more Marzia thought about it, the more she felt a burning in the pit of her stomach. If it really was him, then she would have no choice but to support her cousin. But how could Soraya like him after everything he had put her through? The insults, the bad attitude. The list was virtually endless. It just didn't sit right with her. If it was him, she couldn't let her beloved cousin give her heart to a callous jerk.

"Maybe you should just ask him?" Ameena suggested.

"I can't do that; it would be way too awkward! And I am not emotionally stable enough for a rejection right now!" Soraya said, shaking her head.

"Then I'll do it," Marzia volunteered. "I won't make it obvious or anything, but I *think* I can get it out of him. That is if it turns out it's him."

"Okay, let's all go over together. Casually." Ameena suggested.

"No, no! Don't you dare! Let's just…not do that." Soraya pleaded.

The rest of the party went by without a single hitch. The food was great, Marzia was a dutiful sister of the bride-to-be, and she managed to not spill a single drop on her dress (which for someone as clumsy as Marzia was a miracle).

But something kept bothering her even on the ride home. Did Soraya actually have genuine feelings for Elias? They'd always shared everything about fleeting crushes, but what if this was something more? What if he really was her mystery guy? Could it be possible there was a side of him she didn't know? Marzia was too tired to think more about this at that moment. She decided to ruminate about that particular issue at a later date. Marzia changed into comfortable clothing and went to the washroom to brush her teeth and wipe off her makeup. She opened the door and serendipitously found Elias closing his with a towel over his shoulder. He wordlessly pushed past her to the now unoccupied washroom.

"What do you think of my cousin Soraya?" Marzia asked abruptly.

Elias stopped.

"Why?" he asked cautiously.

"No reason. I- it was just a question," Marzia said, hesitant.

"I think she's cute," he said finally.

"What!?" Marzia blurted out."Do you like her? Like…*like* her?"

"No one has asked me that since grade three. What are we eight?" Elias laughed.

"Forget it." Marzia shook her head, turning to leave.

"Wait, do you really want to know?" Elias asked, raising an eyebrow.

"…Sure?" she replied with vague amusement.

"She's a nice girl, but she's not my type," he answered honestly.

She expected sarcasm but was taken aback by his refreshing candor.

"Oh." She nodded.

"Did you think I liked her? Wait, were you jealous? You were jealous, weren't you? This is rich I-" he began, with a look of intrigue and amusement.

"In your dreams. And maybe not even then." Marzia sighed.

"Don't worry, you're way more fun to piss off," he said.

And it might have been a trick of the light, but Marzia could have sworn she saw him wink.

CHAPTER ELEVEN

⌒

"Oh, Spring! I want to go out and feel you and get inspiration. My old things seem dead. I want fresh contacts, more vital searching."

-Emily Carr

After the fun and festivities were over, Marzia slipped back into the monotony of everyday life, and one of those things was her part-time job. It was a cold and rainy day, making it all the more difficult to get up that morning. Marzia wished she was one of those people who got up every day and had breakfast and then worked on some assignments before heading out to start the day. But that is not who she is, which was why she found herself rushing to stuff her legs into a pair of black jeans before putting on the rest of her uniform. She was just tripping down the stairs with 15 minutes left until she was meant to start her shift.

On her way out the door, her mother handed her a cream cheese bagel and her cup of iced coffee that she normally has without fail every single morning. And today, she was going to need it. It was a school holiday for elementary kids, which means their parents would bring them to Marzia's workplace. While most weekdays were, for the most part, quite uneventful, school holidays were like Black Friday for retail workers. So Marzia was mentally bracing herself for a hellish day. She strolled into work at 9:25, with five minutes to spare before her shift started.

"Hey, Timmy!" Marzia waved at her manager.

"Ready for today?" he asked.

"Ready as I'll ever be!" she replied. She took a large sip of her coffee and headed out onto the floor. As soon as they opened, kids and parents began flooding in like embarrassing memories when you're trying to fall asleep. As the day dragged on, Marzia began talking to her co-workers, which was a good way to pass the time. She strolled over to the photo booth where Karissa and Davis were huddled.

"Me and Davis have a bet going on," Karissa explained. "Those two kids are going at it, and I think the one in the yellow shirt is going to win."

"But my vote goes to the one in the overalls, look at that arm!" Davis said confidently.

"Should we be doing something about that?" Marzia asked. Seconds later, the three of them burst out laughing at the absurdity of the comment. They didn't get paid enough for that. Marzia eyed the two children, sizing them both up.

"Yellow shirt. One hundred percent," Marzia said. "Sorry, Davis!"

Davis gave her an exaggerated look of betrayal.

"You know I thought we were friends, I really-"

"Oh my God, that lady just punched that other lady!" Karissa said in disbelief. Marzia turned her head around just in time to see one lady push another into the ball pit.

"Holy crap! I'll get Timmy!" Marzia said, rushing to the staff room. They *really* didn't get paid enough for this.

"Timmy, there's a situation, and we really need you on the floor. Two moms are punching each other, and I-" Marzia exclaimed, running into the office. She saw several fresh-faced individuals holding newly laminated ID cards and realized she had just walked in on a new hire orientation session.

"I'll be right back, everyone, just a moment!" Timmy said, walking towards the door.

"I'm Marzia, by the way!" Marzia said awkwardly, popping her head in one more time. "Things usually aren't this crazy!"

Once Marzia got back onto the floor, she realized security was already there, taking statements from both women. She'd like to say that this was a one-off and that things were usually pretty quiet there. And for the most part, they were. Except when they weren't. Later during her lunch break, Marzia took great pleasure in re-enacting the altercation for her co-workers.

"And then she went flying backwards into the ball pit!" Marzia said, dramatically pretending to fall over.

"I couldn't believe what I was seeing. One minute everything was fine, and then all hell breaks loose!" Karissa said, shaking her head.

After all the excitement, it came time for Marzia to punch out and head home, but not before taking one of the shortbread cookies that someone had brought for everyone and left in the backroom. She then slowly made her way to her car with all her belongings. Like the superb driver she was, she looked in the mirror before backing out, but all of a sudden, she heard a bump, and her car rumbled.

That was not a good sign. She whipped her head around and saw that she had backed right into a car driving through the parking lot. How had she missed that? Her fight or flight instincts instantly kicked in. It would be stupid to run. Or would it? The people around her began to gawk. Even the seagulls seemed to be giving her the side eye. She immediately called the home phone. No answer. She called both her siblings and her father on their cellphones. Voicemail. She remembered one person she hadn't tried yet. No. Anyone but him.

"Hello?" Elias said, sounding confused to be getting a call from Marzia.

"Yeah, um…so I have good news and bad news," Marzia said.

"Good news first," Elias said.

Interesting choice.

"Okay, so the good news doesn't really make sense without the bad news. The bad news is that I kind of got into a car accident, but I-"

"You got into a damn accident?!" Elias said, the concern in his voice surprising Marzia. "Where are you?"

"I'm at work, but I'm okay, and I'm pretty sure the car is okay. I just wasn't sure what to-"

"Listen to me, okay? Don't say anything, don't apologize, don't say it was your fault. I'm on my way." Elias said, hanging up the phone.

About 15 minutes later, Elias pulled into the parking lot in a red Honda Civic. He circled Marzia's car, surveying the damage. Thankfully, it was only a few scratches.

"What were you doing? Were you even paying attention? You're lucky this wasn't worse!" he said.

"I did it all on purpose!" Marzia declared acidly. "Of course, I was paying attention! It all happened really fast. If I knew there was a car there, I obviously wouldn't have driven into it," Marzia said through gritted teeth.

"You're lucky it wasn't more than a few scratches," he said.

"Whatever, can you just talk to the other guy, please?" Marzia asked.

After a few minutes, the driver of the other car approached them.

"Is this your boyfriend?" The guy in the other car asked, sounding somewhat amused. "We can just forget about it if you give me your number."

"Excuse me?" Marzia asked in disbelief.

"Give me your number, and we'll call it even," he said more persistently.

"How about you say that to me. I'm actually her husband," Elias said, taking a step forward to stand in between Marzia and the strange man.

"Look at Mr. Tough guy!" the man jeered.

"I'm telling you to let it go," Elias said, barely above a whisper but somehow all the more menacing.

"And what if I don't want to?" the man questioned, taking another step closer to Elias.

"Elias, look at me! Let's just give him our insurance information and go," Marzia pleaded.

"Listen to your little wifey here, Elias," the man mocked. "Whatever, you're not worth the trouble." The strange man took one last look at his car, then got in the vehicle and drove off.

"Creep," Marzia said. "The only reason he probably gave up was that you told him we were married. Pathetic. Let's just go home."

Home. That word flowed so easily from her lips. Where was her home?

"Is your car good to drive?" Elias asked.

"I'll be fine," Marzia assured him. Elias gave her a look that said he didn't believe her, but he relented and got into his car.

Even once Marzia got home and finally began to process how shaken up she was, she couldn't shake the feeling she had. She had felt scared and helpless, and that absolutely terrified her. She hated feeling so vulnerable and completely powerless. But Marzia refused to dwell in that dark place any longer. It was over and done with, and Alhamdulillah, she was safe. And yet she was frozen on the couch, paralyzed in thought, with the TV aimlessly playing in the background. That was what she did best.

Marzia thought, and then thought some more, and just a smidge more for good measure. About what, you might ask, dear reader? What happened, what could have happened, worst-case scenarios, and every question in between. She was your typical type 1 Neurotic.

"Do you want to come wedding dress shopping with us?" her sister Nabeela asked.

"Mhmm," was all Marzia could muster.

"Alright, be ready in 15, okay?" her sister said.

"Stop that." Elias sighed, grabbing the remote from the coffee table and settling on the recliner in the corner of the room.

"Huh? I'm just sitting here!" Marzia said, annoyed.

"Yeah, but I can tell you're overthinking what happened today."

"Please, I'm just watching TV, don't act like you can read my mind now," Marzia said.

"You're watching the Spanish network."

"I... maybe I'm trying to pick up a new language! I don't tell you everything, Elias!" Marzia said, visibly irritated.

"You're just mad that I know you better than you know yourself."

Marzia let out an audible scoff. "Your arrogance even leaves *me* without words."

"Please. Even I couldn't do that, Peaches," Elias shot back. "Despite how much I might want to."

Marzia decided she'd had enough verbal sparring for the afternoon and went upstairs to get ready to go wedding dress shopping with her sister. Getting ready entailed grabbing her purse and throwing on an oversized hoodie. This was Marzia's go-to outfit for running errands. Comfortable yet practical. On the way to the dress store, Marzia's mind wandered again as it so often did. The ring of the bell attached to the shop door brought Marzia back to reality.

"Well, hello there! How can we help you?" the cheerful sales associate said.

"She's getting married," Marzia's mother said proudly, gesturing towards Nabeela.

"Hmm… I'm thinking an A-line gown with a sweetheart neckline," the sales associate said airily. They followed her into an elaborate dressing room that was bigger than Marzia's garage. Crown moulding accentuated the perimeter, and a cool chill filled the place with an air of extravagance. Chandeliers lit up the room like a hoard of fireflies. The sales associate pulled a couple dresses from various racks and held them up for Nabeela to choose from. She decided to try on a princess-style ball gown first. The sales associate whisked Nabeela off to try on the dress. When she emerged from behind the curtains, Marzia noticed how stunning she looked. She had always thought her sister was beautiful, but at that moment, Nabeela was ravishing. The gown flowed behind her as she walked up onto the podium.

"I look like a marshmallow!" Nabeela laughed.

"You look gorgeous." Both Marzia and her mother beamed. Nabeela gave a bashful smile and glided back over to the changing room.

"Mom, can you come here and help for a second?" Nabeela beckoned from beyond the curtain. For just a moment, Marzia was left alone in the room. She spied a veil in the corner, and she gingerly snatched it up like a child would with a bag of candy. She placed it on her head and peered at herself in the full-length mirror, imagining what her own wedding day would be like. She would have dozens of roses of all colours. And it would be outdoors. In a park, possibly. For just a moment, Marzia closed her eyes and imagined what it would be like. The chirping birds would harmonize with the cicadas' dull buzz in an enchanting melody to rival that of any composer. She had everything planned out, except for who would be waiting there at her side.

"Marzia? Marzia? Are you listening?" her mother said, returning her to the here and now.

"Sorry, what were you saying?" Marzia asked.

"I said can you pass me the veil. Nabeela wants to try it on with the dress."

"Oh. Yeah, sure, here it is," Marzia said, realizing it was still resting on her head. What had gotten into her? It was like the bridal boutique was clouding her brain.

Pull yourself together! she told herself.

"Don't worry, it'll be your turn soon enough!" the sales associate said, giving Marzia a slight nudge.

Marzia couldn't help but feel her cheeks flush at the thought of it. She pushed that thought away into the darkest recesses of her mind. The idea of someone knowing every part of her; the good, the bad, the bedhead, and everything in between. That level of transparency frankly terrified her. But what terrified her most was the fear of what would happen after they saw her, all of her. She wondered if they would even love her after seeing the parts of her that she was ashamed to admit existed. The parts of her that were lazy, snarky, and selfish. Could they really love someone like that? It remained to be seen.

Marzia's sister couldn't decide on a dress that day, but then again, Nabeela was always the more indecisive sister. While Marzia was often the rasher and more impulsive sister, Nabeela cautioned patience.

A psychological study called The Marshmallow Experiment's basic premise was that a child was offered a choice between a single small but immediate reward or two small rewards if they waited a certain amount of time. Supposedly, the test was correlated to the children's future success. The children who waited for the larger reward turned out to be more successful. In Islam, there is a concept called sabr, literally meaning 'endurance' or more precisely 'persistence' and 'perseverance.' The idea is that if one is steadfast in their faith, they are rewarded with eternal paradise, the likes of which the human mind can hardly grasp. This notion always brought comfort to Marzia, particularly during especially trying times in her life, knowing that no matter how much she struggles, not a single ounce of it will be in vain. Although having sabr for Marzia was sometimes easier said than done.

Marzia went home after the appointment and realized that she had an essay deadline fast approaching. She had just finished the title page when she saw her phone light up with a text notification. She thought it was someone she actually cared about, but it was only notifications for one of her course group chats. She dismissed the faint buzzing because let's be honest, who really keeps up with course group chats unless they had a question?

After working for about an hour on her essay, which truthfully was more like 20 minutes of work and 40 minutes on her phone, Marzia's stomach began to gnaw at her, so she slumped downstairs to get herself a snack. She opened up the fridge when her phone buzzed again in her pocket, and something inside her told her to check it.

"You know I've never really noticed before, but you have really bad posture," Elias said nonchalantly from the kitchen table.

"Take a picture. It'll last longer than my patience with you," Marzia replied.

"Trust me, Peaches, I would if there was anything worth capturing."

When Marzia scrolled through her notifications, she noticed that she has a message request on Facebook. Curiosity overpowered her, and she checked to see who the message was from.

"Holy crap!" she blurted out.

"What is it?" Elias asked, sounding genuinely intrigued.

"I think I just found my aunt!"

CHAPTER TWELVE

～

"It soon became obvious that we were but on the threshold of the discovery."

- Howard Carter

"You're kidding!" Elias exclaimed in a tone between bewilderment and genuine shock. "Damn, I've got to hand it to you. You really did it. You pulled it off!"

"You underestimate me, Elias. It was never a question of if I would do it, but when I would do it," Marzia replied triumphantly.

"Arrogance doesn't suit you, Peaches."

Marzia arranged to meet with her Aunt and cousin the next day with her brother and sister. On the off chance that it was a catfish who wanted to kidnap her, Marzia figured it best not to go alone. Per chance, her long-lost kin were merely an hour away from their house. She had a long day ahead tomorrow, so tonight, Marzia wanted to unwind and relax.

She settled down on the couch in the living room, put her phone on silent, and fired up Netflix. She already knew what she wanted to watch, the 2005 version of Pride and Prejudice. It was a comfort movie of hers, and she insisted that it was the superior version. Partly because she loved Keira Knightly and partly because of the infamous hand flex scene. If you know, you know.

Halfway through the film, Marzia's eyes begin to weigh heavily, and she slips into the sweet land of dreams. When she awakened, all that she remembered from her dream was the flash of a pair of dark eyes. They stared intently at her, like they wanted to tell her something but couldn't quite find the words. She shook herself off the way one does after an eerie nightmare and realized a blanket had been draped over her. She assumed it was her mother or Elias' mother, making sure she didn't catch a cold. She went upstairs to pray the final prayer of the night and settled into her bed. Tomorrow was a big day, and she had to get her beauty sleep.

The next day, Marzia was up bright and early to meet the newest members of her family. Just kidding, she woke up at almost noon. When she finally trudged downstairs, she realized everyone was already having pancakes. Marzia's brother was flipping flapjacks as well as Gordon Ramsay.

"Blueberry or chocolate chip?" Ameer asked.

"Hmmm…blueberries," Marzia answered thoughtfully.

"Coming right up!

Marzia's brother had enjoyed cooking ever since he was a crackly-voiced adolescent. He had been studying law when he had a sudden desire to change paths and enrolled at the local culinary school. Undoubtedly, the entire family was shocked by the sudden change of heart, but nonetheless, they supported his endeavours. Every day he created another concoction. Various meat pies, bisques, and pastas became staples in their household.

Marzia was consumed by her own mind when something out of the corner of her eye caught her attention. She could tell that Bilal was texting away underneath the table. She was both curious and admittedly a little concerned. Although Bilal was always distant, she cared for him as she would her own brother. Something was up with him; she just didn't know what it was yet. But she didn't have time to think about that today. She would be meeting her aunt for the very first time with Nabeela and Ameer. Although, they decided to hold off on telling their mother until they were entirely sure. The last thing Marzia would ever want to do was give her mother hope prematurely.

She grabbed her largest purse, a faux leather bag with a gold clasp on the front. It was a little worn at the seams, but it was one of her favourites, so she couldn't bear to part with it. Her mother called her a hoarder, but it was a title Marzia vehemently denied.

The crisp air nipped at Marzia's skin as she stepped outside, taking in the weather.

"Ready to go? Ameer asked, spinning the car keys around his fingers.

"Yeah, I have the address on my phone," Marzia said, fiddling with her smartphone.

Once in the car with her sister and brother, Marzia closed her eyes and took in the sunshine. She wanted to remember this moment, take a mental snapshot. Marzia had read a book when she was a child about a girl with a photographic memory, capturing a mental image with one simple word; click. How she wished she could do the same with this moment right now. She was suddenly flooded with memories of traveling to Seattle with her parents and siblings to visit family. Despite the lack of sleep and being crammed in one car with her entire family, it was one of her most cherished memories.

It's funny how sometimes your best memories are the most mundane ones.

Halfway to their destination, they stopped at one of the many rest stops that lined the highway. But before she went to relieve herself, she had to indulge in her obligatory iced coffee. She wasn't staring, but she noticed the employee was particularly easy on the eyes; his blond hair swept across his face.

"Vanilla iced coffee?" he asked.

"Yep, that's me. Thank you!" she took her drink.

"You have yourself a great day!" the barista said.

"Love you too!" Marzia replied. And, dear reader, know that at that moment, Marzia wanted nothing more than to take the words she just uttered and stuff them back in her mouth the way she does when she indulges in sour candy. She speedily walked back to the car, refusing to look back at the barista.

"What's wrong? Why are you practically running?" Nabeela asked, slightly confused at her erratic behaviour.

"Just drive. For the love of God, please drive!" Marzia pleaded.

Throughout the long, tedious hour drive, Marzia drifted in and out of consciousness. Finally, when they reached their destination, Nabeela nudged Marzia awake. The house they pulled up to was a beautiful Victorian home atop a grassy hill. As soon as they rang the doorbell, their aunt greeted them with tight hugs.

"You look just like your mother did at your age," she whispered into Marzia's ear as she embraced her. They followed her into the living room, which looked like it's only used for special occasions, the kind you were told to stay out of when you were a kid, but that you snuck into anyway just because you could.

"So…I don't really know where to start." Marzia laughed.

"Does your mother know you're here?" their aunt asked.

"Uh no, actually, we haven't told her yet. We wanted to wait until we actually met you before we talked to her about it. Speaking of which I-" Marzia began.

"I really think you should talk to your mother."

"What do you mean?" Nabeela asked, somewhat taken aback.

"I think there are some things you don't know, and I really don't think I'm the one to be telling you," their aunt replied truthfully.

"What do you mean?" Ameer enquired.

"I'm getting married soon, and I'd love to have you there," Nabeela added.

"And I'd love to be there, Jaanem[17]. But you talk to your mom about it first. She should be the one to explain things to you," their aunt explained.

Their visit, if Marzia was honest, brought up more questions than it answered. Why was her aunt so hesitant to meet with their mother, her own sister? And what could their mother tell them that they didn't already know? Their mother was never one to have secrets, so the fact that there was some aspect of her that Marzia didn't know about was actually quite jarring. What's more was that she didn't quite know how to bring it up to her mother.

---

[17] Jaanem: Dari term of endearment equivalent to"my dear".

How would she explain that she had found her long-lost sister that she hadn't talked to in decades? On the way home, Marzia couldn't help but replay the whole interaction in her head. Was there really something her mother wasn't telling her, and if so, why? By the time they got home, the sun had set, and everyone was having dinner. Marzia walked in and was taken aback by the scene she observed. Two families having a meal as though they were one. She couldn't place the feeling, but something about it felt right; like they were all one big family. She had grown used to them, especially Elias' mother, whom she saw as a secondary maternal figure.

Marzia greeted everyone and then pulled out her phone to see a notification that her statistics exam had been graded. Instantly, her heart began to race, and a lump developed in the pit of her stomach. With shaking hands, she opened the link to assess the damage.

"Exam grades are up," she whispered breathlessly.

Elias looked up lazily from the book he was reading on the couch.

"Why do you look like you just found out someone died?" he asked.

"Statistics," she replied.

"So?" he prodded.

"So what?"

"How'd you do?" he asked, curious.

"Bad," she said, shaking her head. "Go on. I know you're going to say it. Ask me how I could screw up so badly yet again."

"Trust me, Peaches, anything I could possibly say right now doesn't hold a candle to what you're already thinking in that head of yours," Elias said, barely looking up from his book.

"For once, you're actually right about that," Marzia said wryly.

"I never took you for a defeatist," Elias said.

"I'm just accepting my fate," Marzia sighed.

"Fine. I'll do it," he said decidedly.

"Do what?" Marzia asked confused.

"I'll help you study for the next exam."

"Don't talk to me patronizingly like that," Marzia snapped.

"Alright. Have fun retaking stats." Elias shrugged, walking upstairs.

"I don't need you!" Marzia yelled after him.

Marzia decided that she didn't need Elias's help for the next exam. She didn't need another thing for him to hold over her head. She was over his arrogant, holier-than-thou attitude that he always strutted around with. She could do just fine on her own, and she would prove it. She gathered her books and set herself up in the dining room. She always found she worked best in an open space. Before long, Marzia realized she had spent 45 minutes on the same question. Damn it.

"I thought you could use a study snack!" Marzia's mother said sympathetically, laying a plate of sliced apples in front of her.

One question down. This was getting excruciatingly tedious.

"Are you sure you don't want to take a break, Marzia? You haven't even had dinner yet," Elias' mother asked her, her voice dripping with concern.

"Thank you! I'll eat in an hour; I just have to get through a few more questions," Marzia replied graciously.

"Ready to admit defeat, Peaches?" Elias mocked, somehow managing to appear from nowhere.

"Okay. Fine," Marzia said, slamming her head onto her textbook. She had reached absolute rock bottom.

"But first, eat," Elias said sternly, pushing a plate towards her with a sandwich on it cut diagonally into two perfect pieces.

"I don't have time to-" Marzia began, shaking her head.

"You're doing yourself no favours by trying to be a martyr and starving yourself."

"What are you, my mother?" she sulked but still reluctantly took a bite.

"Look, now pay attention. Now to calculate the variance, you need what?

"The mean?" Marzia said uncertainly.

"Yes…then what?"

"Figure out how far each number in the data set is from the mean?" Marzia asked.

"Then you square *each* - are you even listening to me right now?!" Elias snapped. Her eyes caught his staring daggers. Elias saw her texting underneath the table.

"I'm listening, I'm listening!" she insisted.

"Are you freaking kidding me right now? Are you texting while I'm trying to help you not fail your next exam?" Elias asked. "Who are you talking to that's so important?"

Marzia tried to pull her phone away, but Elias was too quick for her and snatched it out of her hands. He saw one name flash on the screen. Mateen.

"You're barely passing, and you're talking to some guy?" Elias asked.

"He's not *some guy*, and it was important. Wedding stuff," she tried to explain.

"Right," Elias said, dripping sarcasm, as he tossed her phone back to her and got up to leave.

"Wait, c'mon, okay, I'm sorry, Elias. Don't go," Marzia pleaded.

"Who needs a degree when you can be a trophy wife, right?" Elias sneered, venom dripping from every syllable.

"Okay, that was rude, even for you. Don't treat me like I'm some vapid, boy crazy-"

"Then *stop* acting like one," Elias retorted.

"You think you have me all figured out, don't you?"

"Yeah, I think I do, actually," Elias said. "You're smart, but you're lazy. And if you can't be the best at something, you won't even bother. That's your problem."

Marzia scoffed.

"That's ridiculous." She shook her head.

"You can't stand that there's something you're not instantly good at, so you're not even going to try," Elias continued.

"That's not true! You don't know what you're talking about, Elias!" Marzia declared defensively.

"And you know what the sad part is?" Elias asked. "If you spent half the amount of time you do avoiding your responsibilities on actually working towards your goals, you'd be pe-"

"Less pathetic?"

"That's not what I was going to say!"

"Yeah, but it's what you meant!"

"Damn, it Marzia, would you just listen to what I'm trying to tell you right now?!" Elias said, exasperated.

"I'm listening," Marzia said, sounding petulant though she was intrigued.

"I'm trying to tell you not to waste your potential," Elias finished.

"Is everything okay?" Elias' mother said, walking into the dining room with two plates of fruit.

"Yeah, um, she's just hopeless with statistics," Elias said, with an awkward laugh.

"Don't study too hard!" his mother said, heading back into the kitchen.

"Spare me your fake concern!" Marzia said, narrowing her eyes at Elias.

"You're actually crazy, you know that?" Elias said.

Marzia grabbed her book and one of the plates of fruit off the table.

"Where are you going?" Elias asked.

"The hell away from *you*!" Marzia said snidely.

"Fine, like I give a damn! Go!" Elias yelled back at her as she walked away.

"I will!"

"Good!"

"Great!"

Marzia felt restless like she had to get out of the house. She quickly shot a text to Reiyna asking if she wanted to get coffee. While she waited for her response, Marzia unconsciously paced back and forth in her room.

Some nerve that boy has. Who does he think he is? Marzia thought.

Her phone buzzed. She would be meeting Reiyna at the Tim's halfway between their houses. She threw on a yellow hoodie and let her parents know she'd be heading out for a bit.

"You have your wallet and keys?" her mother asked.

"Yep! Thanks, Maudarjaan. I'll be back soon. Just needed to get out for a bit with Reiyna."

Marzia didn't see Elias on her way out and was thankful. She really didn't have the emotional capital to deal with him at the moment.

At the coffee shop, she greets Reiyna with a tight hug.

"It's so good to see you!" She exclaimed.

"It's been too long!" Reiyna affirmed. "So, what's been going on with you?"

"Oh, it's everything. I- He-…"

"Deep breaths." Reiyna laughed.

"I have another statistics exam, and I have no idea what I'm doing. I met my aunt for the first time in my life. Oh, and not to mention Elias had the audacity to call me lazy."

"Okay, you're going to have to fill me in!" Reiyna replied curiously.

The two of them sat in that coffee shop for almost three hours, discussing all the woes of their daily lives. It was like an emotional purge, a release of sorts. Marzia took everything she had been bottling up, albeit bottled up badly, and poured her heart out.

"But there's still time to improve, though, right? Like you still have another exam, no?" Reiyna said encouragingly.

"I suppose, but to be honest, I really don't even know where to start. It just constantly feels like I have to try twice as hard just to be average," Marzia lamented.

"Now, I don't want to see you there moping. You know you have a lot of potential. It's just a matter of harnessing it."

"Ha!" Marzia let out a wry laugh. "That's exactly what *he* said."

"Wait, I thought he called you lazy?" Reiyna asked, confused.

"He did. He called me lazy but said that I had a lot of potential," Marzia recalled. "He called me smart too."

"Wait, he did? So, what's the problem?"

"It's not what he said, but how he said it. He honestly thinks he knows me," Marzia said.

"Oh my God, you honestly don't see it. Do you?" Reiyna asked.

"Humour me," Marzia pressed.

"You obviously like him, Marzia," Reiyna said so matter-of-factly you would think she was Bill Nye.

"Please, we can't stand being around each other. We couldn't even get through a study session without fighting," Marzia said dismissively.

"You honestly expect me to believe you don't have feelings for him? I'd sooner believe you got an A in statistics."

"Too soon, Reiyna," Marzia said, stifling a laugh.

Reiyna Haddad always found a way to make Marzia laugh. It was her special superpower. When they were both nine, Marzia had skinned her knee on the tarmac at school. To make her laugh, Reiyna told her knock-knock jokes all the way to the nurse's office. There was a warmth about her that radiated from her, which made her such a good friend.

"So, what's new with you?" Marzia questioned, desperately attempting to change the subject.

"I'm actually glad you asked. I brought something for you to read," Reiyna said ominously, handing her a booklet of paper.

"What's this?" Marzia asked.

"This is something I've been working on for the last little while. It's the first two chapters of my book," Reiyna said bashfully.

"Oh my God! MashAllah! That is amazing! Good for you! I'd be honoured to read it!"

"Promise not to laugh, okay?"

"Never!"

For just a couple hours, Marzia forgot about her problems and gushed over her friend's writing. That night, however, quickly became a restless night for Marzia. It was going to be a sleepless night too. There would be no reprieve. So, after failing to slip into the land of dreams, she pulled out the copy of Reiyna's manuscript and began to read further. She had only read a small portion of it when she was at the coffee shop, but she quickly realized a character bore an eerie resemblance to Marzia. Similar features, a psychology student, and the character even mimicked some of her mannerisms.

All was well until she got to the part where her alleged character was described as cynical. And at that, Marzia became undone. Cynical? Her? Cynical? Maybe she had it all wrong, and that character wasn't based on her at all. Maybe it wasn't that deep.

Maybe...

CHAPTER THIRTEEN

"Love, n. A temporary insanity curable by marriage."

-Ambrose Bierce

Being the introvert that she was, Marzia was never one to really enjoy weddings. Socializing was hard enough but add many family members and distant relatives whom you haven't spoken to in years, and you had the perfect storm of awkwardness. So, suffice to say that her social battery was on borrowed time when her sister's wedding day came around. And it didn't help that there were so many things still on her mind. She still had an exam to study for, she still hadn't worked up the courage to ask her mom about her aunt, and she was still upset with Elias for just being…well, Elias. She woke up at the crack of dawn, also known as 10 am, and made a pot of coffee, which she would most definitely need, especially today. She quickly scarfed down two slices of avocado toast and swallowed her multivitamins.

"We're going early to set things up. Will you be okay, going with Ameer and Elias?" Marzia's mother asked.

"Yeah, I- that's fine. I should be done in an hour," Marzia said reassuringly, although she couldn't get herself to believe it.

"And before you get any ideas, *I'll* be driving," Ameer interjected. "The last time we let you drive us to a family function you rear-ended someone else's car!"

"That was one time! And they were driving under the speed limit!" Marzia argued.

"Look, I want everyone getting along today, okay?" Marzia's father said.

"You have nothing to worry about from me!" Marzia said with a sickly-sweet grin. "Absolutely nothing at all!"

"Wow, for a second there, I almost believed you!" Elias muttered under his breath from the corner of the room.

"Yeah, and for a second there, I almost thought you were a decent person!" Marzia countered. "So I guess it turns out we're both wrong."

"Just remember to buy fresh dates on your way, okay? Fresh dates. They're important," Marzia's mother reminded.

Ameer gave an exaggerated salute in response. Marzia went into her room to get ready. As the sister of the bride, she was going to be in a lot of pictures, and if she looked anything but decent, she would never live it down. She slipped into her dress, grabbed her purse, and was ready to go. The dress she chose was a shimmery blue A-line gown. She walked down the stairs ever so carefully and found her brother, Elias, and Bilal waiting by the door.

"Ready to go?" Ameer asked.

"Yeah, I'm ready. Elias, do you have keys so we can lock up?" Marzia asked. "Elias? I said do you have keys, so no one breaks into the house?"

Elias snapped back to reality as though coming out of a trance.

"Right. Yeah, I do. Relax, okay?"

Marzia could only muster up an exasperated sigh. The four of them, dressed to kill, loaded into the car and drove down to the nearest supermarket to grab dates because otherwise, Marzia's mother would kill her. So, there was Marzia, in a full evening gown in the middle of a No Frills[18] buying dates. She was waiting in the line to check out when she saw a guy staring at her. It peeved her off because she wasn't sure if she was being judged or just stood out wearing a dress in the grocery store.

"It's my sister's wedding okay, take a picture, why don't you!" Marzia said, turning to him.

"You're standing in front of the KitKats," he said, reaching past her to take a candy bar off the rack.

"Oh," Marzia said meekly. "I'm normally a pretty pleasant person!"

---

[18] No Frills: A Canadian grocery store chain.

The man gave her a perplexed look and moved into the other checkout lane. Yet another example of Marzia's stellar social skills. She was definitely on edge. After walking out, and securing what she needed, Marzia plopped into the front seat of the car.

"What's gotten into you?" her brother asked.

"I wish I knew, Ameer. I wish I knew," she responded.

Marzia automatically shifted into daydreaming mode to get her mind off the painfully awkward experience she just endured when her thoughts wandered to Reiyna. Was this what she meant by cynical? Was that really how everyone saw her? Worst yet, was that really what she was like? Always assuming the worst in people? Marzia looked wistfully out the window on their way to the venue when Bonnie Tyler's "Total Eclipse of The Heart" began to play.

"Turn around, every now and then, I get a little bit lonely, and you're never coming 'round, " Marzia hummed.

"Turn around, every now and then, I get a little bit tired of listening to the sound of my tears ," Ameer chimed in melodiously.

Elias rolled his eyes.

"Turn around, every now and then, I get a little bit terrified, and then I see the look in your eyes " Marzia mused a little louder.

"Turn around, bright eyes," Bilal harmonized.

They continued until the chorus.

*"Every now and then, I fall apart. And I need you now tonight. And I need you more than ever. And if you only hold me tight. We'll be holding on forever. "*All four of them, and even, begrudgingly, Elias sang in unison. Badly, might I add.

And just like that, the tension and stress accumulated due to the pending nuptials melted away. It was not often Marzia allowed herself to be silly and let loose, but it felt good, which she hated to admit. Maybe it would be a good day after all.

When they got to the hall, they were met with Marzia's mom looking very concerned.

"What happened?" Marzia asked.

"The imam who is supposed to officiate isn't here yet," she said, with a look of worry.

"It's going to be okay," Marzia said reassuringly. She went up the winding staircase to the second floor, where the bridal suite was, and knocked on the door.

"You look beautiful," Marzia said, looking at her sister. "But if you're having second thoughts, just say the word, and we can be out of here in less than five."

"Thank you for all your help," Nabeela said, pulling Marzia into a tight hug. "Pray with me?"

"I'd love nothing else."

The two of them stood shoulder to shoulder as they went through the motions of worship. And for a few minutes, it was just the two of them against the world, one last time.

Marzia forced back tears, and she closed the door behind her. Marzia went into the private washroom right down the hall from the bridal suite and inspected herself in the mirror. Her eye makeup was a little smudged, but that wasn't anything a simple touch-up couldn't fix, although the sterile lighting did her no favours. A soft knock at the door caught her attention.

"Yeah?" she said, suppressing a sniffle.

"It's Mateen. Your mom asked me to call you," Mateen said timidly.

"Oh, sure, I'll be down in a minute. I'm just... uh freshening up," she said, opening the door.

"Were you just crying?" he asked.

"No, no, I just...weddings make me emotional," she responded dismissively.

"Can I tell you a story? A short anecdote, if you will?"

"Humour me," Marzia said.

"Well, my father has this saying. He would say to me: Mateen Jaan, life is like that machine that shows your heart rate when you're in the hospital. It goes up and down. That's the way of life. If there's no highs and lows, then that means you're dead," Mateen explained, imitating his father's accent.

Marzia broke out in a bemused smile.

"There's the smile I was looking for!" Mateen beamed. "Now keep it that way."

"I'll meet you downstairs." Marzia laughed. "And Mateen?"

"Yeah?"

"Thanks. For trying to cheer me up, I mean."

"Don't mention it."

Marzia took one more look in the mirror and exited the washroom, ready to take on whatever the night had to bring. The corner of her eye caught someone leaning over the balcony that looked over the lobby.

"You really do have a type, Peaches," Elias said, without even looking at her.

"What, nice guys? Somebody should have me committed. I'm out of control," Marzia scoffed.

"You'd think a nice guy would be able to tell when you're lying," Elias said.

"I wasn't lying!" Marzia protested.

"*Weddings just make me emotional!*" Elias mocked.

"It's true!"

"Please, I've only been living with you for a little while, and even I know it goes deeper than that."

"So, you were spying on me?"

"You're changing the subject," Elias pointed out. "And besides, I hardly consider standing in a public space as spying. And that's assuming you were worth spying on."

"Look I'm, tired. I got five hours of sleep. And I have things to do, so if you'll excuse me," Marzia said, pushing past him.

"He's right, by the way," Elias said.

"What?" Marzia replied, crossing her arms across her chest.

"He was right. Things change. It's inevitable. But some things will always be the same. You and your sister, nothing can break that no matter what happens. I know that's why you're sad."

"You don't know anything about me and my sister," Marzia said, lips quivering.

"Whatever you say, Peaches."

"It's just so…so stupid," Marzia said. "I don't know why I feel like crying. I should be happy, right now."

"Yeah, you should be, you dork."

This actually got Marzia to reluctantly let out a stifled laugh.

"I don't want any of it to change. I wish it could be like this forever."

"That's not how life works," Elias said, shaking his head.

"Tell me about it."

"Here's what you're going to do," he said finally, making piercing eye contact. "You're going to go down there, and you're going to be the best sister of the bride you can be. You're going to smile because this is her day. After it's over and she's on her honeymoon, you can fall apart at home, but for right now, you have to be there for her. You owe her that much."

"I think that actually might be good advice," Marzia said, considering her words carefully.

"And one more thing?" Elias said.

"Yeah?"

"Relax, okay? Actually try and enjoy your sister's wedding."

"No promises," Marzia said, holding the hem of her dress as she made her way down the stairs. It must have been the wind because even halfway down the steps, she could still smell his rustic smelling cologne.

"Marzia, there you are. It's almost time for your sister to come out. We have to make sure everyone is in their seats." Marzia's mother said.

"Is the imam here?" Marzia asked.

"Yes, he's here, Alhamdulillah," Marzia's mother said in relief.

Once everyone was in their seats, the timeless Ahesta Bero[19] began to play over the speakers. The lights dimmed, and the guests went silent. A spotlight flashed. Two people pulled the heavy wooden double doors open. Everyone turned their heads and stood up, paying their respects as they saw Nabeela and Mateen's brother Zabi emerge in

---

[19] Ahesta Bero: Dari song that is played at many Afghan weddings as the bride and groom walk down the aisle, translating to"Go Slowly".

the most intricately woven garments that sparkled when they caught the light. It seemed as though time was moving slowly.

The song always had a particularly somber tone, but Marzia never truly took in the meaning until that moment.

"Go slowly, my lovely moon, go slowly."

A song that transcended generations and generations, lamenting the cruelty of the passing of time. A feeling that resonated with Marzia more than anyone knew.

The two made their way to the stage at the other end of the room, where two chairs sat like thrones as they took their place as King and Queen of the night. As they sat, they were cloaked under a decorated shawl. The imam entered, and the two were officially married in the eyes of God and the province of British Columbia.

The newlywed couple was then the first to get food from the overflowing intricately arranged platters. There were at least four different kinds of rice, stews, steaks, and skewers of chicken and beef as far as the eye could see. But Marzia couldn't even think of eating. Her stomach was in too many knots, and she had to make sure nothing went wrong.

"Marzia, you've got to eat something!" Soraya said, approaching her with a plate of food in one hand and a glass of coke balanced on the other.

"Yeah, everything is fine! We haven't even seen you all night. You've been running around like a headless chicken," Ameena said.

Then as though a tornado of chaos, a boy around 18 years old, if Marzia had to guess, bumped into her and spilled what she hoped to God was only cranberry juice all over her dress.

"Damn it!" she yelled.

"Hey, watch it! Pull yourself together before I tell your mom!" Soraya said.

"What am I going to do? We still have pictures, and I can't be in my sister's wedding photos with a stain! She'll kill me!"

"Wait, what size are you?" Ameena asked.

"Five. Why?"

"This dress is a six, but it'll have to do," Soraya chimed in.

"No, I couldn't, I-"

"Shut up and get changed!" Soraya said.

Marzia slid into Soraya's pale rose chiffon gown in the empty bridal suite. Her armpits began to sweat as she pulled the dress over her head. She made a mental note to have it dry cleaned before returning it. When she made her way back into the party, it was time for family photos. Begrudgingly, she posed and complained a little as possible.

She felt a migraine coming on but pushed through and willed herself to overcome it. After the excruciating photo op, Marzia finally got a chance to have dessert. She sat down to have a long-awaited slice of cake, kicking her shoes off under the table.

"Mmmmm, *Vanilla,*" she sighed. "If it were chocolate, I'd have to flip a table."

"This is the best cake I've ever had," Soraya said, with her mouth full.

"I might require seconds," Ameena concurred.

"More slices, anyone?" Mateen said with a wide grin, approaching their table with his hands full of plates.

"You read my mind!" Soraya exclaimed, relieving him of one of the slices.

"Th-thanks!" Marzia stammered, suddenly feeling very self-conscious and unsure of herself. "Uh, so are you having fun?"

"I'm actually a little tired, but that's nothing a little coffee can't fix," Mateen replied.

Is this really happening? Am I really talking to Mateen like it's nothing? Marzia wondered.

In the middle of shoveling her face with cake, she noticed a familiar annoyance from the corner of her eye.

"I'm sorry, is that Dalia over there talking to Elias?" Marzia asked.

"Who's Dalia?" Mateen asked.

"Don't get her started!" Soraya and Ameena harmonized.

"Just someone I have...a history with," Marzia replied, aggressively jabbing a piece of cake with her fork. "I'm going to say hi."

"That's like a snake *just saying hi* to a mouse," Ameena warned.

"Fine. I'll ignore her. Mateen, do you want some tea?" Marzia asked.

"Uh, sure, I'll come with you!" he said enthusiastically.

They made their way to a table littered with little teacups.

"Marzia!" a shrill voice from behind her said.

"Dalia, I didn't expect you to be here," Marzia said, her voice strained.

"Me either! When I saw you, I said to Eli, 'Is that Marzia Rashidi?'"

Marzia raised an eyebrow at Elias. Her expression needed no explanation.

Eli? Marzia thought, barely containing a laugh.

"Yeah. It's my sister's wedding, so I hope I'd be invited."

Dalia let out a strident screech that Marzia assumed to be a laugh.

"You two know each other?" Mateen asked, trying to make conversation.

"We did model UN together in grade eight!" Dalia replied.

"You never told me you were in model UN." Marzia laughed.

"I didn't think I had to," Elias countered.

"Relax. It was a joke, *Eli*," Marzia replied.

Elias relaxed his shoulders as he took a sip of his coffee.

"Can I have some of that?" Dalia asked, turning to Elias.

Marzia grabbed Elias' drink from his hand, chugging the very last of it.

"All yours," Marzia said, handing her the empty cup and then walking away.

"How about I get you another?" Elias said loudly, making sure Marzia heard.

"That was childish. Even for you," Elias said, finding Marzia a few minutes later.

"I don't know what you're talking about," Marzia said, feigning ignorance. "And *Eli* ? Really?"

"I don't understand why you hate her so much. She's actually pretty cool."

"I have my reasons. You know I do!" Marzia said, putting down the tray of cups she was clearing off a table.

"No, I really don't," Elias said plainly.

"She only undermined me my entire childhood," Marzia said, throwing her hands up in the air.

"So that's what this is? A petty childhood grudge?"

"It's not just a petty childhood grudge!" Marzia said defensively. "Everything I did, she had to do it better. She made it her mission to show me up at every turn."

"Hey, is everything okay?" Mateen asked, approaching the very heated argument.

"Yeah, it's fine. Move along, Prince Charming," Elias said dismissively.

"She's obviously upset," Mateen said more assertively.

"She's free to walk away, then. I'm not holding her hostage," Elias countered.

"Could have fooled me with how aggressive you were being." Mateen shrugged.

"You haven't seen me aggressive." Elias laughed.

"I'm not doing this right now," Marzia said decisively, walking away. Before she realized it, everyone began to do the Attan, which essentially marks the wedding's end. Everyone began lining up in a circle and rhythmically clapping to the beat while turning around the circle.

However, Marzia made her way back up into the bridal suite to collect Nabeela's things and make sure that she didn't forget anything important or valuable amid the wedding haze. The rest of the night was a sleep-deprived haze. In fact, she was so tired she barely wiped her makeup off before falling into a deep slumber. But the most important part was that the day was a success. And that, dear reader, made it all worth it.

CHAPTER FOURTEEN

☙

"Smooth seas do not make skillful sailors."

-African Proberb

Marzia was always intimidated by her mother. Nafiza Rashidi was fiercely principled, and the strongest woman Marzia knew. That was why she found the idea of confronting her about what had happened the day she met her aunt felt so daunting. Nafiza once tried to outrun the police to get out of a speeding ticket. When she wants to be, she is terrifying. So Marzia's heart was practically beating out of her chest when she approached her mom, intending to confront her.

"So, you love me, right?" Marzia asked, leaning on the kitchen counter as her mother washed dishes.

"What kind of question is that?" her mother said with a laugh.

"And that wouldn't change even if you were mad at me?"

"Whatever you're going to say, just say it," her mother said, exasperated.

"I found your sister," Marzia said, uncharacteristically quiet.

"What?" her mother said, as though unable to conjure the words to say anything else.

"We went to meet her. Nabeela, Ameer, and I."

Her mother didn't speak for a couple minutes, the silence absolutely deafening.

"Maudarjaan? Aren't you going to say something?" Marzia pressed, disturbed by her mother's reticence.

"You did what now?"

"I met her. She's actually really nice, you should-"

"Bas ast [20] Marzia," her mother said, holding up a hand. "I don't want to hear another word about it."

"But I thought you wanted to reconnect?" Marzia argued, increasingly becoming more confused.

"There are some things that you don't understand and that I can't explain," her mother said cryptically.

What else could Marzia do? She wasn't giving up, but for now, she had to drop it. She wasn't getting anywhere with her mother being this defensive. Besides, she had some serious studying to do if she

---

[20] Bas Ast: Dari for "That's enough."

wanted to pass statistics. She gathered her things scattered all over her room and took the subway to her university campus.

As she stood on the platform, her mind wandered as it so often did. She imagined how this scene would be if she were in a movie. She would trip and nearly fall right onto the train tracks, but luckily there would be a handsome gentleman to heroically save her before falling to her death. The sound of the train approaching grounded her back into reality again. The train whizzed past her as she felt the breeze graze her face.

Marzia got on the train and found a seat with two empty spots on either side. Oddly enough, Marzia was somehow always offended when someone decided not to sit beside her and also equally annoyed if they chose to aggravate her with their presence. Once she got to her stop, she emerged to the surface. One of the perks of her campus was that the subway took her right to it. It almost made up for the muggings and armed robberies that were common in the area. Almost. She walked by the number of food stalls, and the aroma made her stomach growl despite having eaten just an hour earlier. Her favourite place to eat on campus was a Chipotle dupe.

She entered the campus library that vaguely resembled a retirement home, complete with couches with floral print and fake plants galore. She ascended the escalators as she stared out the ceiling to floor window, which revealed a beautiful sunny day.

Too sunny, Marzia thought, as she watched two squirrels chase each other up a tree. Somehow, the weather didn't match how she felt on the inside, which frustrated her. She shook off the bout of pessimism that was bubbling over as she surveyed each floor for the perfect study spot. It had to be close enough to a washroom for her to be able to go when she needed to, but not too close that any less than pleasant odours would offend her sensibilities. Having a window and a plethora of charging ports was an obvious asset. After weaving her way through the labyrinth, Marzia found herself on the fourth floor. It was oddly quiet, which Marzia normally hated, but at that moment, it was exactly what she needed. She cracked open her books and could almost see the tear stains on the pages from the last time she attempted such a feat. But before long, her eyes and hands drifted to her phone, which seemed to be calling her like Odysseus' sirens.

"Marzia?" she heard a voice say from behind her say.

She lifted her head up from her table to see Mateen Heydari staring right at her. Of course, the one day she forwent the makeup was the day she ended up running into someone of some importance. Predictably, Marzia could feel her self-consciousness bubbling over as it so often did.

"Oh, hey Mateen!" Marzia said, trying her very best not to sound alarmed.

"Fancy seeing you here," Mateen said.

"But I go here," Marzia said, a little confused. Did he seriously not know what school she goes to?

"Hey, I'm just kidding! Of course, I know you go here," he teased.

"Oh," Marzia said, fiddling with the zipper on her sweater.

"This seat taken?" he asked, pulling out another chair at the table.

"Be my guest!" Marzia replied.

"So, what are you studying?" he asked, turning her textbook around to read the title." Statistics, yikes."

"Yeah, I'm pretty hopeless." Marzia laughed.

"Nah, I'm sure you'll ace it."

"I've been told I shouldn't waste my potential, so I suppose I have to." Marzia sighed, leaning back into her seat."So, what's that big brick you're carrying?"

"Physics," he replied ominously, the same way one talked about ghosts or the boogie man.

"You're a lot braver than I am," Marzia said.

"I should probably get going. I've got class in five," Mateen said, getting up and tucking his chair back in."It was great seeing you, though, Marzia!"

"Yeah, you too!" Marzia replied.

Marzia decided that it would be prudent to take a study break and get some frozen yogurt. She went to the place by the rotunda, where she always went when craving creamy confection. She ordered two scoops of cookie dough with coconut shavings and dark chocolate crumbles. She sat on an empty seat and watched as students filtered in and out. A tall, freckled girl with strawberry blonde hair walked by, holding a cone in one hand and her boyfriend's hand in the other. He gave her a smirk as he took a bite out of her vanilla cone. Marzia rolled her eyes as she sank further back into her seat. Then, she saw two friends whispering to one another as though they were telling each other their deepest secrets. Suddenly she felt very alone. But that didn't mean she was lonely.

By the time Marzia had finished studying, the clouds were out, and it looked like it was going to rain. But even when she was on her way home from campus, Marzia still felt a haze around her, like TV static that she couldn't quite find the signal for. She put her key in the door and entered to the smell of a home-cooked meal. It smelled like family.

"Oh good, Marzia, your home!" Elias' mother said.

"Salaam everyone!"

"Are you hungry, Marzia?" her father asked.

"Maybe in a bit. I think I'll wash up first," Marzia said, unlacing her shoes.

"You were busy today," Elias said, appearing like a Dementor as Marzia reached the top of the stairs.

"I was, actually. I was studying," Marzia said. "I'll be a trophy wife *and* have degree."

"And I'm sure Mateen was helping you with both," Elias said, his words dripping with sarcasm.

"And what of it? Since when is my life any concern of yours?" Marzia retorted.

"It's not. But his fiancée might care that you were ogling him." Elias laughed.

"He does *not* have a fiancée," Marzia scoffed.

"He most certainly does now. Sorry to burst your bubble, Peaches. His mom called this morning announcing the news."

"Wait, how do you know I ran into him today? Spying on me there, Elias?" Marzia asked.

"You wish you were that interesting," Elias quipped.

"I'm plenty interesting," Marzia countered.

"Whatever helps you sleep at night." He chuckled.

"And you still never answered my question. What were you doing on campus? You don't have class today."

"Keeping tabs on me, there? Since when do you keep track of my schedule?" Elias questioned.

"I don't. You have a habit of making your annoying presence known."

"It is my house, after all."

Marzia's expression changed, and Elias realized he struck a chord.

"Yeah, and you never let me forget it," she muttered, pushing past him.

"Since when were you so sensitive!" he said as she shut the door.

Marzia had way too much to deal with to worry about Mateen and his relationship status. Besides, it was only a silly crush that would have never amounted to anything, she reminded herself bitterly. And so Marzia did what Marzia knew best, avoidance. She decided to text her newly found cousin and probe for some more information about the nature of their mothers' relationship. Hopefully, she had a little more clarity than Marzia, which, considering Marzia knew absolutely nothing, wasn't saying much. She then moved on to some quiet reading that she often turned to when she felt like she was losing control. Just as she finished another chapter, she heard a knock at the door.

"Look, I'm not really in the mood for-" Marzia began.

"I actually have something to tell you," Marzia's mother said, the door creaking open.

"Happy or sad?" Marzia asked.

"Happy. It's actually very good news. The house is ready for us to move back into. They've just about renovated all the damages."

"We're going home?" Marzia said in disbelief. She was quite at a loss for words, which shocked Marzia to her core. Marzia typically had a great deal to say in almost any given situation.

"Aren't you happy?" Marzia's mother asked.

"Oh, I am. I'm just a little caught off guard."

One of Marzia's favourite books has a line that encapsulates her very feeling at that moment. To quote Jane Austen's Pride and Prejudice,

"Elizabeth had never been more at a loss to make her feelings appear what they were not."

Marzia couldn't exactly articulate her thoughts at that moment, but she knew the words would eventually come to her.

The day they moved out of the Hakimzada house was surprisingly bittersweet. Marzia had actually grown to care for them, thought of them as…family…almost. Elias' mother had no daughters, so having a feminine presence was nice while it lasted.

"Oh, do you really have to go?" Elias' mother asked sadly.

"We couldn't possibly impose a minute longer!" Marzia's mother insisted.

"I think I forgot something inside. I'll go run and check," Marzia said abruptly.

Marzia ran upstairs back into what had been her room for the past God knows how long. She opened up the mahogany armoire and stares into the empty abyss as though she could see Narnia on the other side.

"Got everything?" she heard a voice from behind her say. Marzia turned around to see Elias standing in the doorway with his hands crammed into the pockets of his grey sweatpants.

"Yeah, just making sure I haven't forgotten anything," Marzia replied pensively.

"Right."

"You're probably ecstatic right now," Marzia said, breaking the awkward silence.

"Is that even a question?" he responded, but his expression was more playful than malicious.

"Anyways, I should be going. So, I guess I'll see you when I do." Marzia shrugged.

"See you around, Peaches," he replied nonchalantly. He opened his mouth to say something else but seemingly decided against it.

"Hey, Elias?"

"Yeah?"

Marzia paused for a brief moment.

"Don't forget to check the mail," she finally said. "That was always my job, so you'll have to pick up slack from now on."

Before Marzia knew it, she was watching as the house got smaller and smaller as they drove away. It was the end of an era. What kind of era would follow was hard to say, but one thing was for sure: things were going to change. And that scared Marzia.

CHAPTER FIFTEEN

~

"Life is a zoo in a jungle."

- Peter De Vries

Marzia always prided herself on being very in tune with her emotions. But truthfully, if she was being honest, she was a chronic overthinker that specialized in avoidance. One time she baked an entire cake and tray of brownies because she refused to check her mark for an assignment she had been dreading. Some might call that neurotic. If this were a romantic comedy set in the early 2000s, that would be considered cute and endearing. But this was real life, and Marzia did not fit the stereotype of the manic pixie dream girl.

Readjusting to living in her own home after so long had also proven to be a more difficult feat than Marzia had first anticipated. She had never really processed that her house was engulfed in flames, and maybe she preferred it that way. But like a spring, the more you push something down, the harder it will inevitably push back up. Memories included. Life somehow has a way of working out that way; you either move along with it or risk getting left behind. Marzia had a list of disaster worst-case scenarios in her mind that she wouldn't be able to bear should they occur, but the more she went through, the more she realized she was stronger than she gave herself credit for.

The first night back home, she barely got a wink of sleep. It was the room that she had slept in for years but somehow felt incredibly foreign for the first time. It was an odd feeling, being a stranger in her own home. She tossed and turned in unrest. She thought she would never get over this Groundhog Day-style agony. But like everything else she never thought she would get over or recover from, day by day, she got used to the new routine.

One particular night, however, she had a dream that shook her to her core. She was in her very own home, baking cookies in the kitchen. Two children ran through the door and embraced her in a tight hug. Everything seemed fine and wonderful, a perfect dream really. That is, until she turned to see who was standing beside her. None other than Elias. Wearing an apron and whisking batter, she saw him shoot her a warm smile.

Before Marzia knew what hit her, she woke up in a cold sweat. They say that dreams reflected your inner desires, but Marzia always thought that was only something the desperately naïve cling on to. But Marzia didn't have time to grapple with the complexities of her unconscious mind. She was determined to have a productive day. Repression had become an art form at this point. And being productive didn't involve sitting in bed ruminating. She splashed her face with cold water and scraped the crust off the corner of her mouth and eyes.

As Marzia changed into some "going-out" clothing, also known as jeans and a flannel, she heard the familiar buzz of her ringtone coming from her phone.

"Hey Marzia, are you free today? I had a couple ideas for my book that I would love your opinion on!" Reiyna asked on the other line.

"Hey Reiyna, I've got a lot on my plate today, but I'll call you back, okay?" Marzia replied absently. Marzia grabbed her wallet and shoved it into her oversized messenger bag. Her first stop was the local pharmacy, where she had to pick up the medication for the rash on her arm.

"Hey, Shaun!" Marzia said to the pharmacist in the white coat leaning on the counter.

"Hey Marzia, the usual?" he asked.

"The usual," Marzia affirmed. After the wide array of skin ailments that had afflicted Marzia over the years, she was on a first-name basis with all the pharmacists. Whether that was endearing or sad, Marzia couldn't decide. But the pharmacy always sent her a personalized card on her birthday to remind her to get her flu shot. While she was waiting for her prescription to be filled, Marzia flipped through the shelves of magazines and books for sale by the cash register. She scoffed at the melodramatic romance covers with handsome shirtless men and helpless looking scantily clad women. She found those books so unbelievably cheesy. I mean, what were the chances that a Scottish duke would fall in love with her and defy tradition to be with her? Maybe she was just cynical, or perhaps she had come to the realization that she would never experience the whirlwind romance she idolized so highly in books and movies. This was real life, and real-life wasn't that interesting, no matter how much maladaptive daydreaming she engaged in.

A violent buzz in her pocket interrupted her thoughts. The pharmacy pager had gone off to notify her that her prescription was ready. She picked up the white paper bag from the pharmacist and then set off for her next destination, her sister's new condo. She pulled up to the parking garage and into a parking spot next to a shiny silver Mercedes. Usually, that would make her nervous and cause her to doubt herself and subsequently find a place without a single car in sight. Marzia wasn't a bad driver per se, but let's just say she wouldn't bet her life on her vehicular abilities.

She walked into the building and passed by the front desk, where there was a handsome man with tan skin and blue eyes stood. To her surprise, he waved at her. So Marzia, with a big smile on her face, waved back at him. His expression faded to confusion which only perplexed Marzia even more. It was only when she looked behind her that she realized the gravity of her mistake. She turned to see a tall woman in her 50s in a mink coat walking in with her poodle looking just as confused as she was, and then it hit her. The concierge was waving at the woman, not her.

Well, that was one more person she'd never be able to face again in her life. Her face flushed red as she shuffled into the elevator. Marzia somehow had a special talent for embarrassing herself in a myriad of ways she never even thought possible.

Marzia knocked on her sister's door and was greeted by the smell of bubbling pots of delicious goodness.

"Come in, come in!" Nabeela said, gesturing for her to enter.

"I like what you've done with the place." Marzia nodded approvingly.

"I do what I can. There are still a few things left to unpack," Nabeela said, stirring her pot.

Marzia eyed the stacks of boxes in the corner.

"I'd say it's more than a few." She laughed.

"Pshh. Let's see you organize all your stuff into a 1-bedroom apartment," Nabeela retorted.

"Like that'll ever happen. I'll just keep the house after Ameer moves out." Marzia said.

"I don't know, Mar, you might change your mind a few years from now," Nabeela warned.

"I highly doubt it," Marzia assured her. "It'll be me and the cats with mom and dad."

"What about when you get married?"

Marzia nearly choked on the iced coffee Nabeela had placed in front of her.

"Bold of you to assume I'll be getting married."

"To quote our dear mother, the only one meant to be alone is God," Nabeela said, imitating their mother's accent.

"Let's just say I don't see that happening anytime in the near future, if at all," Marzia said, fiddling with her cup.

"Oh, don't be so cynical, Marzia. You never know when the right person will come along," Nabeela said encouragingly.

"I suppose," Marzia conceded. "You know you're the second person who has called me that! I'm really not."

"What about Elias?" Nabeela prodded.

"What about Elias?" Marzia repeated.

"Oh, c'mon, don't play dumb. So, what happened?"

"Absolutely nothing, which is exactly how it should be," Marzia said firmly. "Besides, he doesn't even look at me, the point is that is a dead end."

"Oh, you're no fun!" Nabeela sighed. "What about Mateen? He's a really nice guy."

"Apparently, he's engaged now."

"That doesn't surprise me," Nabeela said. "Are you disappointed?"

"Not really, no," Marzia replied thoughtfully.

"Good for you, Mar. You've come a long way. So, what else have you been up to?"

"Not much, really. School's been eating up most of my time. And frankly, the situation with our aunt that we never knew existed is confusing the hell out of me. I was thinking of calling," Marzia said.

"Maybe you should just let it go? Maybe's there's a reason mom doesn't want you to get too close to her?" Nabeela suggested.

"You know I can't do that," Marzia said, shaking her head.

"I know. I just figured I'd try." Nabeela laughed.

"So, have you learned to cook at all?" Marzia asked, leaning on the kitchen counter."

All of the sudden, the fire alarm went off above the stove.

"Does that answer your question?" Nabeela laughed. "In all seriousness, though. I've been meaning to have a talk with you."

"Very ominous," Marzia remarked.

"Don't ever settle, okay, Mar?"

"I wasn't planning on it."

"I'm serious. And not just for a man. I mean in every aspect of your life. Be it work, school, or even friendships," Nabeela insisted.

"What brought this bout of sisterly advice on?" Marzia asked skeptically, playing with the fake fruit arrangement on the table. She picked up a peach and sized it in her hands.

"Nothing in particular..." Nabeela trailed off. "I just worry about you sometimes. I don't want you to sell yourself short."

"You don't have to be concerned. I'm alright. I'll be alright," Marzia replied pensively.

"Don't give me that look! Now try this!" Nabeela said, shoving a wooden spoon in her mouth.

And believe it or not, Marzia really took her sister's words to heart. She was never really the most secure in herself, but she decided not to accept anything less than she thought she deserved. But not in an arrogant, demanding way. Although she had to admit that it shook her to see her sister concerned about her. Was she really that much of a loose cannon? She never considered herself the reckless type, but then again, she never considered herself cynical either, and yet that's how Reiyna saw her. Not that she was constantly thinking about it, though. Not at all.

Marzia's next stop of the day was campus to attend her developmental psychology lecture. While walking towards her lecture hall, she saw a familiar but loathsome face on several different posters throughout campus. Yet another thing that plagued her sensibilities. And where there's smoke, there's a fire, so no sooner did she turn the corner to see Dalia Alimi in the flesh. The campus wasn't nearly big enough for the both of them. She was just about to pass by unnoticed when…

"Look who it is!" Dalia said.

"Hey, Dalia," Marzia replied flatly.

"I'm running for president of the Student Association," Dalia said, looking pleased with herself.

Didn't ask, didn't care, Marzia thought to herself.

"Good for you," Marzia replied.

"I think I'll be able to do a lot of good for the university. The financial aid services are absolutely lackluster, to say the least."

Marzia was absolutely fuming. How could this girl think she was fit for student government? How could someone so self-centered, so vapid think she could lead? There was only one thing she could think to do at that moment. But first, she had to go to class. Nonetheless, the floodgates of spite were open, and they weren't about to slow down any time soon.

That day's lecture was on attachment styles. But Marzia wasn't paying much attention despite her best efforts. She stared blankly at the video playing on the projector in class, showing an infant crying hysterically after their mother left the room. She tapped her pen rhythmically on her desk.

"Are there any volunteers to help write for me on the chalkboard?" her aging professor asked the class.

Marzia stretched her arm and yawned.

"Marzia, thank you!"

She made her way to the front of the class and palmed a fresh piece of snow-white chalk. She began writing as her professor spoke. Then she heard the unmistakable sound of snickering. She realized she misspelled a word.

"I'm sorry, did you want to come up here instead?" she snapped, at no one in particular and everyone all at once. The class went silent, but Marzia didn't care. She was at her wit's end. And if one more person tested her, she was going to blow into an absolute rage. Call it having a volatile disposition or just plain emotionally unstable, but Marzia was done. In every sense of the word. And she knew exactly what she had to do. She had to run for president of the student association.

And she had to win.

CHAPTER SIXTEEN

≈

"Prosperity is not without many fears and distastes; adversity not without many comforts and hopes."

- Francis Bacon

Marzia was never one for public speaking. But she was pretty damn good at it. Even though her hand trembled and her stomach churned like butter, you could never tell from her face. That was one of Marzia's specialties, hiding how she truly felt at any given moment. Sometimes, even from herself.

Marzia spent the next few weeks campaigning for president of the student association with Soraya and Ameena's help. They put up posters, Instagram stories, you name it. If there's one thing about Marzia that you should know, dear reader, it's that sometimes spite can be her biggest motivator. There's probably a lot to unpack there, but one has to admit Marzia could achieve a lot when she put her mind to it. Sometimes, it even consumed every aspect of her life. That's why Marzia had a particularly hard time concentrating at work when customers approached her.

"I said, what time do you guys close?" a woman with short brown hair asked, hands on her hip.

"Sorry, ma'am. We're open 'till 7," Marzia said, coming out of a dazed stupor. She checked her watch and realized she should have gone on her break about a half-hour ago. She took her lunch out of the refrigerator in the break room and felt an instant sense of relief to be off her feet. Karissa also walked into the back room with a frustrated sigh.

"That's it. I'm serious this time. I'm putting in my two weeks. I'm not joking," she said, plopping herself onto the chair next to Marzia.

"Oh, you say that every other day. I'd be more surprised if you didn't threaten to quit," Davis said dismissively from across the table.

"I swear some people exist just to test me. This woman came in asking for a discount she saw in a flyer…from two years ago," Karissa exclaimed.

"That's a new one." Marzia chuckled.

"That's nothing. I once had a couple break up right in the store because the toy they wanted to buy their son was out of stock," Davis reminisced. "Apparently, the dad was supposed to pre-order it but forgot."

"Retail customers are a different breed." Marzia shook her head, taking a swig of her iced coffee.

"Augustus, sweetheart, save some room for later!" Davis said in a faux German accent.

"Did you just compare me to Augustus Gloop?" Marzia said, feigning offence.

"If the shoe fits." Davis shrugged, grinning.

Just then, Marzia got a call on her phone from an unknown number.

"Hello?" she said, stepping into the service hallway.

"Hi, Marzia?" a meek voice said.

"Yeah, that's me. Who's this?

"This is Neelofar. I'm your cousin. We met briefly a while back."

"Oh yeah, I remember. It's good to hear from you." Marzia said, suddenly feeling awkward.

"Look, I wanted to call you because I think this has gone on long enough. Our moms are sisters, for God's sake, and haven't spoken in decades," Neelofar said.

"I feel the exact same way. I mean, it's ridiculous. They're blood," Marzia replied. "But it seems like they both refuse to talk about it."

"Well, that's where we come in," Neelofar said deviously.

"What were you thinking?" Marzia asked inquisitively.

"I'm not sure just yet, but I will eventually. I'll keep you posted."

"I have to get back to work, but I'll brainstorm too. I think this calls for an intervention," Marzia replied.

Family was one of the things that Marzia valued most. She couldn't imagine not speaking to her siblings for more than a few days, let alone years. She knew that she had to do something to mend this relationship. Some may call it meddling, but Marzia believed that sometimes you have to do something for the greater good, even if the person you're trying to help might not realize it at the time.

Marzia was relieved to punch out at the end of her shift that day. She was physically at work, but mentally she was deep in the recesses of her own mind. When she got in her car, she sat in silence for a couple minutes until the ringing in her ears began to subside.

But her day wasn't through yet. She was volunteering for one of her professors in their lab. It was nothing special, just reviewing and organizing data, but it was a good research experience for her graduate school applications. She enjoyed being in the lab, alone with just her thoughts. Although sometimes that was a recipe for disaster.

She fiddled with the lockbox until she got the door open, then flipped the lights on and set her bag next to one of the computers. The monitors were outdated and had a bigger backside than she did.

Before she knew it, she had spent a good three hours standing, staring at the screen. She checked her phone and realized it was time to pray.

Collecting her things, she headed to the campus prayer room. There was no one else there, so Marzia laid out one of the carpets in the corner of the circular room. As she began her prayer, the rain started to pour down on the glass skylight. When she finished, she hears the creaky door behind her. Glancing over, she saw Elias walk in wearing a red toque and realized he was aware of her presence. He gave her a nod, and she reciprocated as an act of mutual acknowledgment.

"I don't think I've seen you here before," Marzia remarked offhandedly.

"There's a lot you don't know about me," Elias replied.

"I didn't didn't mean to imply-" Marzia said quickly.

"That I'm some kind of heathen, right? Yeah, I think you've made it quite clear what you think of me. I really don't need a recap."

There was an oddly unsettling feeling of familiarity that she just couldn't shake, but she couldn't quite place it.

"Is that a new hat?" Marzia asked abruptly.

"Not particularly, no," he replied with a hint of confusion in his voice.

And then, all of a sudden, the way a rollercoaster plunges after reaching its peak, a memory flooded back into Marzia's mind.

"It was you!" she said, possibly a little too loudly.

"What are you on about? I don't have a lot of time. I-"

"You don't remember, do you?" Marzia asked thoughtfully. "You're the reason I have this scar."

Marzia points to a faint mark just under her eyebrow.

"I think I'd remember-" Elias said. He let out a bemused laugh. "Wait, that was you?"

"You're damn right it was me!" Marzia replied.

"I got detention for a week for that," he said reminiscently.

"Good. You deserved it," Marzia said firmly.

"Is that all?" Elias asked.

Marzia pondered for a moment, something she sometimes neglected to do.

"Yeah," she said finally, realizing the ridiculousness of the conversation. A sudden wave of embarrassment washed over her.

"Oh, and Marzia?" he said, turning back towards her.

"Mhmm?" she said, caught slightly off guard.

"The scar suits you anyways."

And at that, she felt an inkling of a smile creep onto her face. She also felt a peculiar sensation in the pit of her stomach, but before she could grapple with what it all meant, she pushed it back down into the depths of her being. She had no time for distractions. She had no need for anything that detracted from her school and her dreams. Not that there was anything in particular that was distracting her at the moment. She refused to be that weak-willed.

Despite resolving to focus all her efforts into self development for the next few weeks, to Marzia's dismay, she had to attend Mateen's ill-timed engagement party. It felt like there was a party every other week. She was in no mood for social niceties, but her mother convinced her to at least show her face.

It was hosted by the bride's family at an elaborate country club; talk about loaded. She pulled up into a long winding driveway lined with cascades of roses of all colours. Once she reached the main entrance, she was approached by a valet parking attendant. She felt somewhat uneasy when they handed their keys to a fresh-faced blonde in an emerald coat. But then again, she drove a Honda Civic, so she most likely had little to worry about.

If Marzia thought the exterior was breathtaking, the interior left her absolutely speechless. It was an affair of Gatsby-like proportions.

Appetizers flooded the tables with every sort of delicacy imaginable. Her heels clicked on the marble floors as they made their way through the lobby. She spotted her cousins from across the room and sauntered over towards them.

"I thought you weren't going to come," Ameena whispered.

"Don't look at me like I'm a china doll. It was only a crush." Marzia laughed, though she didn't take her eyes off the main entrance, paying close attention to anyone who walked through.

"I'd have called it more of an obsession," Soraya teased.

"I'm telling you I don't even care about Mateen anymore!" Marzia insisted.

"You're right. You've moved onto Elias," Ameena said, dragging out his name.

"Please, his looks are proportional to his arrogance," Marzia said.

"Marzia you-" Soraya began.

"And the annoying part is that he knows it, he knows he's cute, and that's why-"

"Marzia, shut-" Ameena said a little louder and more forcefully.

"No, I have to get this out because, for some reason, he won't get the hell out of my damn dreams!"

"It's nice to know I live rent-free in your head *and* your dreams. It's flattering, really," Elias said from behind her. His arms were crossed in smug satisfaction. He was wearing a jet-black suit with a matching monochromatic black tie and dress shirt.

"I-I knew you were there behind me, you know. You think I'd actually say those things sincerely?" Marzia said, tugging at her dress. "And besides, the only dreams of mine that you would be in would be nightmares."

"That's too bad because you're in mine."

"What?!" Marzia sputtered.

"Nightmares, that is. More like night terrors, really," Elias commented, walking past Marzia into the main ballroom. Marzia hated that she noticed the smell of his cologne.

"Woah, woah, woah, you don't get to walk off all smug like that!" Marzia said, following after him.

"You know normal people take the hint that that's the end of a conversation," Elias said.

"Yeah, and when have you ever known me to be normal?" Marzia snapped.

Elias stifled a laugh. "I mean, there's nothing really left to say. It's obvious what's going on here."

"And that would be?" Marzia pressed.

"It's obvious you like me," he said matter-of-factly.

"I'm sorry, what?"

"You know, a crush, an attachment, an affinity," Elias continued.

"I honestly didn't think you could get any more delusional," Marzia scoffed.

"Look, it's obvious I struck a chord, so as much as I'd love to stand here and have a verbal sparring match, I'm going to-"

"Eli! I was looking for you!" Dalia said, appearing abruptly.

"Are you kidding me right now?" Marzia muttered to herself.

"Everyone's having appetizers outside in the garden by the pool," Dalia said, then added, "Hello, Marzia."

"Hi Dalia," Marzia said, struggling to make eye contact. Dalia was wearing a black sequined dress with a train cascading down the back. Marzia hated to admit it, but she looked good. She would never say it, though. She was way too spiteful for that.

"Appetizers sound great right about now," Elias said, shooting Marzia a knowing glance.

"I'll meet you guys out there," Marzia replied, forcing a smile.

"You didn't think to warn me that he was right behind me?" Marzia asked, walking back towards Ameena and Soraya.

"We tried to, but you were hell-bent on going on your little tirade," Ameena cackled.

"I- it's not funny. I can't believe my big mouth." Marzia sighed.

Soraya and Ameena exchanged a glance.

"What?" Marzia asked expectantly, looking from Soraya to Ameena.

"I think," Soraya said. "That we should get some snacks."

They emerged into the garden and were taken aback by the gorgeous lights that illuminated the entire area. The fountain's gentle roar was drowned out by the many people chatting away about a wide array of topics. Politics, current events, gossip…

Marzia grabbed a plate of spring rolls in one hand and a glass of diet coke in the other. The three of them held their plates and stood by the edge of the pool, marveling at its intricate tiling. Marzia may have also imagined pushing a certain shrill-voiced annoyance into the water. She'd never actually do it, though; despite how much she might want to.

Despite the unpleasant beginning, Marzia was actually having a surprisingly good time. And that was only in part due to the good food. Forest green and gold decorations draped every crevice of the venue. To say they spared no expense would be an understatement. Extravagant flower arrangements adorned every table in crystal centrepieces, and a grand staircase accentuated the centre of the room. It rivaled even the parties in Gossip Girl, one of the many teen dramas Marzia loved to live vicariously through. She loved the formality of it all, men in tuxedos and women in elaborate gowns.

Her thoughts were abruptly interrupted when Mateen and his fiancée made their grand entrance. Marzia had to admit; she was pretty. Her name was Roya Sayed, and she was their age. She was also a business student who had just landed an internship at an accounting firm downtown, according to Instagram, anyways. Her dark brown hair was arranged in a half-up half-down style that perfectly framed her face. She was wearing an emerald green off-the-shoulder dress with a bejeweled belt draped around her waist. And yet, Marzia didn't feel jealous or angry; in fact, she felt nothing at all. Maybe this was growth, or maybe she was just in denial, but she genuinely felt happy for them.

That self-actualization lasted for approximately five minutes before Marzia was annoyed again. She spotted Dalia and Elias from the corner of her eye laughing while eating cake. Why was she even here anyway? Since when did she know Mateen? Did Elias invite her? Either way, Marzia didn't care. Although she did wish she could wipe that smug smile off of her face. But instead, she decided she would go and express her congratulations to Mateen and Roya so as not to be rude.

"Congrats, guys!" Marzia said, approaching the couple.

"Thanks, Marzia! That means a lot coming from you!" Mateen said, grinning widely.

"So, this is the famous Marzia!" Roya said. "I have to admit, I've heard a lot about you."

"All good things, I hope," Marzia replied.

"Oh, nothing but!" Roya assured her.

"Great party, by the way! I'll let you get back to mingling with all the other guests," Marzia said, politely excusing herself.

At the end of the evening, Marzia was waiting in the lobby while her father got the car from valet parking. She felt the rush of cold air hit her face every time someone walked through the doors. She noticed the full moon gleaming brightly surrounded by stars that punctuated the black sky. They were farther from the city, so the stars were remarkably visible. If she looked hard enough, she could see the big dipper.

"Stare hard enough, and you'll burn a hole right through the glass," Elias said from behind her.

"Where's your shadow?" Marzia retorted.

"Ouff, the jealous look does not suit you," Elias said, reaching his hands into his pockets.

"I'm beginning to think you *want* me to be jealous."

"Please, I could feel you staring daggers at me the entire night."

"Hmm, you'd think that if little Miss Wanna-Be President was so great, you wouldn't be so focused on what *I'm* supposedly doing."

"Hey Marzia, you ready to go?" Ameer asked. "Dad's back with the car."

"Yeah, I think it's time I called it a night," Marzia said.

And for a second, Marzia almost wondered what Elias would have said if Ameer hadn't come.

Not that she cared, of course. Never that.

CHAPTER SEVENTEEN

⌒

"I have not failed. I've just found 10,000 ways that won't work."

- Thomas Edison

Marzia never took rejection or failure very well. Once when she got a participation ribbon for an art contest at school, she threw it in the fireplace when she got home. Sometimes this worked to her detriment. She became easily dissuaded when she didn't excel immediately at any given skill that she never gave herself time to learn.

The day she lost the election for student association president was one of those days. She woke up in the morning and felt for her phone sitting on the bedside table. Then she saw the notification flash on her screen. It was an email congratulating the new president of the university's student association, Arden Hargrove. *What kind of name was that anyway*, she thought. The only silver lining in the situation is that Dalia lost too. That only slightly helped her come to terms with the fact that she had failed. Because in her mind, this was a failure. Holding herself to such high standards was exhausting, but she knew nothing else. It was what she was used to, what she was comfortable with.

Regardless of how disappointingly the day may have started, Marzia tried not to let it put a damper on the entire afternoon. She had made plans with Soraya and Ameena to blow off some steam at The Pacific National Exhibition, the local amusement park. Thanks to school, they hadn't hung out in a while, so this excursion would be a well-deserved break from their everyday monotony. The weather was particularly beautiful that day as Marzia arrived at their agreed-upon meet-up spot. She watched a little boy feverishly devouring an ice cream cone and observed as it slipped out of his hand almost in slow motion and plopped onto the ground.

Sometimes her life felt like that cone of ice cream, so much potential but in the wrong hands. She shook her head as though she was banishing the negative thoughts. Suddenly her phone buzzed. Her cousins were approaching the entrance.

"You guys are late!" Marzia laughed.

"You're just early!" Soraya winked.

"I would have been here earlier, but I forgot to fill up gas!" Ameena huffed. "And then I missed the exit, so I had to drive for what felt like forever until the next one!"

"Okay, enough of the theatrics, let's go in!" Marzia said excitedly.

They entered the park, and Marzia was immediately hit with the smell of popcorn, hotdogs, and other various street foods. The sounds of laughter and fun overwhelmed the trio as they navigated through the crowds. They decided to get in line for a particularly menacing-looking wooden roller coaster.

"So, I've been meaning to tell you guys something…" Soraya said, beating around the bush.

"Go on…" Marzia said, fishing for a response.

"So, you remember that guy I said I was talking to, the one who's name I didn't even know?"

"Oh, yeah! You mentioned really liking him," Ameena said.

"It turns out that I know who he is now…"

"And…?" Marzia said encouragingly.

"Okay, you'll never believe who it is!" Soraya exclaimed. "It turns out that my mystery man is Bilal!"

"Wait, wait, wait. Bilal?! As in Elias' brother Bilal Hakimzada?" Marzia asked in astonishment.

"Yes, and there's one more thing… he and his brother are meeting us here today," Soraya said timidly.

"I'm sorry, WHAT?" Marzia choked.

"Look, I'm sorry! I didn't want things to be awkward, so I thought it would be easier if it were a group thing," Soraya explained sheepishly.

"Maybe it'll be fun?" Ameena suggested.

"After the way I made an ass of myself at Mateen's engagement party?" Marzia sighed.

"Well, that's one way to put it," Elias said, walking up to the queue.

"Hi," Bilal stammered.

"Hey," Soraya said quietly, barely making eye contact.

"Let's have a good day today, shall we?" Ameena said, trying to be optimistic.

But as the line advanced and the sun got hotter, the group got antsier by the minute. Elias took off his baseball cap and wiped his brow, catching the beads of sweat from his forehead. Ameena began to fan herself with her map of the park. They were eggs cooking on concrete.

"Maybe we should give up and try a different ride? The line doesn't even seem to be moving," Marzia suggested, attempting to stand on the railings to view the front of the line.

"We've made it this far; we might as well stay." Elias shrugged.

"My foundation is running," Marzia sulked.

"Hey, the line is moving up!" Soraya said.

"Have you been on this ride before?" Bilal asked Soraya awkwardly.

"I come every year, actually. It's sort of like a tradition," Soraya explained.

"Does anyone have an extra water bottle?" Marzia asked.

"Yeah, I brought extra," Elias said, taking a bottle out from his backpack and handing it to her. Marzia hesitated for a second, clearly caught off guard.

"It's not poisoned, Peaches," he smirked.

"Thanks," she replied reluctantly.

This is so damn awkward! Marzia thought to herself.

Ameena fanned herself with her hand.

"You know that actually makes you hotter," Marzia commented.

"Really?" Ameena asked, raising an eyebrow.

Elias audibly sighed.

"If you have something to say to me, just say it. There's no need to be passive-aggressive," Marzia said, irritated.

"Do you always have to talk so much? Or do you just like the sound of your own voice?" Elias asked. "I'm genuinely curious."

"You're welcome to leave. I'm not holding you against your will," Marzia said, turning to face him.

"I think the heat is making everyone cranky," Bilal said awkwardly.

"Oh, it's not just the heat. Elias is *always* cranky." Marzia shrugged.

"What can I say," Elias said. "You just bring out the worst in me."

"Are you guys going to argue the entire time we're here? It's getting to be a real buzzkill," Soraya asked.

"You sound like an old married couple," Ameena laughed.

"The heat must have melted your brains," Marzia said, playfully shoving Ameena.

"Okay, am I the only one who sees the little looks they give each other?" Bilal piped up.

"*Looks?* You've got to be kidding me. I'm being punk'd here, aren't I?" Elias said.

"It's not funny anymore, guys. You know tha-" Marzia started.

"Speaking of jokes. You'll never guess who's walking our way," Ameena said.

"Oh my God. I did not know you guys would be here," Dalia said, feigning surprise.

"It's not like you saw us post on our Instagram stories that we were here or anything," Marzia muttered under her breath.

"Hey," Elias said, with a nod.

"I love this ride!" Dalia said, jumping into line. "Sorry you didn't win the election, by the way. I guess it just wasn't meant for either of us."

"Better luck next year, I guess." Marzia shrugged.

"I've always admired your persistence," Dalia replied.

Was that a subtle jab? Was that implying that Marzia was constantly faced with rejection?

Marzia felt very self-conscious all of a sudden. She picked at her already severely chipped nail polish. Meeting Elias' eyes, she abruptly darted her gaze away.

"I brought Oreos!" Bilal said, desperately trying to ease the palpable tension in the group. He passed the container of Oreos around.

"I can't even see the front of the line from here!" Soraya lamented.

"Let's play a game. Truth or dare?" Dalia suggested.

"I'll go first," Bilal volunteered. "I choose truth."

"What is one embarrassing thing we don't know about you?" Ameena asked.

"I still sleep with stuffed animals," Bilal revealed. "Elias always makes fun of me for it even though he still has that damn stuffed por-"

"My turn. Dare," Elias said abruptly.

"I dare you to scream really loud right now," Dalia said.

Elias raised an eyebrow, and for a second, everyone assumed he wasn't going to do it. But he let out a blood-curdling yell, and the entire group erupted into a hysterical fit of laughter.

"Your voice just went up like three octaves," Marzia said between laughs.

An older woman with a blonde bob shot a disapproving glance in their direction.

"Hey, look, it's our turn next!" Soraya said.

The six of them filed into the ride area and found their seats, which turned into a political incident of epic proportions.

"Elias, this ride freaks me out. Can I sit by you?" Dalia asked, batting her eyes.

"Sorry, Billy over here gets motion sickness. I'm his emotional support brother." He shrugged.

Dalia's face visibly dropped as Marzia attempted to hide the satisfied look on her face. But her tune suddenly changed when Soraya and Ameena plopped themselves down onto the next available seats. The only other seat was next to…

"I guess It's you and me, huh?" Dalia said.

Ameena and Soraya gave Marzia a sympathetic look.

"Looks like it," Marzia said through gritted teeth. She made a mental note to let those two absolutely have it when they left.

They all braced themselves as the mechanical click of the seats locked them in place. Before they knew it, they were ascending. Marzia always hated roller coasters as a child. Her sister once tricked her into going on one of the biggest roller coasters in the park. But one thing she learned that day was that she was stronger than she thought.

After the ride was over, the group was hungry for yet another spike of adrenaline, as young adults often were. So, the next stop on their list of blood-pressure raising rides was the Hellevator. True to its name, it was a tower that slowly ascended riders to the very peak and then abruptly dropped like an elevator whose cables had snapped. Once again, they got in line under the scorching heat. A group of well-to-do teenagers got in line after them. Usually, when Marzia thought people were talking about her, she was able to rationalize that the world didn't revolve around her and that they were probably discussing any number of possible subjects. But this time, she couldn't shake the feeling that they were specifically talking about her. And her suspicions were confirmed when she saw them not so subtly point with their eyes in her direction; if you know, you know. She could also tell that they were ogling Elias. Typical. He was teenage girl fodder.

"Are they talking about me?" Marzia asked Soraya and Ameena in Dari.

"I think they are. I saw them look at you like at least three times in the last five minutes," Ameena replied in Dari.

"Should I say something?" Soraya said, barely containing her contempt for the wannabe influencers. "Because I'll do it, just say the word."

"Hey, babe, where should we have lunch?" Elias said to Marzia, giving her a look that she struggled to decipher.

"Did you hit your head or something? What are you talking about?" Marzia asked in Dari.

"You want to give those girls something to talk about? Play along," Elias replied back in Dari.

"We should go somewhere nice. A restaurant?" Marzia said, switching back to English.

"Sounds good. Love you," Elias said.

Marzia flinched. She knew it was all just good fun but still... it was the way he said it. And anyway, saying "love you" was completely different than saying "I love you." Though those two similar-sounding phrases had two completely different meanings. So, did he even mean it at all? One thing she knew for sure, however, was that little scene of theirs' worked. The girls looked at each other in scorned indignation. They almost seemed jealous. Marzia admittedly felt very pleased with herself.

"Love you too," she played along.

Soraya and Ameena stifled their bubbling laughter while Dalia furrowed her brow, oblivious to the rouse.

Once the group got off the ride, they figured it was time to break for lunch. The one thing they could unanimously agree on was pizza. Marzia took one bite before her phone suddenly rang, jolting her into alertness.

"Hello?" she said.

"Are you going to be home anytime soon?" Ameer asked, urgency in his voice.

"I was going to head home in a few hours. Why?"

"Uh...I would highly suggest you get home as soon as you can."

"Okay, now you're scaring me. What's going on?"

"Our aunt and cousin are here. You know the ones we didn't even know existed until a little while ago? And mom has no idea," Ameer said.

"What!?" Marzia asked in disbelief.

"Look, how quick can you get here?" Ameer pressed, urgency lacing every word.

"I'll be there as soon as I can!" Marzia said, hanging up the phone.

"What happened?" Ameena asked.

"Are you okay?" Soraya added.

"It's... I- have something I have to take care of at home. I can't really explain right now, but I have to go."

"So soon?" Dalia said.

"Yes, it's- it's a family thing. But you guys have fun." Marzia waved, departing from her little ragtag group of…friends? Elias looked like he was going to say something but ended up deciding against it.

When Marzia got home, she saw a silver Subaru parked by the curb. She noticed the front door wide open. As she approached, she heard voices coming from inside the house.

"You know what you did!" she heard her aunt say.

"I will not have this in my house. We aren't teenagers anymore, Saba!" her mother countered.

"When you said you had a plan, I didn't think it would include an ambush!" Marzia said to her cousin, visibly flustered.

"I didn't mean for this to happen. I thought you'd be home, I-I-" Neelofar replied.

"We're going," her aunt said curtly.

"Why won't you tell me what happened with her all those years ago?" Marzia pleaded with her mother.

"There are some things that are best left unsaid."

That was all her mother had to say. What started out as a carefree day turned into a stressful mess, one that she would eventually need to untangle.

But not tonight.

CHAPTER EIGHTEEN

∽

"The best time to make friends is before you need them."

-Ethel Barrymore

Marzia liked to think she was a good friend. In fact, in grade 1, she almost got into a fight with a boy who destroyed Reiyna's sandcastle. Before she could really let him have it, a teacher quickly put a stop to whatever WWE moment would have transpired. She was subsequently sent to the office, where her dad had to come and pick her up in the middle of the day.

"Was he bothering you?" he asked Marzia in Dari when he came to pick her up.

"He was bothering my friend," she replied.

"Good job," he said to her with a sly smile as they exited the school doors.

However, despite her heart always being in (generally) the right place, its execution sometimes proved to be a bit elusive. In light of recent events, Marzia unintentionally put her friendship with Reiyna on the backburner. For someone who claimed to be so perceptive, Marzia could be really oblivious sometimes. To add to the perfect storm, Reiyna was also not the confrontational type. So, I suppose you could say they were in between a rock and a hard place. Marzia didn't realize Reiyna was hurt, and Reiyna refused to admit she was. But like a tea kettle on the cusp of whistling, there is only so long you can hold something in before it begins to eat away at you.

Marzia had practically spent the entire morning in the lab and eventually lost track of how long she had been there in the glow of computer light. Her eyes began to feel strained, but she just rubbed them tiredly and went back to work. Her phone buzzed, alerting her to several missed calls, but she ignored it. She took another gulp of the large vanilla iced coffee sitting beside her when her finger slipped, and the creamy mixture cascaded across the shiny black keyboard sitting in front of her. It all happened so quickly she wasn't able to do anything to stop it, and yet it appeared to be in slow motion as she watched the screen fade to black.

Oh no. Oh no. Oh no, no, no, no.

In a delayed response, Marzia finally realized the gravity of the situation. Her brain had short-circuited the same way the computer did. Before she could put her thoughts into action, Reiyna walked in through the door with a bag of food in her hand and a tray of drinks.

"I've been calling you. Why do you look like someone died?" she laughed.

"Because someone has," Marzia replied with a blank expression, gesturing towards her monitor.

"Oh. I see," she said, taking in the gravity of the situation. "It's fine. I can fix this."

"I think this is beyond fixing, to be honest. I've just lost all my data," Marzia said in disbelief.

"So, to quote…well, I don't exactly know who said it, but it's not over 'till the fat lady sings," Reiyna said, putting down the food and her maroon backpack donned with decorative pins. Marzia put her head in her hands in resigned hopelessness.

"I'm finished," she sighed.

"There's no time for theatrics," Reiyna said decisively. She grabbed a rag from the cupboard and began fiddling with the computer and keyboard. Then, she pulled out a hairdryer from her backpack.

"Well, that's oddly convenient," Marzia said. "Why do you have a hairdryer?"

"I was going to work out and shower at the gym, but I hate having wet hair." Reiyna shrugged. "No talking, I need absolute quiet concentration."

Marzia resorted to rhythmically banging her head on the table, repeatedly whispering a desperate supplication to herself. Reiyna used the hairdryer, evaporating the moisture from the computer.

"You belong in a straight jacket," Reiyna said teasingly.

"I belong in a noose," Marzia sulked.

"Just wait one more second…" Reiyna replied, turning the device on and off again. "It turned on!"

"What?!" Marzia said, her head shooting up.

"You're welcome," Reiyna said with a look of satisfaction.

"Since when were you so good with computers?" Marzia asked.

"I'm surprised that you know anything about me at all these days."

"What's that supposed to mean?" Marzia asked, sensing her accusatory tone.

"I mean, you've barely had time to return any of my texts lately. It seems all you have time for lately is school, work, and fighting with Elias," Reiyna said.

"Elias has *nothing* to do with this. I don't even know why you're bringing h-"

"Oh, it has everything to do with him! You're spending every waking moment avoiding the obvious feelings you have for him."

"What is this really about?" Marzia asked.

"You know, sometimes you can be really selfish. Besides all that, have you even read my manuscript?" Reiyna asked.

"I, well...I read the part where you said you think I'm cynical!" Marzia pointed out.

"Those characters are only loosely based on the people in my life! And the character you're talking about, you didn't read the part where I also call her brave, and kind, and fiercely protective of her friends and the people she cares about."

"I'm...sorry. I've been so preoccupied that I really haven't been fair to you," Marzia said. "I guess I never realized that I've been neglecting our friendship. I've been so busy wrapped up in my own drama."

"I mean, it's a two-way street," Reiyna admitted.

"Well, you were wrong about one thing, though," Marzia said.

"And what might that be?" Reiyna asked, raising an eyebrow.

"I do *not* have feelings for Elias," Marzia insisted, throwing a crumpled-up piece of paper at Reiyna.

"I want whatever will make you happy," Reiyna said diplomatically, considering her words carefully.

"You know there is something I hadn't told anyone else..." Marzia started.

"Which is?" Reiyna replied encouragingly.

"My data wasn't the only thing I was worried about losing on my computer. I was in the middle of applying for an internship. In Korea," Marzia continued.

"Woah, really? I'm surprised! But I'm happy for you. I hope you get it. But that doesn't mean I won't miss you," Reiyna replied.

"I mean, I don't know if I'll get it, but I wanted to at least try. It's getting a little...suffocating here. Not to mention, I've barely seen the world yet. Can you believe I've never even left the country, Reiyna?" Marzia said wistfully.

"Well, you're going to have to watch a lot of K-dramas if you want to have a lay of the land and the people," Reiyna teased.

When Marzia got home, she heard her mother speaking quite intently on the phone, obviously discussing something of importance. She had a worried expression painted across her face when she went to greet Marzia. She noticed the cats quietly sleeping on the couch and that the house felt odd and tense, even the floorboards refused to make a sound in that moment.

"What's going on?" Marzia asked.

"Elias' mother told me Bilal was considering a girl."

"Oh?" Marzia said, feigning ignorance.

"Yes, but it won't work out. They are incompatible, so he said. He has moved on."

"What?! And why is that?" Marzia asked anxiously but acting as though she hardly cared for the answer.

"Elias advised him that she didn't seem all that interested and that he should protect his interests," her mother replied.

"His interests? What does Elias know about relationships?" Marzia scoffed.

"I just hope you all get married, as any mother would. And I would hope during my lifetime," Marzia's mother said longingly.

"I'm sure there's plenty of time for all of that," Marzia replied, kissing her mother on the cheek as she departed upstairs. Once in the confines of her own room, she called Soraya and Ameena immediately on a three-way call.

"I heard," Marzia said.

"I guess I should have figured word would travel fast," Soraya replied wryly.

"This is all Elias' fault. I heard my mother say he was the one who convinced Bilal not to continue courting you," Marzia replied.

"It doesn't matter. Despite how much I actually liked Bilal…It'll be okay. Like the cliché goes, there's plenty of fish in the sea," Soraya said.

"But I don't understand what went wrong. You guys seemed like you got along amazingly," Ameena pondered.

"He says you seemed disinterested," Marzia replied.

"That couldn't be further from the truth!" Soraya protested.

" *We* know that. But evidently, someone doesn't," Ameena said.

"Don't you worry, Soraya; I'll have this sorted out. Don't count yourself out just yet," Marzia said, hanging up with blazing determination. The next call she made would not be so pleasant.

"Hello?" a wary Elias replied."I'm surprised you still have my number."

"Believe me, so am I," Marzia replied. "But I didn't call you to pour my heart out."

"So why did you call me, Peaches?" he asked.

"You know what you did! How can you sit there when you- well, I don't exactly know that you're sitting because I can't see you right now, but- that's not the point. How can you not feel guilty when you cost one of the closest people to me a chance at true happiness?" Marzia said accusingly.

"If you're talking about Bilal and Soraya, I don't regret what I did, and I don't think I was wrong either," he said unapologetically after a thoughtful pause.

"You know nothing about her, Elias! You had no right to-"

"I had *every* right. He's my brother, and I won't stand by and watch him makes one of the biggest mistakes of his life."

"Mistake? Soraya is kind and caring. Anyone would be lucky to have her! And she's also smart and funny...and yet you still think she isn't good enough for your family," Marzia said.

"That's not true. I just think that-"

"So, do you think I'm beneath you too?" Marzia snapped.

"That's- that's irrelevant you're not the one-"

"Are you really that cold-hearted?"

"It seems like you've already made up your mind about me, so I guess there's nothing more for us to say," Elias said, his tone hardening.

"I guess so," Marzia affirmed.

They both hung up after a brief silence that felt excruciatingly long. Marzia felt her cheeks flush with anger. How could he do this? She knew he loathed her, but she never thought that he would take it out on her cousin. It was times like these that Marzia required wise council. And who better to talk to than her older brother. He was a guy, wasn't he? So maybe, just maybe, he could make sense of the turbulent complexities of the male species. She entered his room and laid down on his bed, putting her chin in her hands.

"Can I help you?" Ameer asked, peering at her from over his laptop.

"I need your insight on something."

"Proceed," he responded.

"Do men really have no empathy?" Marzia asked philosophically.

"I feel like there is a back story to this."

"Like, do some of you not have any critical thinking skills at all?"

Ameer sighed, closed his laptop, and turned his chair to face her.

"What's this really about?" he asked.

"What this is about is that there has been a *grave* injustice," Marzia said. "And the root cause was Elias Hakimzada."

"What did he do this time?"

"Where do I start? I mean, he's been an ass since we met, and- I digress. Bilal and Soraya were actually getting to know each other, and they seemed pretty compatible too. Well, anyways, Elias convinced him to break it off."

"Well, did you ask him why?" he replied.

"Well, no, but he had no right to just interfere like that!" Marzia insisted.

"In that case, I think you're asking the wrong guy." He shrugged."If you wanted to know what his reasons were, why didn't you just ask him?"

"I...well..."

"And there's your answer," Ameer said.

"But you didn't answer my question?"

"If you have to ask, then you're not ready for the answer."

"Huh?" Marzia said.

"What?"

"Ameer, sometimes I need you to actually be serious for once."

"Okay, here's my honest to God answer," Ameer said. "I think you need to sort this out with the people involved and actually have an open mind and hear what they have to say when they tell you."

And so Marzia went to sleep that night the way she went to sleep most nights; unsure how everything was going to unfold. Ameer always told her exactly what she needed to hear.

CHAPTER NINETEEN

❧

"The best things in life are often waiting for you at the exit ramp of your comfort zone."

-*Karen Salmansohn*

There were certain moments in Marzia's life when she remembered being distinctly proud of herself. One of those times was in elementary school when the entire class was tasked with a creative writing exercise. She wrote about a mysterious package being left at the doorstep of the school. She loved mysteries so much that she incorporated them into almost everything she wrote. Her heart leapt when she heard her teacher reading her short story out to the class. She beamed with pride when the teacher congratulated her on her stellar work.

And that is also how she felt the morning she found out she actually got the internship she had applied for. She had slept in, like most days when she didn't have class or work. She checked her phone and saw the email with her eyes still adjusting to the morning light. A wave of happiness washed over her, but it was quickly replaced with creeping anxiety. She had never been away from home. In fact, she had never even left the country before. And suddenly, she wondered if she had made a huge mistake by applying. She subsequently went about her day in a haze as though there was a dark cloud over her head. She couldn't even concentrate when she was grabbing her daily obligatory vanilla iced coffee.

"Ma'am?" the cashier asked timidly.

"Sorry, what was that?" Marzia shook her head, almost like she was trying to remove the intrusive thoughts from her mind.

"Your drink," she said, gesturing to the cup in her hand.

"Sorry! Thanks!" she said, flustered. She grabbed her drink and rushed out the door to catch her lecture, which she was somehow always chronically late to. The lecture was about defense mechanisms. She was tuning in and out, but the only one she really paid any attention to was *denial*.

Once class was over, she found herself wandering aimlessly around campus. She saw so many people walking past her, laughing, unaware of the monumental decision that was before her. How was everyone so calm when she was dealing with something so life-changing? She knew what she had to do. She had to talk to Soraya and Ameena. She patched them both through on a three-way call and waited expectantly as it rang.

"I'm making popcorn. What's up?" Soraya said. Marzia could hear the microwave humming in the background.

"I got an internship!" Marzia said excitedly.

"That's amazing, Marzia!" Ameena said.

"We're so happy for you!" Soraya affirmed.

"But the only thing is that it's in Korea. I would be gone the whole summer."

"A whole summer is a long time. But this is such a good opportunity for you," Ameena said.

"Yeah, if you don't do this, you'll regret it for the rest of your life!"

"You guys aren't going to forget about me, are you?" Marzia asked, seeking reassurance.

"Are you crazy? How could we possibly ever forget about you?" Soraya laughed. "What is it they say? Absence makes the heart grow fonder?"

"It'll be a big change," Marzia continued.

"That you'll get used to," Ameena insisted.

"What about everything I'll be leaving behind?" Marzia fretted.

"It'll all be waiting for you when you get back," Soraya assured.

"Well, then I guess I'll need an English to Korean dictionary," Marzia said, uncertainty edging into her tone.

"Have you told your parents?" Ameena asked.

"Ummm…. no. I haven't really thought that far ahead, to be honest," Marzia said thoughtfully.

"I'm sure they'll be fine with it if you explain how enriching of an experience it'll be," Ameena said encouragingly.

"Yeah, you're right. I'll go do that. I gotta go but thank you for the encouragement. I don't know what I would do without you guys," Marzia said, hanging up.

Marzia had a lot to mull over, and one thing that, without fail, comforted her in times like these was her favourite sour candy. Thankfully, a place on campus had them; in fact, she went there so often that the employees there practically knew her by name. She tossed a few of them in her mouth and chewed with purpose as she was consumed by her internal thoughts. She checked her phone and realized that it was about time to pray. So she made her way to the prayer room and walked through the narrow hallway to a row of prayer mats. She saw other people finishing up their prayers and thought for a second how crazy it would be if she ran into Elias again. And just as soon as the thought crossed her mind, she saw a tall figure get up from tying his shoelaces. She wondered if he was like Beetlejuice; if she said his name enough times, he would just appear.

"Hi," she said, breaking the silence.

"Hey," he replied with muted enthusiasm.

"How… how are you?" he asked. Marzia began to fiddle with her beaded bracelet. At that moment, the bracelet seemed like the most interesting thing in the world to look at. Or maybe it was just to avoid making eye contact with a certain brooding brown-eyed boy.

"Good," he replied. "How are you?"

"I'm doing great, actually. I got offered an internship," Marzia said abruptly. "It's in Korea."

"Good for you," Elias said, his tone indecipherable.

"Really? That's all you're going to say?"

"You're unbelievable," he said, half to himself.

"*I'm* unbelievable?" Marzia replied, aghast.

"Yeah, you're unbelievable, Peaches. I mean, what am I supposed to say to that? Do you want me to tell you to stay? Is that what you want to hear? Do you want me to beg you not to go? Because I'm not going to do that, you're not going to get that from me."

"Don't worry, I wouldn't dare assume you cared enough to even bother," Marzia scoffed. "And besides, I would imagine you have your attention occupied by your little fan club of one."

"And who is that?" Elias asked, humouring her.

"Dalia." Marzia almost laughed. "Don't pretend like you don't see the way she looks at you, the way she talks to you."

"I don't know what you're talking about," Elias said, shaking his head.

"I'm sure it doesn't hurt that her father is the CEO of a venture capital firm. You have to secure the bag, am I right?"

"You think I need her family's money?" Elias asked, sounding a bit more arrogant than he meant to.

"Right, how could I forget. You never miss a moment to remind me how much more fortunate you are than I am," Marzia said bitterly. "How could a charity case like me understand?"

"That's not what I meant," Elias protested. "I don't give a damn about money."

"How noble," Marzia retorted mockingly.

"How long will you be gone?" he asked, a little quieter.

"The whole summer."

"Well, then you should make sure you pack a bathing suit," Elias replied.

"I never said I was going to take it," Marzia said.

"Well, are you?"

"I don't know…probably." Marzia shrugged.

"It's a great opportunity."

"It is."

"What's the problem then?"

"It's just…this one thing."

And at that moment, their silence said more than words ever could.

"We're doing a marriage seminar next week. You should come!" an enthusiastic girl in a floral hijab handed them both a flier.

"Thank you," Marzia said, still a little dazed.

"Uh, thanks," Elias replied, trying to sound genuine.

The girl cheerily walked off to hand out more fliers to the other students.

"You know you're not as mean as you think you are," Marzia said abruptly.

"You seem be the only one who thinks that Peaches," Elias replied wryly.

"Why do you do that?" Marzia asked, "Act so tough all the time, I mean."

Marzia expected a sarcastic comment but was shocked when Elias let his guard down.

"I guess it's easier to hurt others than to give others the opportunity to hurt you," he replied.

"Why do you think people will hurt you?"

"Because they already have," Elias said, barely above a whisper, "When you've been bullied all your life, I guess you come to expect it."

"Do you think *I'm* going to hurt you?" Marzia asked him.

"No," Elias replied, "Actually you're one of the few people I'd never think would ever intentionally hurt someone. But I guess old habits die hard."

"The first step to recovery is admitting you have a problem," Marzia replied.

"Thanks Doc," Elias laughed.

Marzia couldn't remember the last time she saw him laugh, but it looked good on him.

"So, I guess I'll see you…when I do," Marzia said.

"Yeah, maybe," Elias replied, hands in his pockets.

"Goodbye, Elias."

"Safe travels, Peaches."

She heard the door close behind her as Elias left the prayer room. An echoing silence filled the room, radiating through every corner and crevice. She didn't know what she expected from that conversation, but nonetheless, it felt incomplete. But then again, maybe she did, and she didn't know how to put it into words, and maybe a part of her didn't want to.

The ride home for Marzia was silent and deafening at the same time. She turned up her podcast volume to drown out the sound of her own thoughts, the maladaptive coping mechanism of her choice.

"What's wrong, Marzia you've barely touched your dinner," her mother asked.

"I have something to announce. But don't worry, it's actually good news," Marzia assured."I received an offer for a research internship in Korea."

"Korea?" Marzia's mother said with intrigue.

"Yes, and I know it's across the world, but it's a really good opportunity for experience," Marzia said with all the determination she could muster."And it would only be for the summer."

"I think it's time you make your own way in the world. So, if this is what will make you happy, then you should go with our blessing," her father said.

"Although we will miss you terribly," her mother lamented. "But there is a lot to prepare for. You have a lot to pack, and wash and-"

"Don't worry, there's still lots of time," Marzia laughed.

"You know what I always say, don't put off until tomorrow what you can do today!" Marzia's mother said.

"I think Benjamin Franklin said that," Marzia laughed.

"Nonetheless, the sentiment is the same," her mother affirmed.

"Are you sure you're not just going to get pickpocketed and lose all your money?" Ameer teased.

"I'm perfectly capable of navigating a new city without being robbed; thank you very much!"

"You once left your house keys inside the actual door," Ameer said.

"That was one time!" Marzia sighed.

"Everyone knows you're the most aloof sibling," Ameer said matter-of-factly.

"I am the most aware person in this entire family. I might as well have eyes at the back of my head, Ameer! I'm always watching and listening! Even when you think I'm not watching, I'm still watching!"

"Ameer, don't tease your sister," their father scolded half-heartedly.

For once, she decided to heed her mother's advice and took stock of her clothes and what she wanted to take with her. She ruffled through her closets, examining the collection she had amassed over the years. Some pieces she wore frequently, and others hardly fit. She tried to busy herself, but she couldn't escape the feeling that something was amiss. Her cats observed her sleepily from their spot in corner of the room.

One thing was for sure, however. Before she left, she had to make sure things were resolved between her mother and her aunt. Marzia hated loose ends, and she was determined to tie this particular one up with a nice bow. The first phase of this plan was to orchestrate another ambush. But this time, she would have to be prepared. She would have to do it right this time.

She texted her cousin Neelofar and arranged for both of them to bring their moms to a particular park halfway between their houses. It was a flower garden similar to the one they both played in when they were children. Marzia didn't know all that much about her mother's life in Afghanistan, but she knew she loved that garden and would spend much of her time there with her siblings and cousins. So

Neelofar and Marzia agreed to bring both of their mothers to the park at exactly 2 p.m. one Friday afternoon. Despite having thoroughly planned it out, Marzia still fretted over the execution. She was never one for confrontation, so to be staging an intervention of sorts was daunting. The sun was shining, which was a juxtaposition to the internal turmoil occurring within her. She watched as two squirrels chased each other up a tree.

"You ready to go?" Marzia asked her mother, grabbing her purse and keys.

"Just about, I just have to refill the cats' bowls. What's the hurry?"

"Oh, no hurry," Marzia said, checking the time on her phone.

1:30 p.m. She tried to hide the urgency in her voice. Once they pulled up to the parking lot, Marzia got a text message from Neelofar saying she had just arrived as well. Everything was going to plan...so far. Marzia continued with cautious optimism as she and her mother took a turn about the pond situated in the middle of the park. She saw Neelofar and her mother approaching from the distance, and Marzia looked at her mother, who was feeding the ducks with stale pieces of bread. It was now or never. The two of them would have it out, for better or for worse.

"Marzia, what's going on?" her mother asked skeptically, following her line of sight.

"Okay, don't be mad, but… this had to happen. There's only so long you can go without talking to your own sister," Marzia reasoned.

"That was not your business to be getting into. I am the mother here, not you!" her mother reproached sternly.

"I'm sorry, but I did what I thought was right. And I won't apologize for trying to bring you two together," Marzia said, holding firm to her convictions.

"Salaam Khalajaan. It's nice to properly meet you, finally," Neelofar said, as charming as ever.

Marzia admired how she could stand there so composed and respectful in such an awkward and stressful situation. If she was nervous or uncomfortable, she didn't let it show. That was one thing she admired about her new cousin. She seemed to always know what to say to people to get them to like her.

"I think the girls are right. It's been too long, Nafiza Jaan," her aunt said.

"I was never the problem," Marzia's mother shot back.

Her mother's candidness shocked Marzia. She was so used to her polite hospitality in front of other people that it felt weirdly off-putting when she was anything but pleasant. It was the Afghan way to be hospitable, but that doesn't mean they can't be vindictive. What was that overused quote from Alexander the Great?

"May God keep you away from the venom of the cobra, the teeth of the tiger, and the revenge of the Afghans.."

There was an awkward pause where both mothers struggled to make eye contact. You'd think one of them was Medusa.

"If no one else will address it, then I will. What happened all those years ago that you guys can't even stand to be in the same room together?" Marzia asked, miraculously feeling emboldened.

"I hate to bring you kids into this, but the truth is the truth. Back in Afghanistan, long ago, back when I had no grey hairs, I was going to get married to the man I loved. We were going to pay someone to smuggle us out of Kabul. I almost didn't make it out because your mother, how do you say it in English? She sold us out to the soviet soldiers. We almost didn't make it out, but his father bribed the officers to let us go, and then we made our way to Pakistan," her aunt said, a haunting sorrow in her eyes.

"That's what you thought happened all these years?" Marzia's mother asked, clearly bewildered by the accusation. "I never betrayed you! You were the one who left without so much as a single word! Do you know how that made me feel?"

"There was no time! You knew Hakim was in danger! We had to get out! And I wrote you letters! Didn't you get them?"

"I didn't get any letters!" Marzia's mother said.

"You honestly thought I wouldn't say goodbye to my only sister? We moved a few weeks later after father was taken in for questioning. That's probably why we didn't get any of your correspondences," Marzia's mother said reflectively.

"Woah, wait, grandfather was interrogated?" Marzia asked.

"It was a time of great suspicion. It was a time where your own neighbours would report you for anti-government sentiments," Marzia's mother lamented.

"I wrote you guys for months. But after a while, I lost hope of ever getting in contact again. I thought you really wanted nothing to do with me. I thought you hated me."

"You're my sister. I never could…I would never hate you," Marzia's mother said.

At this point, both women had tears streaming down their faces. And maybe it was the high tensions, and perhaps it was all the emotional revelations, but Marzia's eyes began to water too. She couldn't imagine that a simple misunderstanding led to two sisters being estranged for decades, decades they could never get back. But that wasn't important, because you can't change the past. And there's nothing more futile than expending energy on what is out of the realm of your control. But what *was* in her control was today's events, and for that, she was proud of herself, proud that she made it happen.

CHAPTER TWENTY

∽

"I dislike feeling at home when I am abroad."

–George Bernard Shaw

And so, Marzia departed on an adventure she could have never imagined in her wildest dreams. Getting there was all a blur. Before leaving the house, she was in a neurotic stupor, double and triple-checking everything she needed. She checked the expiration date on her passport, and she even made sure she had three forms of government-issued ID just for good measure. All of a sudden, however, her face flushed white. She was forgetting something.

"My watch, the one with the leather wristband, do either one of you know where it is?" Marzia asked her parents.

"I don't remember seeing it since we moved back into the house," her mother replied.

"I can't believe this; I need that watch!" Marzia said, trying her best not to sound whiney but continuing to do so anyway.

"Maybe you should ask the Hakimzadas. You might have left it at their house when we moved," her father suggested.

"I…are they even home?" Marzia asked, checking the time on her phone.

"I'll give them a call," her mother replied.

"Thank you! I'm going to make sure I didn't forget anything upstairs," Marzia said, running up the stairs.

She glanced through her room one last time, noting that it looked more bare than what she was used to seeing. She was lost in thought for what seemed like forever until she heard her mother's voice hurling her back into reality.

"Marzia! Elias' mother said it might still be in your old room. We can stop by on the way to check."

"Uh… okay. Sounds good," Marzia replied.

The route to Elias' house felt weirdly nostalgic, and Marzia was reminded of the very first time they drove over there after the fire. Looking back, it felt like eons ago. Marzia was greeted by Elias' mom and the smell of a freshly cooked meal.

"You must stay for lunch, Marzia Jaan!" Elias' mother said, warmth resonating with every word.

"Thank you so much, but we're actually headed to the airport! I just wanted to quickly stop by and see if I left my favourite watch here accidentally! Thank you, by the way. I know this is very short notice!" Marzia said apologetically.

She made her way up the flight of stairs that she had ascended countless times while they had stayed there. She passed Elias' room; his door left ajar. Her curiosity got the better of her, and she stood at the door, daring to peer inside. As soon as she did, something caught her eye. She eyed the mahogany bedside table, but the quality marksmanship of its construction was not what caught her attention. What did catch her off guard was what rested on top, a stuffed porcupine. The very same one she threw at Elias when she was angry with him the day that she ran into him at the fall fair. He kept it. Why had he kept it?

"He's not home," Elias' mother said quietly. Marzia hadn't noticed her come up behind her.

"Oh, I- I wasn't, I was just-" she stuttered.

"My mistake," she said sweetly and then excused herself to go put away the laundry that was in the basket she was holding.

Marzia realized she had been standing there for way too long, so she continued on to what had been her room for the better half of a few months. She gingerly pushed the door open, a wave of nostalgia hitting her like a ton of bricks. The furniture had changed, and the lighting seemed different, but it was still the same room she spent all those nights in. Nights spent pouring her heart out to Soraya and Ameena, pulling all-nighters to finish essays that she left until the last possible minute, and nights she spent enjoying her own company. She noticed the light hitting something wedged underneath the bed. It was her watch. She knew that was why she came over initially, but she honestly didn't expect to actually find it. Which, in retrospect, was rather asinine considering she was supposed to be getting on a flight to Seoul. She grabbed it off the floor and carefully examined it. Other than a little dust, all it was really in need of were new batteries.

"Find what you were looking for?" Elias' mother asked.

"I did, thank you! I was just reliving some old memories." Marzia laughed. "And I just wanted to thank you again for taking us in. I don't know how I'll ever repay your kindness."

"The pleasure was all mine. It was nice to have some feminine energy in the house. It's actually been pretty quiet with all of you gone. The boys are always out with their friends, and their father works late more days than not."

Marzia gave her a tight hug as she got back into the car to depart on a perilous journey across the world. Finally, when she reached the Vancouver airport, Marzia began to feel rocks in her stomach, and suddenly she was less confident and a lot less sure of herself.

"Maybe I'm making a mistake. Maybe I should-" Marzia began.

"You've made it this far. And we believe in you. If you don't do this now, you will regret it for the rest of your life," her mother replied.

"You'll always wonder what could have been. Trust me, you don't want to live with that kind of regret," her father added.

"Don't you dare second guess yourself now!" Ameer said, attempting to sound stern but failing.

After all was said and done and many tears were subsequently shed, Marzia bid farewell (for the time being) to the place she had known all her life. The next few months were a question mark, but it was a mystery she was looking forward to exploring. She decided then and there that she would make the most of it and leave behind every worry and negative thought she had accumulated over the past year. Before she knew it, she was on a flight, and there was no turning back. When she looked out the tiny window, she didn't see the sky but opportunity and, most importantly, hope.

"What's waiting for you in Seoul? Or should I ask who's waiting for you?" a friendly elderly woman sitting beside her asked.

"Nobody," Marzia replied wistfully. "Just a research internship."

"Do me one favour, hun."

"What's that?" Marzia asked curiously.

"Never settle for anything less than you deserve," the woman replied. She said this in such a serious tone that it took Marzia by surprise. She wondered what brought on such advice but nodded anyway.

Marzia fell asleep after indulging in several movies, snacks, and magazines. Later she woke up to the sound of the plane landing. She wiped the drool that pooled at the corner of her mouth as she came back to her senses. Near baggage claim, she saw a girl holding a white sign that said "Rashidi" in big block letters. She was rather tall and had a highlighter yellow jacket that Marzia spotted from miles away.

"Hi there! I'm Son-Ha Park! I'll be working with you at the lab and will also be your guide while you're here in Seoul!"

"Hi, Son-Ha!" Marzia said, exhausted from the taxing journey. "Is there anywhere around here to eat?"

"I know just the place!" Son-Ha said with a knowing grin. A taxi ride later, and the two of them were in Itaewon, Seoul's International District, and home to many foreigners. It was like a whole other world, and definitely nothing like Vancouver.

"Toto, I have a feeling we aren't in Canada anymore," Marzia said, half to herself.

As they walked through the streets of Itaewon, Marzia remained dazzled by the sheer number of things going on at the same time. She was used to the suburbs. But here, people were talking, cars were honking, the smell of food wafted through the streets...and yet, it was orderly chaos. The neon sights glowed brightly in the night sky, like the North star guiding them through the darkness. An orange taxicab whizzed by, snapping Marzia out of a daydream. They entered one of the brightly lit doorways, and Son-Ha said something to an elderly man behind the counter.

"We can take a seat in the corner over there!" she said, pointing to a corner with a window. Almost instantaneously, a server brought over two menus in both English and Korean.

"*Gam sahamnida!*" Son-Ha said cheerfully in Korean.

"That means thank you, right?" Marzia asked, flipping through her English to Korean dictionary.

"Yes, you're learning!" she said excitedly.

"*Dubu-gangjeong,*" Marzia read off of the menu. "Sweet and crunchy tofu."

"Make that two!" Son-Ha affirmed.

When their food finally came out, Marzia was unspeakably famished; the kind of hunger that leaves you shaking. The steam coming from the food entered Marzia's senses as she took her first bite.

"The flavour...it's..."

"Amazing, isn't it?" Son-Ha smiled. "I'm so glad you like it."

"So, tell me, Son-Ha, what is it going to be like at the lab?" Marzia asked, her mouth full of food.

"It's a lot of data entry, I won't lie. But it's an amazing chance to network and work closely with some amazing researchers."

"I'm no stranger to busywork." Marzia shrugged. "Mostly I'm just glad to be here."

"Well, with me by your side, I'm sure we'll have a lot of fun this summer!"

The two continued their meal and traded jokes and childhood stories until Marzia noticed someone glancing over at her newly minted friend. A young man sipping a coffee with chestnut hair looked over at them, seemingly trying to catch Son-Ha's eye.

"Hey, I think you have a fan club," Marzia said, her voice low.

"Huh? Who?"

"Eleven o'clock!"

"What happens at eleven o'clock?" she asked.

"Twelve, eleven, ten. Eleven o'clock!" Marzia laughed, demonstrating with her arm that the hands of the clock corresponded to the cardinal directions.

"That's the Last Crusade, no?" Son-Ha giggled.

"You've seen Indiana Jones? You know you're the first person who's gotten that reference," Marzia declared.

"We're in South Korea, not North Korea." She winked.

"Okay, but seriously, eleven o'clock, that guy is honest to God checking you out!" Marzia said insistently.

"Oh, I don't think so, I really don't-"

"Hi," the chestnut-haired mystery boy said, approaching their table.

"He's cute. You should ask him to sit!" Marzia said.

"I don't know, Marzia-"

"Hi, I'm Marzia, and this is Son-Ha," Marzia said, turning to face him.

"Young-Do," he said with a toothy grin.

"Ask him to sit down. He doesn't look like he's a serial killer," Marzia joked.

"I'm glad you don't find me threatening," Young-Do said with a breathy laugh in perfectly unaccented English. "You know in Itaewon, a lot of us speak English."

"Oh, I- I didn't mean to imply that-" Marzia sputtered, her face quickly turning as red as a fire truck.

"It's really okay. I'm only joking!" Young-Do consoled her.

"Would you like to sit down?" Son-Ha asked.

"I actually have work in a half-hour, but maybe I'll run into you again," he said, as he picked up his to-go order and gave Son-Ha a wink.

"What in the Wattpad just happened!?" Marzia asked, amazed and bewildered.

"Wattpad?" Son-Ha asked, confused.

"It's a website where people write fanfiction- anyways, that's not the point. That guy was very cute and very much into you!"

"I don't think so, but I appreciate the compliment," Son-Ha replied bashfully.

"Then what is this?" Marzia replied, pulling out a slip of paper tucked under Son-Ha's cup. "This looks like a number."

Son-Ha let out a shocked, laugh-croaking noise hybrid.

When Marzia got home to the apartment she would be inhabiting for the summer, it was almost 9 o'clock, which to Marzia was practically the middle of the night. Along with jet lag and the general achy feeling that pulsated through every muscle of her body, she was itching to knock out. But her racing thoughts kept her up. Back home, it was well into the afternoon. She launched WhatsApp and tried to call her mom's cellphone.

"Hello, Marzia? Can you hear us?" her mother asked, speaking loudly.

"Yes, Maudarjaan, I can hear you!" Marzia laughed. She already missed hearing her mother's voice. She never truly appreciated it until this very moment, when she wasn't able to hear it in person.

"Have you arrived safely? How was the flight?" her father asked in the background.

"The flight was long, but I got here safely! Everyone here is very nice. But it's very different from home."

"Make sure you lock your door!" her mother cautioned.

"I will!"

"And don't forget to buy groceries. You can't just be eating out for two entire months!" her father said.

"It's important to know how to cook! You never know when you'll find your hands tied!" her mother added.

"I can cook. I'll even show you guys next time I make myself a meal!"

"And not just noodles!" her father added.

"I can make more than noodles!" Marzia insisted.

"We'll see about that!" her mother replied.

"What are you guys up to right now?" Marzia asked. Her mother and father began to speak, but the signal kept cutting out, so all Marzia heard were choppy half sentences. Then, the line went dead. Her apartment must have very terrible Wi-Fi.

At that moment, all alone in a tiny one-bedroom apartment, Marzia felt more alone than she had ever been in her life. She was far from home, without anyone she knew, and she didn't even know the language. She could be kidnapped or killed, and no one would know for probably weeks. She shook her head, trying to rid herself of these thoughts. And so, because she had nothing else to do, she stuffed her earbuds in her ears, put on a podcast, and went to sleep. Tomorrow would be a better day, but for now, she just had to get through the night.

CHAPTER TWENTY-ONE

"I am not afraid of storms for I am learning how to sail my ship."

–Louisa May Alcott

It is a truth universally acknowledged that a single woman in possession of mediocre cooking skills will be in want of good food. And after nearly burning down her kitchen at least three times, Marzia decided to take a break from trying to be Gordan Ramsay and went to the Starbucks down the street for breakfast. Usually, she could find at least one employee who could speak English there, which felt like a relief when she would finally be able to communicate in a language she understood. It really got her thinking about what it must have felt like for her parents to come to Canada with little more than the clothes on their backs. Although her experiences could never truly compare, Marzia felt a newfound appreciation for the struggle her parents underwent, all to give her and her siblings a better life. But if they could do it, then so could she.

After eating breakfast at Starbucks, she made her way down to the lab, where she met with Son-Ha.

"How'd you sleep?" she asked.

"Very minimally. I never do before the first day." She sighed.

"First days are always nerve-wracking, but thankfully you only have to experience them once, right?" Son-Ha joked.

"I suppose that's the only silver lining to be being the new girl!" Marzia concurred.

The lab was similar to the university back home, but the feel was a lot sleeker and technology based. There was a bench lined with iMacs, each one littered with post-it notes. A whiteboard lined the wall by the window, which had indiscriminate Korean and English phrases written in various colours.

"Welcome to the Hanyang Behavioural Science Lab!" Son-Ha said excitedly.

"I'm Dr. So, the principal investigator for the study you'll be helping us with. But you can just call me Tae-Sung!" a spectacled man greeted Marzia cheerfully, his hair noticeably askew.

"I'm so excited to be working with you guys over the summer!" Marzia said graciously.

"I'll mostly be around, but Son-Ha is who will let you know what to do. Anyways, I better get going, but I hope we'll be seeing more of you!" Tae-Sung replied, tapping away at the iPad in his hand as he walked away absent-mindedly.

"Dr. So's a little aloof, but you'll get used to him," Son-Ha said.

"Everyone seems really nice!" Marzia assured her.

"I'm glad! So, for now, I'll just have you input the BMI ratings into Excel." Son-Ha said."And then just run a two-way ANOVA in SPSS. It should all be there on the desktop."

"Got it! I'll get right on that!" Marzia said, attempting to exude confidence despite her wavering voice.

Not long after, Marzia realized she was way out of her depth. She was able to input numbers just fine, but she was completely lost when it came to SPSS. She had only used it once, and even then, a professor had been walking her through it. She had no idea how to do what was asked of her. She had close to zero experience with any sort of statistics softwares. So, she did what everyone does when they have absolutely no idea what they're doing; she googled it. But before she could, she somehow locked herself out of the computer. She couldn't read Korean, but she assumed it was asking for a password.

"Do you need any help?" Son-Ha asked, peering over her computer.

"I think…I need a password," Marzia said a little sheepishly.

"Oh, you must have gotten locked out. Here I'll help," she said, leaning over and tapping something on the keyboard. Once the computer was unlocked, Son-Ha took in the google page left open on the home screen.

"Is this your first time using SPSS?" Son-Ha asked curiously.

"I-I…I've only used it once before, actually. When you were explaining what to do, I was trying to find the right time to ask…but then it was too late," Marzia said nervously, mindlessly tugging at one of the threads on her shirt.

Son-Ha was more than happy to help Marzia, which was a relief because Marzia had spent practically all of the last hour trying to work up the courage to ask. It was one of the things she disliked about herself. She always felt incredibly uncomfortable asking for help or asking for anything for that matter. In fact, one time at a sleepover, she went hungry the entire night because she was too awkward to ask for a snack before bed. Of course, over the years, she had gotten a lot better at communicating her feelings, but it was still a weak spot of hers.

Like a young child learning to ride a bike, Marzia very quickly learned to use the software with ease. Weeks went by and Marzia became an integral part of the research team. Soon enough she was even training newer members. She established a routine for herself and began to feel like she wasn't as lost as when she first came to Seoul.

One evening after spending hours imputing values into an excel spreadsheet, Marzia's eyes began to tire as the time to head home approached. But strangely enough, she wasn't looking forward to it.

She knew there would be no one there waiting for her, no family, no cats, just an empty apartment. The thought felt incredibly lonely. Maybe she was being dramatic, or maybe she was feeling particularly melancholy. But at that moment, she wanted to be anywhere but there. So, she decided she would indulge in some sightseeing.

She made her way to one of the sights she had researched before she left home, Lotte World Mall. She input the directions into her phone and resolved to walk all the way there, which wasn't very far, but it still felt like a huge accomplishment in Marzia's eyes when she eventually got there. It was one of the first moments where she felt the vaguest semblance of home. And that's on capitalism, baby. The upbeat pop music and the recognizable logos like Zara and Mac brought her a sense of comfort. It was funny that she came to a foreign country to go to a mall, but it was nice not to feel so out of her depth.

She stepped into Mac and took in the familiar scent of cosmetics. The only difference, really, was that all the signs were in Korean. She scanned the aisles, taking in the merchandise. She didn't even need anything, but she just liked looking at everything they had to offer.

After a sufficiently thorough mall crawl, Marzia met Son-Ha at one of the local cat cafes. She figured that if anything were to cheer her up, it would be the company of a furry feline or two. Son-Ha smiled and waved wildly at her when Marzia walked in the door, a little bell ringing above it as she entered.

"I'm so glad you called! I've been craving caffeine!" Son-Ha exclaimed. She went up to the counter and ordered them both something, speaking rapid Korean.

"What did you order?"

"I ordered us both something, and it's a surprise," Son-Ha said, smirking. She came back to their table with two fancy-looking drinks.

"This is a cinnamon vanilla latte," Son-Ha said, placing one of the frothy creations in front of Marzia.

"This almost looks too good to drink!" Marzia said, taking a giant gulp with her straw.

"Almost!" Son-Ha said, doing the same.

A fluffy Persian rubbed up against Marzia's feet, and she picked up the ferocious beast and plopped it onto her lap. At first, it was quite startled, but then it settled itself as it curled up into a ball. Son-Ha coaxed a slender-looking Calico, to no avail. Marzia absent-mindedly swiped through her Instagram stories, stroking the magnificent Persian beauty behind the ears.

But suddenly, Marzia almost choked on her latte. She saw a group photo with a few people she didn't recognize and Dalia standing a little too close to Elias.

"Are you okay?" Son-Ha asked, a look of concern washing over her face.

"I'm-I'm fine, I just forgot to swallow," Marzia replied dismissively.

"You know I haven't known you very long, but even I can tell when there's something on your mind," Son-Ha said.

"It's silly, really...I just thought I knew someone. But it took me until just now to realize that I really didn't know them at all," Marzia said, shaking her head.

"Do we really know anyone?" Son-Ha shrugged. "Most of us barely even know ourselves."

"Doesn't that unnerve you? I mean, you could meet someone and think they're as sweet as pie and not even know that they were, say...a serial killer!" Marzia asked.

"I think everyone has an inner intuition about these things. That person who you thought you knew, what was your first impression of them?"

"I thought he was arrogant and conceited," Marzia replied.

"And that isn't what you think of him now?"

"I mean...I did...and then I didn't...but then I did again because he did something incredibly stupid. I don't even know if I even fully understand it myself," Marzia said, putting her head on the table, narrowly missing her cup.

"You know what I think you need?"

"What's that?" Marzia asked, intrigued.

"I think you need to see some nature," Son-Ha said decisively.

"In the middle of Seoul?" Marzia asked.

"You'd be surprised what you'll find in this city," she replied cryptically.

The two of them finished their drinks, said goodbye to their feline friends, and then made their way to what seemed like a park. Marzia was taken aback by the beautiful scenery. She felt a sort of serene silence wash over her as they walked along one of the cobblestone paths.

"It's… so beautiful!" she said, in awe.

They walked onto a bridge that sat atop a pond, and Marzia stopped and leaned over the side. At first, she didn't see them, but upon closer inspection, she noticed that dozens of tiny fish were swimming about the body of water, to her surprise.

"You know, it's at times like these that I always am reminded of how little my problems are," Son-Ha commented.

"How so?" Marzia asked.

"Well, how can you worry when you're surrounded by all this beauty?"

"I don't know if a few flowers and a pond can really solve my problems," Marzia laughed.

"You just need a change of perspective," Son-Ha said, pointing behind her. Marzia looked behind her and saw a huge mountain in the distance. She marveled at its stature. Suddenly, everything she was worried about felt so small. She was just a speck of dust in the endless abyss. Was she having an existential crisis? Possibly.

"I think that you've seen one too many movies!" Marzia laughed.

"That may be so, but my point still stands," Son-Ha retorted.

"And I suppose a rugged soldier will show up any minute and declare his undying love for me!" Marzia said, unable to contain her laughter.

"Naturally!" Son-Ha replied.

"Son-Ha, do you think I'm a likable person?" Marzia asked abruptly.

"Where did that come from?" Son-Ha asked, a little taken aback by her candor.

"I just...wanted to know. Like, honestly, coming from someone who didn't know me until a couple weeks ago," Marzia said.

"I think…" Son-Ha said, considering her words very carefully. "That you care too much about what other people think."

"That's not true!" Marzia protested. "Okay, maybe it's a little true."

"And that's not a bad thing!" Son-Ha said, taking a rock and skipping it on the pond. "But coming from someone who has only recently met you, you have nothing to be insecure about."

"I think some people would disagree with that," Marzia said offhandedly.

"You know something my mom always tells me? She would say, *Son-Ha, the sun doesn't ask the permission of humans to shine, nor would it believe someone who called it dull,* " she said. "It sounded better in Korean."

"I'm not sure I follow."

"The moral is that when you know your worth, you're not concerned with what others have to say," Son-Ha explained. "Do you get what I mean?"

"I'm starting to," Marzia said, looking reflectively out at the distant towering mountains.

Marzia went home that evening feeling a lot better than when she woke up. She was bewildered at how Son-Ha knew just the right thing to say. She began to brush her teeth while listening to one of the plethora of podcasts in her repertoire, and she got so into it that she didn't even notice her phone ringing. She spat the toothpaste out into the sink and frantically picked up the phone.

"Hello?" she said.

"Marzia Jan?" she heard her mother's voice say, sounding slightly off in her cadence.

"Is everything alright?"

"Your grandmother just passed away."

CHAPTER TWENTY-TWO

~

"For death is no more than a turning of us over from time to eternity."

-William Penn

Marzia had never really experienced death. The closest thing she came to feeling loss was when her hamster died when she was seven. In fact, at first, she wasn't even all that sure he was gone. Once, she had thought she killed him when she dropped him. He actually had fainted, probably from the shock of a near-death experience. Marzia had cried her little seven-year-old eyes out. Come to think about it, everyone who has had a hamster has probably had some kind of traumatic experience with the animal.

Marzia's internship gave her time off to fly back home for the funeral and spend some much needed time with her family. The flight back was oddly quiet. There were only a handful of people on the plane and none of them so much as made eye contact with her. Not that Marzia had a problem with that. Marzia wasn't particularly close with her grandmother, but somehow hearing that she passed away caused her to face her own mortality. Maybe it was morbid of her to think this way, but it truly made her acutely aware of how she and everyone she ever knew would be dead and in the ground one day. It was a depressing thought, yet somehow comforting. Knowing that everyone, no matter how wealthy or famous, would all inevitably meet the same fate. It was…humanizing. Her brother picked her up from the airport, giving her a gentle hug.

"How is mom?" she asked.

"She's a strong woman, so she puts on a brave face. But I know it's hitting her hard," Ameer said.

Hearing that made her stomach churn. Her mother had always been her rock, so thinking of her in that way made her deeply upset. When they got back to the house, Marzia felt the warm feeling of home overcome her. It felt like it had been so long since she had been back in her parents' house. She greeted them with a hug and kiss. She really had missed them and was truly glad to be home. Although, she wished her return could have been under better circumstances. She spotted her sister in the corner and enveloped her in a big bear hug. She noticed that everyone was there, even distant relatives. They had all come to pay their respects. It truly warmed her heart, not so much for her but for her mother's sake.

After quickly offering her hellos to the guests, she went upstairs to put her things away and freshen up. Her room was just as she left it, even the purple sweater that was left askew atop her desk chair. It smelled like home. She hauled her giant suitcase into the corner and propped it up against the wall. She promised herself she would deal with that later when she was less tired and jet lagged. She saw her cats curled up on her bed and nearly cried. She couldn't believe she had gone so long without their furry embrace.

She honestly wished she could spend the rest of the night up here, but she knew that would be incredibly rude. So, she sighed, went to the washroom, splashed some water on her face, and went back downstairs. She could fall apart later, but for now, she had to pull it together.

When Marzia trudged back down the stairs, she sat down next to Soraya and Ameena, who gave her a sympathetic expression.

"How is your mother?" Soraya asked.

"And how are you doing? How was Seoul?" Ameena added.

"She's good. As good as she can be, anyways. And…I'm good too. Seoul was amazing. I've never really seen any place like it," Marzia replied. "And I met the nicest people."

"You're so lucky! I've always wanted to travel!" Soraya lamented.

Marzia was so enthralled in her conversation with her cousins that she hardly heard the front door open.

"Look who's here," Ameena motioned with her eyes.

Both Marzia and Soraya whipped their heads around to see Elias, along with his brother and parents, walk through the door.

"Zindagi saret basha[21]!" Elias' mother said to Marzia, pulling her into a firm but gentle hug.

"Thank you," she replied sincerely.

Time seemed to stand still as Marzia met Elias' eyes. They seemed demure yet searching. Searching for what? He seemed as though he was analyzing her every expression. But maybe she was overthinking it. Maybe her anxiety was creating situations that were not based on reality at all.

"I'm sorry for your loss," he said.

"Thanks."

She was going to say something more but decided against it and settled for a polite half-smile—one where her eyes didn't crinkle.

"He hardly even looked at me," Soraya spat.

"Who, Bilal?" Ameena asked.

"Yes, of course, who else!" Soraya responded. "Look at him acting like it was all nothing to him."

"Forget him!" Marzia insisted.

---

[21] Zindagi saret basha: Dari phrase roughly translating to "may life be upon you." It is often said to a mourning person.

She suddenly felt extremely restless and excused herself to go make some more tea in the kitchen. She poured water into the kettle and placed it onto the stove.

"I've been sent for tea" She heard a familiar voice from behind her. She didn't have to turn around to know who it was.

"I just turned on the kettle," Marzia said in reply.

"Oh," Elias replied, his hand tapping the side of his leg.

"Should be done in like five minutes."

"Right," Elias said awkwardly.

The two of them stood there in silence for what seemed like ages.

"So, you're just going to wait?" Marzia asked, a little harsher than she had meant to.

"I see. I can take a hint," he replied coolly. "I'll tell them it'll be a minute."

"No- I-I wasn't saying you should go, I just-"

"It's fine," he said quickly.

"So, how have you been?" Marzia said, trying to busy herself by wiping down the already spotless counter.

"I'm… I'm good. And you?"

"Well, I'm at a funeral, so I've seen better days."

Both of them let out stifled laughs.

"Did you enjoy Seoul?" he asked her.

"Yeah, it was really great. Definitely an experience I'll never forget."

The air of awkwardness was painfully obvious, both of them almost crawling out of their skin as they waited for the kettle to boil, a perfect representation of their growing discomfort. Marzia fiddled with the zipper of her sweater, trying to seem busy. Elias typed something on his phone. Texting someone, maybe?

"I-Is your mom doing okay?" he finally asked, shoving his phone into his pocket.

"She's hanging in there."

"That's good," he nodded.

Marzia could have sworn that Elias was going to say something else, but just then, the kettle whistled, bringing her back to reality. First, she scooped a few spoonfuls of loose green tea leaves into a beautiful floral printed thermos. Then, she went to pour the boiling water into the concoction.

"I've got it," Elias said, attempting to take the kettle from her.

"I can do it," Marzia insisted, pulling it back.

"You're going to spill-"

"OWWWW!"

Marzia let a couple expletives escape as boiling water streamed down her arm.

"I told you I could do it!" she said angrily.

"I didn't know you were going to grab it like that!" Elias explained.

"There goes my career as a hand model," she said sarcastically, nursing her raw hand.

"Ha. Ha. Where's the ice?" he asked.

"Freezer. Bottom corner," Marzia said, still holding her tender hand gingerly.

He opened the freezer and shuffles through some frozen TV dinners to find an ice tray.

"Ziplock bags?"

"Cabinet. Top right," she replied.

Elias grabbed a plastic bag from the cabinet and emptied the loose ice cubes into it.

"Marzia, what happened to your hand?" her mother exclaimed, taking in the frantic scene.

"Nothing, just… you know, clumsy old me," Marzia replied.

Elias wordlessly handed her the makeshift icepack and grabbed the thermos to take to the other guests.

"Are you okay?" her mother asked again, with worry in her eyes.

"I'm perfectly fine!" Marzia assured, trying to hide the grimace on her face as she placed the ice on her hand. "I'm just going to go to the washroom. I'll bring out the rest of the tea in a few minutes!"

Marzia turned the corner into the dimly lit hallway where the washroom was. She noticed the light was on, so she pulled out her phone with her uninjured hand and scrolled through Tiktok while she waited. The flush of the toilet and sound of the tap running caught her attention, and when the door opened, she was startled as she stood face to face with Bilal.

"Washroom's free," he said.

She wasn't going to say anything. She really wasn't. In fact, she was doing everything she could to stop herself but, in the end, she just couldn't help what she said next:

"You know you'll never find someone as good as Soraya, right?" she said.

"What?" he sputtered, eyes widening.

"She's the type of girl who a lot of guys don't appreciate because they think that when they're ready to settle down, there'll be plenty more like her. But just because you don't recognize how great she is, doesn't mean someone else won't. And by then, it'll be too late. And you'll regret it for the rest of your life."

He paused a second, taking in her words.

"I didn't mean to hurt her," he said finally.

"And I didn't mean to burn my hand with boiling water, but that didn't stop it from hurting!" she retorted. "Excuse me," Marzia added, pushing past him before he had a chance to respond.

She was proud of herself for speaking her mind. Normally, she would just let it go and pretend like nothing happened. But something inside her just couldn't take it anymore. She had to tell him what he would be missing out on. But part of her wondered if she had only made things worse.

The next few weeks were filled with people giving their condolences. Marzia knew they meant well, but it began to get a little exhausting after the first dozen calls. One thing she was grateful for however, was that her mother had her aunt by her side. She had been such a support throughout the entire funeral process. She had been by almost everyday, preparing food, washing dishes, and any other task that needed to be done. Marzia had only seen her aunt cry once, in the kitchen when she thought no one else was home. Sometimes others are so strong so that you have the space to fall apart.

The tone of the household was still very somber for a long time afterwards. It felt like the lights had dimmed ever so slightly. She couldn't imagine things ever going back to the way they were, but like most things, one has no choice but to make the best of what we're given. It was times like this that Marzia remembered a quote from one of her favourite movies, The Lord of The Rings. Frodo tells Gandalf that he wished the ring had never come to him and that none of the pain and suffering they had endured had ever happened.

"So do all who live to see such times, but that is not for them to decide. All we have to decide is what to do with the time that is given to us."

So Marzia did the only thing she knew how to do. Take it one day at a time. She made certain to spend time with her mother to make sure she didn't feel alone. They watched the news, discovered an interesting Turkish drama, and they took up knitting. Although Marzia's stitches were far from perfect, it felt good making something with her own two hands. It kept her busy. It kept her from overthinking and allowing her mind to wander. One day, she was daydreaming about one of the imaginary scenarios she often conjured up when her phone buzzed on the coffee table. She put down her needles and thread and answered the call. It was Soraya.

"Hey guys, are you both on the line now?" Soraya asked.

"I'm here!" Ameena said.

"I'm here too. What's up?" Marzia asked.

"Okay. So, you'll never believe what just happened," Soraya said.

"What?!" both girls responded, their curiosity piqued.

"Bilal asked me to marry him! His family is coming over this weekend to make it official!" she blurted out, hardly able to contain the excitement radiating in her voice.

"But I thought it was over?" Marzia asked in disbelief. Had Bilal really taken what she said to heart?

"I haven't a clue what could have possibly transpired for him to change his mind all of a sudden, but I'm not one to question a good thing," Soraya replied.

"Well, however it came about, I'm so happy for you. I can't believe how many people are getting married this year! You, Mateen…" Ameena said.

"Well, this is definitely a cause for celebration," Marzia replied.

"I don't know the specifics just yet, but I definitely want a party. And a big one at that. You only get married once, right?"

"I mean..." Ameena said.

"At least, I hope that it's only once," Soraya said with a laugh.

Marzia couldn't say that she saw it coming, nor could she say she was particularly thrilled. If Bilal was so easily swayed, how could he possibly be a loyal husband to her beloved cousin? But she couldn't very well say that without either coming off as jealous or incredibly cynical. So her only option was to be supportive, hold her tongue, and pray for the best. That might prove to be a challenge, but Marzia was determined not to be another obstacle to Soraya's happiness. She couldn't bear the thought of being the only obstacle between her and what she'd wanted for so long.

And like Marzia always liked to remind herself, whatever was meant to be would be.

CHAPTER TWENTY-THREE

❧

"Self-love seems so often unrequited."

- Anthony Powell

A few weeks eventually went by, and Marzia was slowly adjusting to being back at home. Her internship had been gracious enough to give her some time off to be with her family in light of her grandmother's death, but she still kept in touch with Son-Ha and the rest of the research team about the study's progress. Although she was glad about her time in Seoul, she was happy to be back home in Vancouver.

When Reiyna heard the news, she called Marzia and offered her condolences. Her mother also sent some Lebanese delicacies over to their house, which was the first time Marzia's mother had genuinely smiled since losing her mother. Realizing it had been way too long, Marzia and Reiyna decided to meet up at their favourite coffee shop to catch up on the goings-on of their lives. Which, suffice it to say, could fill an entire novel. The two of them weren't always able to see each other as often as they would have liked, but when they did, they picked up exactly where they left off.

"I'm so sorry about your grandmother, Marzia," Reiyna said in a low and somber voice.

"Thank you. It gets easier, honestly, but my mom is so strong. She's really the strongest woman I know," Marzia said.

"She's one of the strongest women I know too," Reiyna said sympathetically.

"So, what's new with you?" Marzia asked, trying to lighten up the mood from the previous melancholy.

"I'm great, it's weird talking about my successes when your family's going through such a rough time, but my book was actually picked up by a publisher," Reiyna replied. Marzia could see the excitement and glee in her eyes.

"That's absolutely amazing, Reiyna! I'm so incredibly proud of you!" Marzia exclaimed. And she meant it. Reiyna was one of her oldest and truest friends, so naturally, she was happy for her success. But, a very small part of her, the part that was ugly and vindictive, the part she made sure to keep locked up inside her, was jealous. She was embarrassed that she even felt this way, but the truth was she did. And she hated herself for it. So she did the only thing she knew to do when the green-eyed monster reared its ugly head. She concealed it; telling herself, don't feel it. Just let it go.

Haha. See what I did there?

Marzia was once again deep in thought when her phone lit up with an email from her university. She opened it up and saw that her final marks were in. But only one truly concerned her, stats. She felt a lump in her throat and her stomach twisted into knots as she clicked the link to her doom.

Loading...

71%

She got a B-. Normally this would be a travesty but considering a few months ago, she wasn't even sure if she would pass or not, this was actually good news. For once, a B- was great. It was more than great, actually.

"You look like you just saw a ghost. Is everything alright?" Reiyna asked, concern flashing on her face.

"Actually, I just got some good news of my own," Marzia said. "I actually passed statistics!"

Marzia was still in a state of disbelief. If you think I'm being dramatic, Marzia had spent many nights (and days) going over practice problems and holding onto her sanity by the hairs on her neck. Well, actually, the back of her neck was pretty hairy, so maybe not that, but you get what I mean.

"Wow! And you were so worried too! Now you'll be able to graduate on schedule!" Reiyna said.

"I just feel like a weight has been lifted off my shoulders." Marzia sighed, taking a gargantuan bite out of the peanut butter cookie in front of her.

"Well, you should. You've earned it!" Reiyna said.

"Did I?" Marzia said all of a sudden. "What if it was a mistake, or what if that last test was ridiculously easy?"

"Nope. You're not going to do that," Reiyna said.

"Do what?"

"Diminish your accomplishments," Reina replied.

There's a theory in psychology called Attribution Theory that explains the cause of any given occurrence. A Dispositional Attribution assigns the cause of behaviour to the person themselves. While on the other hand, a Situational Attribution assigns the cause to some external force outside the person's control. Marzia was one of those people who always had a way to explain it all away when she accomplished something. Chalking it up to a fluke, or just plain luck, Marzia, for some reason, always had a chip on her shoulder. I'm sure there's a lot to unpack there, but we don't have time to get into that.

"What's really bothering you?" Reiyna asked.

"What?" Marzia said, just a little bit startled. "What do you mean?"

"Marzia Rashidi, I have known you since we were seven years old. I can tell when there is something that's bothering you that you're not telling me. So, spill," Reiyna said sternly.

"I honestly don't know, to tell you the truth. It's like something is hanging over me, but I have no clue what it is. And it's annoying."

"Maybe it's delayed grief. People deal with death in different ways," Reiyna suggested.

"Yeah, maybe. I've just been feeling completely out of sorts lately, and I can't put my figure on why," Marzia reflected.

"I think what you need is a drive," Reiyna said decisively. "C'mon, let's go. Get up."

Reiyna grabbed her keys and pre-emptively unlocked her car from behind the glass window. The two of them got into Reiyna's car as she blasted the AC.

"It's like a freezer in here," Marzia joked.

"I sweat like a pig, so AC's really my only option!"

"You'd think summers would be a little milder considering it's Canada. And yet, every year, I'm still surprised."

"You know what this calls for?" Reiyna asked.

"What?" Marzia replied curiously.

"Ice cream. And lots of it," Reiyna said, making a sharp turn around the corner. Reiyna was usually a very safe and risk-averse driver, but sometimes she would turn into what Marzia called Roadrunner mode, whizzing around, weaving through streets and sideroads. That is, until they heard the familiar siren of an unmarked police car pull up behind them.

"Wait, is that a cop?" Marzia asked.

"Oh God, we're getting pulled over, aren't we?" Reiyna said, her voice cracking.

"Okay, okay, just be chill and pull over," Marzia said.

"My parents are going to kill me if I get another ticket!" Reiyna said mournfully, pulling over to the side of the road.

A freakishly tall officer with black hair and a buzz cut approached the car and tapped on the driver side window.

"Do you know how fast you were going, ma'am?"

"Uh, very?" Reiyna offered.

"You were going 70 kilometers in a 50-kilometer zone."

And like the flip of a light switch, Reiyna began to sob rather uncontrollably. Marzia was quite startled by this. She had not seen her cry since they were little.

"Ma'am? Are you okay?" the officer asked, also obviously taken aback.

"I…can't…get…another…ticket…I…just…can't!" Reiyna choked out between sobs.

Marzia shifted uncomfortably in the back seat, unsure exactly what she was witnessing.

"Ma'am, I'm going to let you off with a warning today, seeing as how you're…distressed right now. But next time, there *will* be a fine," the officer said sternly.

"I completely understand, officer. Thank you so much!" Reiyna said, still sniffling profusely.

Once the officer got back into his car and left, Reiyna burst out into a fit of laughter.

"Sorry, I should have warned you, but your face was priceless!" she said. "Like I said, I could *not* get another ticket."

"You're going to have to teach me how to do that!" Marzia said.

Marzia aimlessly scrolled through her phone, and an ad for career counselling came up. She audibly sighed.

"What is it now?" Reiyna asked, intrigued by what could have caused such a drastic shift in Marzia's mood.

"I just got a reminder that I have no idea what I want to do with my life. Not to mention I'm a little over a year away from graduating."

"You'll figure it out, I'm sure of it," Reiyna assured her.

"Will I, though? I mean, it seems like everyone else has already got their lives planned out. Even Dalia knows what she wants to do!"

"What is she *really* going to do with a degree in fine arts, though?" Reiyna said.

"She always said she wanted to open up her own gallery." Marzia shrugged.

"Marzia, there's only one person you should be competing with," Reiyna advised.

"And who's that?"

"Yourself."

"Where'd you get that nugget of advice from?" Marzia asked.

"Arthur," Reiyna replied matter of factly.

"Arthur?" Marzia asked.

"Arthur, as in the cartoon," Reiyna affirmed.

"But seriously though, it feels like everyone is moving on with their lives, and I'm being left behind. Everyone's getting married, or writing a book, or…well I can't think of anything else at the moment, but you know what I mean."

"I'm telling you, everyone else feels the exact same way."

"I'm having a hard time believing that," Marzia replied.

"You know how many times J.K Rowling's manuscript was rejected? Twelve times before she finally published The Sorcerer's Stone. Things tend to work out the way they're meant to in the end. One way or another."

"Since when are you the wise one?" Marzia quipped.

"I was always the wise one. It just took you 'till now to appreciate the depths of my wisdom."

Marzia got home that day to find a familiar car in her driveway. She walked through the door to see Elias' mom sitting at the kitchen table talking to her mother as she cooked.

"Marzia, it's so good to see you!" she said, pulling her in for a warm embrace.

"It's great to see you too!"

"How was your day?" her mother asked.

"Not bad, but whatever you're cooking just made it a whole lot better by the smell of it," Marzia said.

Marzia grabbed a cookie from the cupboard, keeping one ear open like the Nosey Nelly that she was.

"And so, Elias had a whole talk with Bilal and convinced him it was just cold feet," Elias' mom said, as though continuing a previous conversation.

"I'm telling you, sometimes a young man just needs some sensible advice from someone he trusts," Marzia's mother affirmed.

Marzia was having a bit of a hard time making sense of what she had just heard. Wasn't Elias completely against Bilal and Soraya getting together? And now, all of a sudden, he wanted to play cupid? Nuh-uh. That wasn't how this works. He wouldn't be able to get off the hook so easily. Marzia had to physically restrain herself from saying anything, which wasn't easy by any stretch of the imagination.

"Marzia, are you going out?" her mother asked her, snapping her out of her trance-like state.

"I can if you need me to!" she replied.

"Can you go to Kabul Market and get some roht[22]?"

"Sure, I can go now."

---

[22] Roht: A sweet bread made in the shape of a circle.

Reader, Kabul Market, as you probably have guessed, is the local Afghan supermarket that Marzia's family patron, along with just about every Afghan within a 5-mile radius. Marzia had never been to Afghanistan. The store was just about as close as she would ever get. She walked in and greeted the cheery cashier, who was a girl just about her age. She had Air Pods in, and to be honest, Marzia didn't blame her. Marzia made her way to the back of the store where the bakery was. She approached the stacks of rising bread arranged awkwardly on racks and was a little alarmed when an older man with salt and pepper hair popped out from behind one of them.

"One roht, please!" she asked politely in Dari.

"It'll be about 10 minutes," he replied, nodding his head in approval.

It looked like Marzia had some time to kill, so she wandered the narrow aisles, analyzing their contents. She imagined that this might be what it was like to live in Afghanistan. There was sense of unspoken comradery with her *wataandaars* [23]. It should be noted, however, that Marzia was by no means the nationalistic type. It just sometimes felt comforting being around people that reminded her of family. Marzia absently trailed through the aisles, touching the various different foods and spices that lined them. She heared the bell ring as another customer entered the store.

---

[23] Wataandaar: Dari for "fellow countrymen"

At first, she barely noticed it. Who would pay attention to who entered a grocery store? But Marzia's life wasn't that simple or uncomplicated. She only noticed who it was when they began perusing the top shelves just down the aisles from her. Elias. Why did he seem to be everywhere and nowhere all at the same time? What kind of bizarre happenstance was this? Their eyes met, and Marzia dropped the jar of pickled chili peppers she was holding in her hands. She held her breath, and miraculously the jar remained intact. Thank God. Marzia didn't know if she could emotionally handle being completely and utterly humiliated today. Elias was at the other end of the aisle, but Marzia could tell the corners of his mouth twisted into a condescending smile.

"Looks like Peaches over here has got butter fingers." He laughed, sauntering over.

"I have perfectly good coordination, thanks," Marzia said dryly.

"Righhhtt." Elias nodded, bending down and picking up the runway jar of chili peppers.

"Thanks," she said, quickly snatching the jar from him.

"Looks like we'll be seeing a lot more of each other."

"So it seems," Marzia replied, turning around again to face him.

"Do you really still hate me?" Elias said bluntly.

"I-I never hated you," Marzia replied.

"You honestly think that by now, I haven't figured out what your lying face looks like?" he shot back.

"Well, it's not like I can hate you after what you did for Soraya." Marzia shrugged.

"How'd you know?" he said, seeming genuinely shocked that Marzia had any idea.

"Your mom was over, and I overheard her talking to my mom," Marzia said. "And I guess I should say congratulations."

"Likewise," he said.

"Oh, and Elias?"

"Yeah?"

"Thank you."

"I was just undoing what I had done earlier." He shrugged before continuing on with his shopping.

"One roht!" Marzia heard the baker call out.

CHAPTER TWENTY-FOUR

"In three words I can sum up everything I've learned about life: it goes on."

–Robert Frost

By this point, you're probably wondering how many weddings could there possibly be? Well, when your family is huge and Afghan, there's bound to be several weddings and engagements in any given year. Though it was pretty quickly planned by Afghan standards, Mateen's wedding had approached rapidly. Marzia had decided to re-wear another dress because she frankly couldn't be bothered with buying a new one. Was it lazy? Yeah. But did she care? No, not really. And it wasn't like anyone would notice as long as she changed up her accessories.

This time it was a venue she hadn't been to yet. It was what they called a Manor; very well-to-do. Marzia was surprised by the extravagance. Which, admittedly, didn't happen very often. It seemed old and drafty, but the lights and candles, along with the multitude of decorations, gave the venue a new life.

The first thing Marzia always did at a party or wedding was scan the room, figuring out who to avoid and who to stick to like glue. For

Marzia, that was almost always Soraya and Ameena. But she had the misfortune of first being spotted by Dalia Alimi. Why, oh, why did it seem like she was always at these things? How was it that she somehow knew anyone and everyone? Or her family did, anyway. It was barely afternoon, and Marzia already knew she needed another coffee.

"Marzia, your dress looks great! You seem to look even prettier than the first time you wore it!" Dalia said, appearing at her side like a specter.

"Thank you, Elias chose it," Marzia retorted, smiling through gritted teeth. That technically wasn't a lie. It *was* the one he chose when she couldn't figure out what to wear. She took an almost criminal amount of joy in Dalia's smug smile transforming into a contorted frown.

"You guys don't live together anymore, right? I guess that was the only thing you had over me," Dalia said, trying to sound like she was joking, but they both knew it was a subtle jab.

"Yeah, you're right. If, in fact, I was competing for him," Marzia replied. "Excuse me, but I'd rather be anywhere but here right now."

All of a sudden, the lights dimmed, and a huge spotlight shined on the double doors at the front of the room. It was a strange feeling, watching Mateen and his fiancée walk in. This was the guy she had been obsessing over for as long as she could remember. And yet, she wasn't mad. In fact, she was happy for them. She was...content. She knew that even if she happened to end up alone for the rest of her life, that she wasn't such a bad person to spend her time with.

Is this the part of the story where the main character goes through a period of introspection and self-reflection to figure out what she truly wants in life? Maybe. But it is also the time when the main character finally stops giving her nemesis power over her—sort of.

"Marzia, let's go sit down!" Ameena said, leading her to their table.

Marzia began mindlessly snacking on the assortment of nuts neatly placed on a platter.

"Can you believe Dalia is following him around like a sad little puppy?" Marzia said, tossing an aggressive mouthful of salted almonds into her mouth.

"Who?" Soraya asked, looking up from her phone.

"Elias!" Marzia said, mouth still full. "I mean, she's not even his type!"

"Why do you care?" Soraya asked, intrigued.

"Yeah, you can hardly stand either of them. They deserve each other if you ask me," Soraya said.

"Oh, I'll tell you what those two deserve..." Marzia muttered, pouring some Perrier into her crystal glass.

Ameena and Soraya exchanged a knowing look.

"I mean, who does he think he is? Who does *she* think she is?" Marzia continued ranting. "Do you know what he did?"

"What did he do?" Ameena asked.

"Apparently, he was the one who talked to Bilal and made him realize all that was really wrong was that he had cold feet," Marzia said.

"Wait, really? But that's a good thing, no?" Soraya mused.

"I mean, on the surface, yes. But he just did that so he can continue to be his self-righteous self," Marzia protested, crossing her arms.

"Look, I get that you hate the guy but don't do it on my account. I'm really over it. Everything turned out alright in the end," Soraya assured.

"But what if it didn't?" Marzia countered. "And besides, it's not just that…it's everything."

"Sometimes some things are just not worth holding on to," Ameena said gently.

"I'm being a buzzkill right now, aren't I?" Marzia asked, suddenly becoming soberingly self-aware.

"I mean…" Soraya began.

"You're not *not* being a buzzkill," Ameena added.

"What we mean to say is that we get you're feeling a lot right now," Soraya explained.

"Oh God, I'm one of those complainers, now aren't I?" Marzia sighed.

"Have you spent the entire night thus far complaining? Yes. And are you doing this because you aren't able to fully deal with your feelings yet? Also, yes. But the important thing is that you will eventually get over it," Soraya said.

"Woah, wait, what do you mean by *feelings*?" Marzia questioned.

"Well, I mean, I thought it was pretty obvious at this point," Soraya said simply.

"I'm still not following."

"Okay, why do you think you're so upset that Dalia is hanging all over Elias?" Ameena asked helpfully.

"Because I can't stand her. We've gone over this," Marzia said, beginning to get a little irritated.

"Or..." Soraya prodded.

"Or?" Marzia said.

"Or maybe you're just in love with Elias." Soraya finished.

"That's funny. Thank you, I've been in a terrible mood, and that almost made me crack a smile," Marzia replied.

"See, I told you she wasn't ready to deal with it yet," Ameena said, shaking her head at Soraya.

"Wait, you've been discussing this?" Marzia said.

"We love you, okay? And you're usually pretty self-aware," Soraya explained.

"But when it comes to Elias, you have a bit of a blind spot," Ameena reasoned.

"I do *not*," Marzia protested, awkwardly taking a sip of her carbonated water.

"You talk about him constantly," Soraya pointed out.

"Because he just infuriates me that much," Marzia countered.

"And you always make excuses to be around him," Ameena added.

Marzia began to get progressively more flustered as she struggled to find the right words to convey what she was feeling at that very moment.

"But we can't go through a single conversation without getting in a few digs at each other. He constantly insults me-"

"Oh, don't even get me started on him! He's a whole other ball of crazy," Ameena began."The guy kept a damn stuffed animal that you threw at him."

"But he was the reason why you and Bilal almost didn't get engaged!" Marzia declared.

"People change and grow. He also made amends and righted his wrong," Soraya replied.

"No one changes that much." Marzia sighed.

"Look, we're not saying go marry the guy. We're just saying that it's time you deal with your feelings instead of bottling them up," Ameena said.

"I guess we'll have to agree to disagree," Marzia grumbled.

"Look, why don't we take some pictures? It could be a good opportunity for a new Instagram post," Soraya suggested.

"Yes! My feed's been looking a little dull," Ameena concurred.

The three of them went outside, where there was a beautifully luscious bush of lilacs. Marzia admittedly didn't really take in the magnificence of the venue. Over her short life so far, she had already been to more weddings than she could remember. In truth, after a certain point, they all began to blend together—sort of like how a surgeon becomes desensitized to blood after working so many years in a hospital.

"Marzia, you go first!" Ameena said, pulling out her phone and positioning the perfect shot.

Marzia awkwardly put her hand on her hip and ever so slightly tilted her head. That's how models did it, right?

"Okay... less constipated, more *'I'm happy that I'm at a wedding surrounded by love,'* " Ameena said.

Marzia frowned slightly but complied. She was never naturally photogenic, so she wasn't in a position to be giving any orders. Her smile faded when she heard a familiar antagonizing sharp voice.

"Is someone doing a photo shoot?" Dalia said, getting in the shot. She put her arm on Marzia's shoulder, highlighting their difference in stature.

Alright. This is what we're doing, then? I'm game, Marzia thought to herself.

"Eli, can you get us from this angle?" Dalia asked Elias, her voice sickeningly sweet as she gestured to her left.

Marzia physically restrained herself from rolling her eyes so hard that they fall out. Elias complied, pulling out his phone and taking several burst shots of the pair. At that moment, it suddenly occurred to Marzia why Dalia was doing this. She was obviously trying to show her up in some weird, twisted way, so she looked better than her in front of Elias. But that didn't make sense, she told herself. This was a competition she had zero interest in being in.

"Aww, your heels are so cute. What are they five inches tall?" Dalia said, smiling into the camera.

"Four and a half, actually," Marzia retorted. "It's funny. At this height, I'm face to face with your little mustache. You bleach, right?"

"Are you making fun of me?" Dalia asked.

"On the contrary, I commend you. It takes such confidence to go out in a dress like that," Marzia said, smiling disingenuously.

"You know that's not going to get his attention, right?" Dalia smirked.

"You're right," Marzia conceded. She pulled Dalia in close as Elias took more candid shots of the two of them together. "Because I lived with him for months, and if I really wanted his attention, I would have it."

Dalia crinkled her nose as she broke away from her. Marzia admittedly took way too much pleasure in how riled up Dalia got.

"C'mon, let's go get dessert," she quickly said to Elias.

"You go ahead. I'm not hungry," he replied, pulling out his phone again. He walks off to make what was presumably a phone call.

After a few seconds of awkward silence, Dalia smoothed her dress and went back inside. Marzia really didn't enjoy being snarky or mean. She was really typically a charming person to be around. But something about that girl really brought the worst out in her. And not to mention, completely unprovoked. Now, this is where many would argue that it was just jealousy, which might have some truth to it, but some people honestly just get a kick out of making others feel as bad as they do.

"What the hell was that?" Soraya asked.

"I honestly have no idea," Marzia replied.

That night was one of the most restless ones Marzia had in years. She paced back and forth in her room until she made herself dizzy. Eventually, Marzia trudged her wide-awake self to the kitchen for an impromptu midnight snack. She grabbed an unopened bag of hot Cheetos and plopped herself at the kitchen table. Her cats thought the rustling was the sound of their cereal, so they were disappointed when they got to the kitchen and found it was just Marzia stuffing her face with the red powdered delicacies.

She put on a YouTube video of some girl talking about her horrible roommate. After about half an hour, Marzia began to feel her eyes getting heavy, so she realized her late-night excursion was probably working. She lazily went to the washroom to brush her teeth, ears still ringing from the deafening music at the wedding. She normally didn't like the quiet, though. In fact, most times, she hated being alone with her thoughts. Was there some avoidance and escapism going on here? Most definitely. But we don't have time to get into it.

Marzia flossed her teeth as she examined herself in the mirror. She was now incredibly tired, and she looked it too. The whole day was exhausting; Dalia, Elias, everyone. She felt her face flush with anger as she replayed the day's events in her head. She went over what else she might have said...what she should have done. Why was Elias even hanging around Dalia in the first place? What could he possibly have in common what that vapid pick-me anyway? Not that she cared. Why would she? It wasn't like either of them were worth the thought.

Yet, her mind continued drifting. Why had Elias convinced his brother to give Soraya another chance after expressly giving him the opposite advice? And just when she thought she was ready to go to sleep again, her mind continued whirring like a well-oiled machine. Or was it the opposite? Did well-oiled machines even make noises? If a machine whirrs in the middle of the forest and no one's there to hear it, does it even make a sound?

It was only when she got back into bed, and everything was quiet and still that her mind felt calm. And for the first time in what seemed like forever, she knew what it was telling her.

She was in love with Elias.

Hopelessly, unequivocally in love.

And she had been for a lot longer than she allowed herself to believe.

CHAPTER TWENTY-FIVE

⁓

"To love and be loved is to feel the sun from both sides."

-David Viscott

Falling in love is like breathing air. You don't even realize it's happening until you stop for a second and hold your breath.

Marzia spent the entire night agonizing over her revelation. She had no idea what it was she wanted to do next. Should she tell him? And even if she did, who's to say he would feel the same way? Maybe she misinterpreted her own feelings. I mean, what did she know? She was only in her twenties. And besides, she could just end up embarrassing herself. She really had no reason to believe he thought of her as anything other than a nuisance. Well, that depended on who you asked. Maybe he really *had* grown.

Maybe she was asking too many questions. But what was it she really wanted? Marzia was always happy having things just as they were, and she didn't know if she wanted to risk rocking the boat. She didn't want to risk getting her heart broken. They say it's better to have loved and lost than to have never loved at all, but Marzia wholeheartedly disagreed with that. You see, her thought process was that you can't really miss what you've never experienced. Marzia realized she had been sitting in her living room for the past hour just staring out the window.

"Marzia?" her mother repeated.

"Hmm? Oh, I'm sorry, I didn't realize you were talking to me," Marzia replied, slightly startled.

"I was just asking if you could take the garbage out to the curb. I don't want it stinking up the garage," her mother responded.

"Oh yeah, sure. I'll do it right now," Marzia said, struggling to ground herself in reality again.

Marzia went to the dingy crevices of their garage to collect the bags of trash their family had accumulated over the week. She dragged them to the curb one by one. Then she heard someone call her name.

"Hiya, Marzia!" an elderly man with thick-rimmed glasses said.

That was Marzia's neighbour, Antonio. His hobbies included tending to his plants and sitting on the front porch watching people walk by. Not to mention talking the ear off anyone in shouting distance.

"Hi, Mr. DeLuca! Are those weeds giving you a hard time?" Marzia replied.

"Nothing I can't handle! My knees aren't what they used to be, but I'll manage!" he replied. "You know, in 1993, this place wasn't even developed. It was all farmland. That's why there's such good quality soil."

"Who would have thought." Marzia nodded, trying to politely and subtly end the conversation. It was not that she didn't like her neighbours. Well, she didn't particularly like them, either. I guess you could say she was pretty neutral. But sometimes, she just had zero social battery for idle small talk.

"You know, when I first moved into this neighbourhood, they still had a drive-in."

Yeah, and segregation, Marzia thought to herself. But that's not what she said, of course.

"Interesting. I've never been to a drive-in," Marzia replied. She tried to subtly walk back towards her house.

Just slowly walk away.

"You know, Marzia, people don't really talk to their neighbours anymore. Especially young people like you. Other kids don't take the time to talk to an old geezer like me."

"Oh, it's always a fun time talking to you, Mr. DeLuca," Marzia assured him, albeit disingenuously.

"That's so good to hear. You know, the other day..."

It was at this point that Marzia began tuning out of the conversation. She didn't mean to, but the words just all started to jumble together. And the more she tried to pay attention to what he was saying, the more lost she got. All she could manage to do was smile and nod at the elderly gentleman. She couldn't bring herself to tell him she hadn't been listening to a word he said. She just had way too much to work out in her brain to expend any more energy on socialization.

"I have to go. Helen made paella. How exotic!" he said excitedly. "But I'm so glad we had this talk!"

"Me too! See you around, Mr. DeLuca!" Marzia said, more relieved than she would have liked to admit.

Once Marzia went back inside, she decided she was due for a healthy dose of escapism. Now was avoiding working through her feelings the healthiest thing to do? No. Was Marzia still going to do it? Absolutely. So Marzia got into bed, pulled out her phone, and swiped through Instagram stories. She was pretty blasé about it all for a good fifteen minutes until a familiar name popped up on her screen. Elias had posted a story of himself doing work on his laptop. To the untrained eye, it was just a regular picture capturing a moment in his day. But Marzia's inner FBI agent noticed one of the tabs on his computer. It looked like a course website, and the title had the course code and section.

PSYC 201 Section B.

So as any normal person would do, Marzia went to the university's course catalog and typed the code into the search bar. And just like that, she figured out where he would be every Monday at 11:30 for the rest of the semester. Now, I don't condone these actions, this probably breaks some stalking laws, but Marzia figured desperate times called for desperate measures. She checked the time on her phone.

10:38 am.

She could make it in time to catch him just as his lecture started. She could probably go to his house, but that seemed a whole lot more confrontational. She didn't know exactly how it would go or even what she would say, but she figured she would work that out on the way.

Carpe Diem?

She grabbed her keys, and before she realized what she was doing, she was driving down to crash Elias' lecture. She couldn't help but roll her eyes at the cliché-ness of it all. She felt like she was in an early 2000s rom-com.

What am I doing? she thought to herself, halfway to her destination.

What, indeed.

It wasn't too late. She could turn around, and no one would know that she'd had such a colossal, monumental lapse of judgment. Or maybe it was temporary insanity? Either way, she arrived at the university and pulled into one of the closest on-campus parking lots. But as she circled around the myriad of stationary vehicles, she realized that this lot was full. Okay, next one. They couldn't all be full. She couldn't fathom why it was so busy. Almost every parking lot she pulled into was at maximum capacity. She finally found one that was nearly a 10-minute walk from the building where Elias' class would be taking place.

11:19 am.

She would have to run. And fast. Dear reader, this was not a promising thought. Marzia competed in the 100-metre race in elementary school at her school's annual track and field day. She came in dead last. But with adrenaline pumping through her veins, she ran through the various corridors of their university campus until she got to the right room.

By the time she got there, puddles of sweat had developed underneath her arms, but at that moment, it didn't matter. She was going to do something that would either go very well or abysmally.

She walked into the lecture hall as everyone was filing in, her eyes scanning the rows for Elias. She spotted him a couple rows from the front, his backpack sitting on the seat next to him. He was probably saving a seat for a friend. She was just about to run down the steps when she suddenly stopped dead in her tracks.

As though in slow motion, Marzia watched as Elias waved to someone out of view. Marzia felt like she was watching a car wreck, and there was nothing she could do to stop it. She soon saw Dalia approach the row that Elias was sitting in.

No. Is this happening? Marzia thought to herself.

Elias waved her over and took his backpack off of the seat. Marzia felt her heart drop as Dalia took the seat next to him.

They laughed.

Marzia felt like there was a lump in her throat. She pushed the door, unable to get out of that room fast enough.

Stupid.

She was so stupid. She couldn't believe she even thought for a second that Elias would ever feel the same way. She cringed at the very thought. Her vision began to blur, and she ran out of the building, cheeks burning. The only silver lining of this ridiculous situation was that she could pretend like none of this had ever happened. She could walk back to her car, go home, and everyone would be none the wiser. No harm, no foul, right? If only.

Marzia knew very well that she would replay this in her head for weeks to come. But at least she still had her pride. I mean, it was hanging on by a thread, but nonetheless, it was still there.

She really didn't know what to do next. She hadn't thought that far ahead. Maybe it was poor planning, or maybe it was arrogance. Marzia picked up her phone and called Reiyna because she knew she was the only one who wouldn't be in class right now.

"Hello?" Reiyna replied on the other line.

"Hey, are you busy right now?" Marzia asked.

"I'm at the bookstore, Chapters. Why don't you stop by!"

"Sure, I'll see you there in ten!"

When Marzia walked into the store, she was shocked to find her friend sitting at a table signing books. Her book!

"Are we at a book signing? Are we at *your* book signing?" Marzia asked, her tone clearly displaying her shock and confusion.

"Yeah, it kind of is," Reiyna said bashfully.

"When you said you were at the bookstore, I thought you meant you were buying books, not signing them for people!" Marzia replied.

"You seemed upset; I didn't want to leave you hanging," Reiyna said simply, as though it was the most logical thing in the world.

"Well, I can call you later, really it's fine-"

"Marzia, pull up a chair," Reiyna said.

Marzia sheepishly took a fold-out chair and set it up off to the side of the table so as not to attract too much attention. Like crashing your friend's book signing didn't already do that. Right.

"Hey, since you're here, can you hand me some books from that stack over there?" Reiyna asked nonchalantly.

Marzia took a book from the stack of novels with her friend's face plastered on the back of it. To say this was surreal would be an understatement.

"Sure!" Marzia said, handing the paperback to Reiyna, who promptly signed it and gave it to the next person waiting in line for a copy.

"So, what is it that's got you looking like that," Reiyna asked.

"I really love your work!" a gangly teenage girl said as she gleefully snatched a book from Reiyna.

"Thank you! Your support means so much to me," Reiyna replied appreciatively.

"So... I think I love Elias," she blurted.

"WHAT?!" Reiyna demanded, almost spitting the coffee out of her mouth. "Wait, Elias, as in, *Elias,* Elias? Elias Hakimzada?"

"The very one," Marzia said, starting to get a little embarrassed.

"I have several questions. Firstly- Hi, thanks for coming! - How?" Reiyna said in between signing books.

"I-I honestly don't know, I just- It's like a switch flipped," Marzia replied.

What changed your mind?" Reiyna asked curiously.

"He…wasn't who I thought he was. I guess he reminded me that people are complex," Marzia said thoughtfully. "But then he turned out to be exactly the type of guy I thought he was."

"So…you don't love him?" Reiyna said, confused.

"I do, but there's nothing I can do about it now. He's not interested. And I would be deluding myself if I tried to convince myself that he was."

"So that's it?! That's the end? You love someone, and you're just going to let them go?" Reiyna responded.

"It never started to begin with. And I think I'm okay with that," Marzia said.

"So, you're not even going to try and tell him?"

"Why bother." Marzia shrugged.

"Are you kidding me right now? After all this time, after what happened with your cousin, you're just going to let it go?"

"Yeah, I am. Because I know when to quit."

"Are you saying that because you really feel that way, or are you just scared?" Reiyna said pointedly.

And to tell you the truth, dear reader, it was the latter.

When Marzia got home, she had an overwhelming feeling that she had to express herself. She was going to write a letter to Elias. Yes, a physical letter. She procured a sheet of paper and a pen and let her thoughts flow.

Elias.

I don't really know why I'm writing this, and maybe I'll regret it as soon as I put down the pen. And perhaps you won't even end up reading this. But there are some things I have to say, and I don't expect an answer from you, but I just ask that you read this in its entirety before you formulate any thoughts.

I'd like to say that I've loved you from the first moment I saw you, but I would be lying if I did. You challenged my self-deprecation, called me out when I was selfish and arrogant, and at times relayed some hard truths. I thought you were an ass, and you still kind of are. But you're also one of the only people who can tell I'm lying when I say that I'm okay. It's actually annoying how well you know me. You made me

realize that I'd be okay on my own but that I don't want to be. I know
you hate cliches, so I'll end with this;

There's no one else I'd rather argue with.

Marzia.

She really didn't know what she was doing. It made no sense, and she couldn't explain her actions if she tried. She really should have let it go. I guess she realized that regardless of what happened she wanted to leave nothing unsaid. After finishing it, she read it over and then over again. She folded up the paper and sealed it in an envelope. It was almost like her body had a life of its own. She wasn't in control anymore. Before she could talk herself out of it or even fully process the ramifications of what she was about to do, she got in her car to deliver the note in person. Was she insane? Probably. But that didn't stop her from knocking on Elias' front door.

"Salaam. This is for Elias," Marzia said, quickly handing the note to his mother and swiftly fleeing back to her car.

There was no going back now. It was only when Marzia began the drive back home that the gravity of what she had just done hit her right in the gut.

"What the hell did I just do?" she said out loud to herself.

But it was too late now. There was no taking it back. Maybe she could turn back and tell Elias' mother it was a mistake, and the note wasn't meant for him? What if he had already read it? She pulled over to the side of the road and whipped out her phone, dialing Soraya and Ameena into a three-way call.

"Guys, I think I just did something stupid."

CHAPTER TWENTY-SIX

❧

"Every new beginning comes from some other beginning's end."

-Seneca

Marzia was never good at saying goodbye. It always felt like she was losing a part of herself that she would never get back. Like they say, parting is such sweet sorrow. It had been at least a week since Marzia had written her letter to Elias, and she hadn't heard back. Now, I don't want to say Marzia was spiraling, but she was spiraling. In fact, so much so that she decided it was time to go back to Seoul to finish her internship.

Now some might call this avoiding her problems, and it is, but Marzia had gotten it into her head that the only way to move on was to move forward...on the other side of the globe. She figured that if she was on a completely different continent, maybe the things weighing on her would seem less significant. Her internship said she could take all the time she needed to be with her family, but Marzia was feeling impatient to continue her research. Also, it might not be helpful seeing the guy who most likely rejected you around town, at least for a little while. He hadn't even so much as sent her a text, so

Marzia assumed that alone was an answer, and she had made peace with that. She was at a point where she knew within herself that she was a kind and caring person, and if Elias didn't see that, then it was his loss. She was feeling good. She was keeping up with her courses and doing well at work. You'd be surprised how well you can do when you have a clear mind.

On this particular day, Marzia's mom sent her to the grocery store to pick up some essentials. She didn't bother with any makeup. What were the chances she would run into somebody she knew? She entered the store with her notes app open to her shopping list and a determined look in her eyes. In and out. What could possibly go wrong?

She was making her way through the aisles when she silently noticed how all the employees looked so intimidating. They looked like the type of kids at school who would treat the shy and quiet kid like a pet. Most of them didn't look older than 19. She felt a little embarrassed for being so out of sorts around a bunch of teenagers working at a grocery store, but adolescents can be pretty scary in her defense. She noticed a girl about her age down the aisle from her make eye contact. She smiled at Marzia, which just left her feeling confused. Did she know her from somewhere? The girl began walking closer. Was she about to…socialize?

"Oh my God, hi!" she said with unabashed enthusiasm.

"Uh…Hey! It's, ah, great to see you!" Marzia replied, unsure of where this conversation was going.

It was obvious at this point that the girl had mistaken her for someone else, but it was too late now. Marzia was in too deep.

"You should come over for dinner one of these nights! We have to catch up!"

"Right, totally! I haven't seen you in like forever, girl!" Marzia said, realizing she was digging herself deeper and deeper into a hole, but there was nothing she could do about it.

"So, how's the baby?" the girl asked.

"Great! Lots of- uh crying. But you know, still blessed," Marzia replied.

"How's she latching?"

"Really well, super latched, the most latched. Couldn't do it without my mom's help!" Marzia said.

The girl got a confused look on her face like she just smelled compost juice.

"I thought Helen passed away last year?"

"I-I… you know what, I think you have the wrong person, but you have a nice day!" Marzia sputtered quickly as she speed-walked down the aisle away from the strange woman. She took one last look at her and saw the expression of absolute confusion as the woman faded out of view.

You know what? It was Marzia's fault. It was her fault for thinking she could survive a simple grocery trip without embarrassing herself. Her bad. At least there was a good chance she would never see that woman again.

When Marzia got back to her house with the groceries, something caught her eye in the rear-view mirror. Lo and behold, there was an obscene pimple on her chin, a blemish, a spot, a zit. No matter which way the dice fell, it was there, staring her smack dab in the face.

Well, at least no one I actually care about will see me like this, Marzia thought to herself.

As soon as she put the key in the door, she had a gut feeling. Call it a sixth sense. Something just didn't feel right. She opened the door to find an unusually dark foyer. Where was everybody? Didn't anyone care that she would be leaving in a couple weeks? She puts the groceries down in the kitchen when she heard some noises coming from the dining room. She had watched enough Criminal Minds to know how this was going to go down. But first, she needed a weapon. She was suddenly very grateful that she had the pepper spray her sister had encouraged her to get. She took it out of her bag, poised to spray at any possible intruder.

When she finally plucked up the courage to investigate the source of the sound, she timidly entered the dining room. The next couple minutes all happened so fast, each progressively worse than the last. Marzia entered the room where the lights suddenly turn on, and before she knew what she was doing, she dispensed the pepper spray. Then she realized… it was just her cousins and friends trying to throw her a surprise going away party. And you thought this day couldn't get any more embarrassing. The room erupted into a fit of coughs as the spray wafted through the air.

"Oh my God, is that pepper spray?!" Ameena asked, mascara running down her eyes.

"I thought someone broke in," Marzia said, a little panicky. "I'll grab some water and damp washcloths!"

So that's how they spent the next forty minutes trying to soothe everyone's irritated orifices. Thankfully the effects went away after a little while, and aside from the slight awkwardness of accidentally pepper-spraying her closest friends, Marzia was actually having a good time.

"I cannot believe that we got pepper-sprayed while trying to throw you a surprise going away party," Soraya began hysterically laughing.

"I mean, I haven't been a part of the family for very long, but I'm assuming this isn't a normal occurrence," Neelofar said.

"Actually, you'd be surprised," Ameena nudged her with her elbow. "Marzia always played a little rough. I once got a nosebleed when we were playing."

"Woah, woah, that was one time! And I think I've mellowed out a lot since then." Marzia laughed.

"What about the time I needed stitches because you thought it would be a good idea to play gymnastics with a couple of wooden planks and some lawn chairs?" Soraya asked.

"What can I say? I was a daredevil."

"Are there any stories that don't have to do with one of you guys getting injured?" Neelofar chuckled.

"I can answer this one. Back when I used to live in an apartment, we used to play Nicky Nicky nine doors," Marzia added.

"Huh?" Neelofar asked, her brow furrowing.

"It's basically Ding-Dong ditch," Soraya explained.

Although the explanation made sense, Neelofar got very quiet and had a look on her face that Marzia couldn't quite read.

"Sorry, where's the washroom?" Neelofar asked suddenly.

"Down the hall. First door on the left," Ameena offered.

The pizza later arrived, and everyone was digging in, but Marzia suddenly got an unsettling feeling in the pit of her stomach. Neelofar still hadn't come back yet. She excused herself and went down the hall to where the washroom door remained locked, a faint light spilling out from the crack underneath.

"Hey, are you good?" Marzia asked timidly.

"Yeah. I'm good, don't worry."

"Are you sure, because if you need like a pad or something…" Marzia offered.

When the door opened, Neelofar emerged slightly blotchy and puffy-eyed.

"What happened?" Marzia asked, concern filling her features.

"Oh, nothing, don't worry I-"

"I know we haven't known each other very long, but I'm always here for you, okay?" Marzia said.

"It's just… seeing you with everyone, talking about childhood stories, it just reminds me that I didn't have that. I didn't know anyone besides my immediate family, and I guess I just realized how lonely it was. I don't even know where your washroom is!"

"I didn't even realize how isolating that must have felt," Marzia reflected. "We can't change what happened. But we can do our best moving forward."

When Marzia first got home, she was in absolutely no mood to do anything even vaguely resembling socialization. She was in one of *those* moods—the kind of mood where you just feel like sitting at home feeling sorry for yourself. Now, don't get me wrong, that's still a favourite pastime of hers, but Marzia actually really enjoyed the company. In fact, it was exactly what she needed that day. Regardless of whether Elias responded to her letter or ignored her until the day she died, she would keep it moving. She didn't hate Elias. Okay, maybe she hated him just a little. And alright, maybe she wouldn't hate it if he spontaneously sprouted multiple painful boils on his face. So no, Marzia wasn't angry or jaded whatsoever. And she certainly wasn't going to let it ruin her last few days before she left for Seoul.

"Soraya, I cannot believe you're going to be the first one of us to get married," Ameena commented.

"I'm actually really nervous. I mean, don't more than half of marriages end in divorce?" Soraya said.

"That's true. But you can't go into it with a defeatist mindset," Marzia replied.

"Woah, woah, when did Marzia become the therapist here?" Soraya laughed heartily.

"I don't know, in case you guys forgot, I'm so much more cultured now that I've been to *Korea*," Marzia said, feigning an air of importance and sophistication.

"Right, how could we possibly forget. You only mention it every other sentence," Ameena teased.

"Okay, guys," Soraya said. "It's time to pick which movie we're going to watch!"

"I vote You've Got Mail!" Marzia said.

"You've seen it like a thousand times!" Ameena said.

"And it gets better every time!" Marzia replied.

"What about A Cinderella Story?" Soraya suggested.

"I'm down!" Karissa said.

The rest of the girls nodded in agreement. I mean, who could resist a classic and Chad Michael Murray?

However, despite it being one of Marzia's favourites, she was having an excruciatingly difficult time paying attention this particular evening. Marzia always had a difficult time paying attention but never during movies she loved. And not to mention, Hillary Duff's monologue in the boy's locker room hit particularly close to home.

"Because waiting for you is like waiting for rain in this drought. Useless and disappointing."

Ha. How fitting. Marzia was definitely not comparing her life to a fictional film. She wouldn't do that because she was a rational adult who maturely dealt with her feelings rather than using media as a form of escapism to avoid being left alone with her own thoughts.

I could say Marzia enjoyed the rest of her evening, but I would be lying.

When all was said and done, and everyone had gone home for the night, Marzia felt oddly empty. She felt like when your friends finally go home the morning after a sleepover. And unrelated, but why are those mornings the days you feel greasiest like you haven't showered in days?

Anyway, I digress.

Marzia sat in the silence that was filled with laughter merely an hour ago. Not in a sad way, though, more of a pensive, self-reflective kind of way. She realized she had left the TV on. The room seemed darker, and less colourful. A rogue mug sat on the coffee table, devoid of any beverage.

"You were sitting there so long I thought you had a stroke," Ameer said, passing through on his way to the kitchen.

"Hey, do you think I'm a likable person?" she asked him.

"Are you a likable person?" he repeated.

"Yes, am I likable? Am I cool, fun to be around?"

"Of course, you're likable. That's such a weird thing to ask," he replied.

"Are you sure you're not just saying that because you're my brother?" Marzia pressed.

"Do you want the truth?" he asked.

"Obviously!"

"Well, I can't really be objective, now can I?"

"I suppose," Marzia replied.

"But that doesn't mean you're not a likable person. I mean, some people are sociopaths. You're definitely more likable than they are. And then there are the murderers and child molesters," Ameer replied facetiously.

"Thank you. Wow. You know that's just what I needed for my self-esteem," Marzia said sarcastically.

"In all honesty, though, you're fine, okay? Don't overthink it," he said, biting off a piece of a sour straw.

"Thanks."

Marzia prayed, and she prayed that whatever was meant for her would find her soon. Then, she subsequently spent the rest of the evening watching Extreme Couponing and eating all dressed flavoured chips. And for just a moment, her problems seemed to fade away.

CHAPTER TWENTY-SEVEN

"When you reach the end of your rope, tie a knot in it and hang on."

-Franklin D. Roosevelt

Marzia spent the next four days tying up loose ends before leaving for Seoul. And by loose ends, I mean eating enough Chipotle to last her the entire time she'd be away. South Korea had a few dupes, but nothing beat the original. One thing would be different than the first time she left. This time she was absolutely sure nothing, and no one was holding her back. This time she knew just about everything to expect. She knew what to pack, what gate she would be going to, and even which Starbucks she would stop at on the way to the airport.

But another one of the loose ends she had to tie up was handing one last assignment in to one of her professors in person before she left. As much as she didn't really feel like going anywhere, Marzia knew the sooner she did this, the sooner she would be able to go back home. It's funny really, Marzia never realized how nostalgic she could feel over a place she hadn't even left yet. Leave it to her to turn handing in an assignment into an emotional experience.

The sun was shining, and Marzia resolved to make it a good day. On her way to the psychology department, Marzia walked by the library. She noted how busy it looked. It was midterm season, so it was undoubtedly a full house. But something caught her eye as she walked by one of the windows. It was Elias in a bright red hoodie, sitting across from…

Dalia.

Why? Why was it always them?

Suddenly, Marzia experienced a wave of curiosity. She decided she had enough time to spare for a little detour. She casually passed through the automatic doors and walked towards one of the shelves stacked with books. From between the shelves, she could see both of them in broad daylight, coffee cups in hand. Marzia tried to look natural. She would periodically pick up a book and skim through it haphazardly. She saw Elias get up, but without taking his bag. How curious. Apparently, Marzia wasn't natural enough because she heard a familiar shriek from behind her.

"Marzia, is that you?" Dalia asked, addressing her.

Maybe there was another Marzia?

"Hey. You guys studying too?" she asked, trying to sound nonchalant.

"Yeah, you know, I have to keep up my A average," Dalia replied smugly. "Elias just went to the washroom."

"And what were you planning on doing after undergrad, anyway?" Marzia asked, putting the book down and walking towards them.

"Oh, I don't know, maybe some influencing work. Media can be such a multifaceted discipline."

"Well then, I guess you don't have to hurt yourself too badly, right?" Marzia shot back.

Now I'll be the first to admit, that was pretty below the belt. But Marzia couldn't deny the satisfaction it gave her, wiping that smug smile off of her face.

"You're right, but it's just so much fun if you have the right company," Dalia said, smirking.

Oh, she knew exactly what she was doing. And then, she saw it; her note, sticking out of Elias' backpack stuck in between several other loose sheets of paper. Typical guy move. Had he still not opened it? Or maybe he had and frankly couldn't give less of a damn. Marzia's eyes betrayed her because Dalia followed her line of vision.

"Anyways, I'm going to go," Marzia said abruptly.

"I'll make *sure* to tell Elias that you stopped by," Dalia said.

Stopped by? It's not like this is your house. What is this, the Brady Bunch? Marzia thought as she made her swift escape. This was unfortunate because if she had stayed just a little longer, she would have seen Dalia snatch the note from his bag and stuff it into the trash can. Even without that, though, Marzia was absolutely seething. There were very few people who could incite this kind of rage in her. Dalia was one of them.

Throughout all that excitement, she almost forgot what she had come there for in the first place. Marzia speed-walked to her professor's office; she had to hand in her assignment before 3 pm, and it was exactly 2:55 pm. Which meant she had exactly five minutes to get there before her professor left for the day. But she made one mistake, she walked through the *warzone*. Or at least, that's what she liked to call it. Why, you might ask? Well, this is where all the university's different clubs would set their tables up to try and entice more people to join. Now, this seemed innocent enough, but things got heated when the school's Environmental Club would be right across from the Capitalist Student Association. On that particular day, the Feeding Orphans Coalition was trying to get more donations.

"Hi, would you like to make a donation?" a perky redheaded first year asked

This place will chew you up and spit you out, Marzia thought.

"I'm sorry. I don't have my wallet on me!" she said, checking her phone again for the time.

2:56 pm.

"How did you get here then?" she asked, her dimples as prominent as two craters.

"I took the bus," Marzia replied quickly.

"With what money?" the girl quizzed.

"I had just enough for the fare," Marzia replied.

"What about ID?"

"I didn't bring my wallet. I'm just dropping off an assignment, I don't need my ID today."

"You don't bring your wallet places?" The girl asked judgmentally.

"It's been a busy day. I forgot, okay? Look, I have to go. I'll feed all the orphans another day, okay?" Marzia replied. She didn't bother looking at her face as she walked away, but if she had, she would have seen a disappointed scowl. I guess some people just don't know how to take no for an answer.

2:57 pm.

Marzia could feel the perspiration materializing in her armpits. But that was a sacrifice that Marzia would have to be okay with for her GPA and all mankind. Okay, just kidding about the last part, but my point still stands.

Marzia darted and weaved through the halls until she finally got to the psychology department. She ran through the corridor, looking for room 132.

2:59 pm.

125, 130…

When she finally knocked on her professor's door, she was practically out of breath.

"Handing in an assignment? You're just in time. I was just about to head out!" he said cheerfully.

"Thanks…I…ran…" Marzia said in between breaths. She gave him her assignment and took a couple seconds to catch her breath.

"I know you. You always sit up front, right?" he asked.

"Yeah, that's me," Marzia said, a little taken aback that he recognized her in a lecture hall of over a hundred people. But then again, Marzia was always the one to ask questions to get those class participation marks, even if the comment was inconsequential. She was sure lots of people found it annoying, but she didn't care.

"Hey, you're doing a great job, by the way. Keep it up!" he said.

"Thanks, you too!" Marzia replied reflexively.

You too? Really, Marzia? she thought, mentally kicking herself.

She awkwardly shuffled out of the office before he could reply. She could only hope that he wouldn't remember her name the next time she was in class. You'd think she would be used to being so socially inept, but she still managed to surprise herself sometimes. Thankfully she would soon be in Korea, so the next time wouldn't be for a while.

When Marzia got back home, she reluctantly began the gruelling task of packing once again. You'd think she would've gotten the hang of it by now, but you would be sorely mistaken. She spent the next hour looking through all the clothes she had. She realized that she probably hadn't worn a third of them in over a year. But would she throw them out? You would sooner pry them from her lifeless fingers than see her part with a single one of them. I'm sure there's a lot to analyze there, but this is not a psychology textbook.

She was admiring one of her crimson t-shirts that was probably a little too small for her now when she heard a knock at the door.

"Is anyone downstairs?" she called out. "Hello?"

This house would truly fall apart without me, she thought to herself.

She set the clothes down on her bed and went to answer the door.

"This is an intervention," Soraya said simply, pushing past her and walking through the foyer.

"Wait, what? Intervention? What for?" Marzia asked, stunned and confused.

"So, you're just going to pour your heart out to him and then get on a plane to go halfway across the country before he can even respond?" Ameena asked, arms crossed.

"It's been days now. He would have replied by now if he had any intention to. And I'm finishing up my internship. It's not exactly like I'm running away or something," Marzia countered defensively.

"That's hardly enough time!" Soraya argued. "Maybe he hasn't read it."

"Maybe he doesn't want to," Marzia suggested.

"C'mon. Everyone can see the way he looks at you," Ameena said.

"I don't know what you're talking about," Marzia said.

"Bull," Ameena said firmly.

"Even if that were the case, it's obvious that he's moved on. I even heard that he's getting engaged."

"To who?" Soraya asked.

"Dalia."

"That cannot be true," Ameena said.

"I saw them studying together today. It's not as far-fetched as you might think. So whatever might have been there…or whatever you guys thought was there…that's in the past," Marzia said.

"You have to talk to him. *In person,*" Ameena insisted.

"What's the point?" Marzia asked defeatedly.

"What is the point?" Soraya repeated. "You might let the possible love of your life pass you by!"

"Love!" Marzia scoffed. "What has that ever gotten me?"

"Oh, don't go all humbug on us now!" Ameena said.

"We're just saying you have to deal with it. One way or another," Soraya added.

"I *am* dealing with it. By going to Korea," Marzia said. "Sometimes you have to cut your losses."

"But I'm sure there's a reasonable explanation-" Soraya began.

"Really, and how would you know that? I'm the one he made feel like complete crap, so excuse me if I'm not jumping at the chance to give him another opportunity to do so," Marzia said.

"But do you like him?" Ameena asked abruptly.

"What? What do you mean?" Marzia sputtered.

"I mean, do you like him. Do you have feelings for Elias?" Ameena continues.

"What a ridiculous question, I...yes. Yes, I do." Marzia responded thoughtfully.

"Do you love him?" Soraya prodded.

"Yeah, I love him. And I think I've loved him for a lot longer than I realized," Marzia replied.

"Well, then you can't leave without being sure about how he feels about you!" Ameena said.

"I think he made himself pretty clear. Besides, I've said everything that needs to be said. I know when to accept defeat. This isn't a movie, and I'm not the main character. No matter how much I wish I were," Marzia replied, barely curving her lips into a smile. "Trust me, I'll be fine."

"Hey, let's go get some food to cheer you up," Soraya suggested.

"I told you guys, I don't need cheering up. I'm completely fine. I am, however, always down for Chipotle," Marzia replied.

"I'll drive!" Ameena said.

The three of them piled into Ameena's car, and they drove to satiate their white-washed Mexican food craving. They walked into the establishment in a fit of laughter. Everyone else must have found them insufferable, but they were too preoccupied to be bothered with them. But Marzia's easy-going air quickly dissipated when she saw who was standing in line.

"You set me up!" Marzia exclaimed in a hushed voice.

"I may have asked Bilal where Elias would be this afternoon," Soraya replied sheepishly.

"Et tu, Brute?" Marzia said melodramatically.

"You can't leave now; he's already seen you," Ameena pointed out.

"What part of 'I'm fine' don't you guys understand?!" Marzia asked through gritted teeth.

"I don't know about you, but that iced coffee really went right through me. I gotta go to the washroom," Ameena said.

"I'll join you," said Soraya said as they both scurried off to use the facilities.

Marzia remained frozen for a minute, unsure of what to do, until Elias finally broke the awkward silence.

"Hey," he said, nodding his head.

"Hi," she responded.

"So, I heard you're going back to Seoul to finish your internship," he said. "My mom told me. I mean, not that I was asking about you."

"Yeah, I am. It'll be good for me, new environment and all."

"How- how have you been? How's school?" he asked.

"It's good, I'm, I'm good. And you?" Marzia replied.

"I'm great, thanks. It's just been kind of hectic with all the wedding planning and all," Elias replied, his eyes quickly widening once he realized what he said. "I mean not my wedding; I'm not getting married."

"Oh, good- I mean, it's great that everything worked out, and they're making it official," Marzia replied.

"Yeah, I guess everything works out the way it's supposed to in the end."

"Right."

"Here you go, sir," an employee said, handing Elias a brown paper bag with his food in it.

"Good luck, Marzia," he said.

"Thank you. I'll see you around."

"Marzia?" he said, turning back around to face her.

"Yeah?"

"…tell your parents I said hi."

"For sure," Marzia replied.

Marzia watched him leave out of the corner of her eye. Maybe it's true what they say; maybe some things are better left unsaid.

CHAPTER TWENTY-EIGHT

❧

"The course of true love never did run smooth."

-William Shakespeare

Marzia always enjoyed spending time by herself. She was a firm believer in the idea that being alone doesn't have to mean you're lonely. That's why she found herself hiking all by herself a few days before she was to leave for Korea. She wasn't planning on it, but in a spur-of-the-moment decision, she chose to spend one more day in the great outdoors before she left. Now, this was a little out of the ordinary because she wasn't the most outdoorsy girl. She could appreciate a tree as much as the next girl, but was she ever going to be Bear Grylls? Most definitely not. However, she could still enjoy a good sunset without having to rough it overnight outdoors.

She set off down the gravel path with her brand-new running shoes, which would almost certainly get scuffed at some point during the perilous trek. Reusable water bottle in hand, she jogged along the path, maintaining a respectable pace. That lasted for about five minutes. Slow and steady wins the race.

Marzia began to feel beads of sweat form on her forehead with the sun beating down on her.

I should do that laser treatment that makes it so that you don't sweat, she thought to herself.

Nonetheless, she persisted with an annoying pep in her step. Her phone vibrated, and she checked to see what it was. Only a Twitter notification, but what alarmed her was that she only had 20% battery left. That was kind of cutting it close, but as long as she didn't use it, she figured she should be fine. What was the worst that could happen on a hiking trip that shouldn't take more than an hour max?

A cardinal perched on a Blue Spruce gave her a quizzical look. Or maybe it didn't, and Marzia was just delirious from heat exhaustion. She was fixated on the fledgling when she tripped on a tree root. That would have been fine if she hadn't horribly skinned her knee. She had to sterilize it, right? What if it got infected and they had to cut her leg off? I mean, you never know what kind of germs are outside. Thinking quickly, she took out her water bottle and poured some onto her knee.

That should do it, she affirmed to nobody in particular.

Alright, that stung a bit, and she was off to a rocky start, but that was okay. Adversity builds character. She could clean it out properly when she got home. She passed by a couple holding hands, which reminded her of something that always crossed her mind when she saw a couple. When do they let go of each others' hands? Do they keep holding hands the whole hike? What if their hands get sweaty? Who initiates the disengagement of handholding? It was all so convoluted. Could you even effectively hike when you're glued at the hip like that? I mean, talk about co-dependent, am I right? It was still a beautiful day, though.

Marzia got progressively more breathless the longer and the higher she climbed. But she was getting closer to the top, which kept her motivated. She pulled out her phone to take a picture of the beautiful scenery; she was in complete awe of the towering trees and the rushing stream running alongside her. She passed her hand through the water and felt instantly refreshed. A breeze grazed her face as she closed her eyes to listen to the buzzing cicadas. If only her face wasn't so itchy...and her arms...and her legs. She pulled out her phone and looked at herself in the camera. There were angry pink bumps all over her face. She had been bitten by mosquitos. See, this is what happens when you try to do something nice. You try to go out in nature, disconnect for an hour, and this is where it gets you.

It's fine. This is fine, she thought.

The end was in sight. She just had to go a little further. She was almost there. She could taste the air at the peak.

Until...

Marzia's stomach began feeling a little unsettled. Why did she decide to do this again? Was she trying to pull some kind of Eat, Pray,

Love, self-discovery crap? She looked around and spotted a few bushes far out from the main path. There was no one else there, and it was pretty secluded. After she mentally prepared herself for what she had to do and finally relieved herself, she figured a few leaves would do the trick. She was lost in thought about who knows what (are we even really surprised at this point?) when she suddenly looked at the leaves she was using—specifically the number of leaves.

Leaves of three, let them be.

I'm sure at this point, dear reader, you can most likely deduce what just happened. Marzia had used poison ivy as toilet paper. You know when you're in such shock that you're basically frozen in place? Yeah, that was Marzia. She didn't know what else to do but try and use the rest of her water to…wash it off? Does that even work? At this point, you probably think she'd definitely turn back now. Well, you'd be wrong. She eventually made it to the top, and boy, was it worth it, battle scars and all. She saw where the blue water met the clearest sky she had seen in weeks. There was something poetic about finally reaching the top despite the adversity she faced along the way. Someone should write a poem or something about that. In fact, a wise person once said, "*There's always gonna be another mountain. I'm always gonna wanna make it move.*"

Now, I'll spare you the details of what the next few days consisted of, but let's just say that it involved more calamine lotion than she ever thought possible. To say it was uncomfortable would be an understatement. However, like I said, moving on, the day came when it was finally time for Marzia to fly back to Seoul. She did a full walk-through of her room, double and triple-checking that she hadn't overlooked anything she had planned on taking with her. Somehow though, she still couldn't shake the feeling that she was missing something.

"You're going to be late for your flight!" her father called from the bottom of the stairs.

"Coming!" she replied, grabbing her carry-on bag and luggage.

She noticed her cats sleeping soundly on her bed, and a sudden wave of sadness washed over her. They didn't know she would be leaving, and there was no way for her to tell them. How could she tell them that she wasn't abandoning them? They would just wake up and see that she wasn't there. She told herself she would be back soon, dismissing her sad intrusive thoughts.

She snacked on some trail mix in the car, although there were more pieces of chocolate than actual nuts. In Marzia's opinion, that was the best part. As the car passed by the scene of an accident, Marzia was reminded of how one is more likely to die on the way to the airport than on the actual airplane. She never understood why people used that example like it was supposed to make anxious flyers feel better. Wouldn't it just make them more anxious about driving and being on the road? She figured there was a good chance that the car they just passed by might have been part of that statistic.

"It might be cold there; did you bring enough warm clothing?" Marzia's mother asked her.

"Don't worry, I have enough for every season," Marzia assured her.

"What's wrong? Are you not happy to be completing your internship?" her father asked.

"Yeah, I'm happy. I'm just tired. I was up really early packing," she replied. "By the way, did I get any mail, by any chance?"

"Nope, not that I saw," her father replied.

"Oh."

...

Meanwhile, Ameena and Soraya were plotting. They conspired to ambush Elias on campus and do what Marzia was too afraid to. They waited outside his lecture hall, and when they saw him emerge, they pounced.

"Can we talk to you?" Soraya asked.

"Yeah? Why?" Elias said, leading them to an area of the corridor that was less crowded.

"Do you have anything to say for yourself?" Ameena asked, arms crossed.

"Huh?" Elias responded, not sure if this was some kind of joke or hidden camera show.

"You had the nerve to ignore Marzia's letter, and you're just going to stand here like you have no idea what's going on? Sure, buddy," Soraya scoffed.

"Wait, what letter are you talking about? I didn't get any letters, let alone one from her," he said, genuinely confused.

The girls came to the conclusion that he really was clueless.

"You're lucky she sent us a copy," Ameena said, pulling out her phone and handing it to him.

At first, he was perplexed and, to be honest, a little annoyed. But as he read on, he realized what Marzia's words were saying.

"Where is she now?" he asked frantically.

"The airport. Her parents are dropping her off right now!" Ameena replied.

"I gotta go," he said. "And thank you. Both of you."

He slung his backpack over his shoulder and began a mad dash to the airport. Elias frantically called an uber from the parking lot. Somehow always having the most atrocious timing, Dalia approached, presumably also just getting out of class.

"You seem like you're in a hurry," she observed.

"Yeah, there's something I have to do that's time-sensitive," he said, not looking up from his phone.

"Maybe we can go for coffee afterwards?" she suggested, fluttering her eyelashes.

"Look, Dalia, I'm sorry, but I really have to go," he said, just as his Uber arrived.

Okay, okay, I know what you're thinking. *Really? He rushes to the airport to stop her? How cliché.* But trust me this isn't a Ross and Rachel type situation.

Unlike in the movies, when Elias got there, they didn't let him through security without a ticket for obvious reasons. He was going to have to get creative.

...

Marzia checked her phone. Thankfully, she was ahead of schedule. She passed through security without a hitch. Her stomach began to growl again. She was thankful she had those snacks in the car. Otherwise, she would have been even more famished. She figured she could grab a bite to eat by her gate. Just kidding, she would never buy food at the airport. With those ridiculous prices? Please. She had a sandwich tucked away in her purse that her mother had made her for later. Just as she collected all her things again after putting them through the scanner, her phone began to ring.

"Hello? Elias?" she said, puzzled. "I'm about to board my flight. Can this wait?"

"No," he said simply. "I read your letter."

"What?" she said."I can't hear you. It's too loud."

"Look behind you," he said.

Marzia spun around and saw Elias just on the other side of the security checkpoint. She couldn't help but notice he was wearing a red flannel. He always looked so good in red.

"I said I read your letter!" he repeated.

"Look, it's okay, you don't have to-"

"Do you know why I was always so mean to you? Why I would constantly berate and insult you?" he continued."Because being mean was a lot easier than admitting…than admitting that I'm in love with you."

"What? What about Dalia? You two are all but engaged? I've seen you around with her. In class, at the library…"

"We're not engaged, and we're not planning to be either. I know what you think you saw, but that was more her just following me around like a damn shadow! I was just too nice to tell her off. Until today."

"So, you have no problem being nice to her, then? It's nice to know you're actually able to be kind when you want to be," Marzia retorted. "Answer one question for me, Elias. Why did you interfere with Soraya and Bilal?"

"I- I was wrong. I thought I knew everything, but I was being arrogant. I judged Soraya too harshly, and I'm sorry."

"Is that all you came to say?" Marzia asked.

"I'm in love with you, Marzia Mahnaz Rashidi. I'm sorry that I ever made you feel otherwise," he said, his voice steadying.

"You know my middle name?" was all she managed to say.

"Yeah. And I also know that you're still scared of the dark, so you always sleep with a light on. I know that ASPCA commercials always make you cry, and I also know that I don't want to stop you from going to Korea to finish your internship. Just know that I'll be here when you get back."

"Hey, Elias?" Marzia said.

"Yeah?"

"Let's get married," Marzia replied abruptly.

"There's nothing I'd like more."

"Until we meet again," she said.

"Until we meet again."

Sitting in a cramped seat, Marzia realized that things were probably never going to be the same. And for the first time in her life, she didn't want them to be.

CHAPTER TWENTY-NINE

"There are no happy endings. Endings are the saddest part, so just give me a happy middle and a very happy start."

-Shel Silverstein

Now at this point, dear reader, you're probably wondering what happens next. Do they live happily ever after? Do they grow old in a house that has a picket fence, surrounded by their children? The next two chapters are two different endings, but the catch is I'm not going to tell you which one is real. So, as to the question of what comes next, well, I'll leave that one up to you.

The next few weeks after Marzia got back from her internship were truly a whirlwind and included lots of wedding preparations which, frankly, Marzia couldn't have cared less about. In fact, it terrified her being the center of so much attention. She didn't care about the flowers, or party favours, or even the generous gifts they would be receiving. All she cared about was that she was going to get to spend the rest of her life with someone who understood her.

Marzia couldn't quite believe it was real life when everything went to plan (well, as much as any wedding could). Of course, she looked forward to all the big events like the wedding and honeymoon in Turkey. But what she was most looking forward to were the little things, like going to Walmart together at 10 pm or driving for an hour without having a clue where they were going. But it was only when she was sitting on a breezy patio in the coastal city of Marmaris when it truly hit her how much her life really had changed. She sat back in her chair as she watched the massive boats drift by.

"What are you thinking about?" Elias asked, putting his elbow on the table and resting his chin on his hand.

"I'm thinking about how we'll never be able to explore everything under the sea," Marzia replied thoughtfully.

"I've never thought of that. I wonder if they've ever tried," Elias replied. "Like just…drain an ocean and figure out what's going on under there."

"Exactly!" Marzia exclaimed. "Oh, you're making fun of me, aren't you?"

"No, I am totally in support of your dreams of nautical exploration," Elias replied, taking her hand and kissing it.

"Well, as long as you're sincere," Marzia rolled her eyes, a smile forming on her lips.

A comfortable silence remained as they both continued eating their breakfast.

"Hey, can I ask you something?" Marzia said abruptly.

"I imagine you're going to anyway," Elias quipped but broke into a smile. Marzia noted how much the expression suited him.

"Why would you always wear sunscreen even when it was winter, and you weren't going out?"

Elias shifted in his seat, putting a hand behind his neck.

"Do you really want to know?" he asked.

"Yes, I really do. It's honestly been killing me." Marzia laughed.

"You said once that winters depress you," Elias explained.

"Definitely sounds like me," Marzia affirmed.

"I thought it would cheer you up to be reminded of the beach and summer," he replied. "I had all sorts of different scents too."

"You...you...did that for me?" Marzia asked in bewilderment, weaving her fingers through his.

"I thought it was kind of obvious." He shrugged.

"Huh. I just realized something."

"And what is that?"

"That meant that you fell for me long before I even *thought* about you," Marzia said with a smug smile.

"Oh, I don't know about that. Weren't you the one who practically *begged* me to help you with statistics just so that you'd have an excuse to be near me?" He grinned, planting a kiss on her nose.

"I was also failing the course, you know!" Marzia laughed. "But...yes."

"You really were hopeless." Elias chuckled.

"I still passed, though," Marzia reminded him.

"That's one of the things I love about you, you know," Elias commented. "You're stubborn, but in the best way possible."

"And don't you forget it." Marzia smiled, giving him an affectionate kiss.

The two of them later went for a walk along the coast by the beautiful beach that had been their view for the past two weeks. Marzia could smell the salt in her nostrils, and she wanted to bottle this moment and keep it in her pocket. She wanted to keep it for when things got hard, for when things weren't going their way or when they were feeling sad or down. She wanted to remember this moment when they were old and grey, and no longer had the strength or patience to travel. It was truly a remarkable feeling, being in a moment that you know one day will be the fuel for your nostalgia. Dear reader, one piece of advice I would give to you is to recognize these moments. Secondly, savour them, enjoy it, and not in a way where you're too busy trying to capture the moment and you let it pass you by.

"Hey, do you think we're going to be one of those old couples who argue all the time?" Marzia asked, looking at an elderly couple sitting on a bench sharing a sandwich.

"Most definitely," Elias replied. "And do you think you're going to get sick of me?"

"Oh, most assuredly," Marzia replied.

"Then I guess it's a good thing we're stuck with each other."

The two of them walked silently for a few minutes, but the quiet was like the comfort of a warm hug, subtle but all-enveloping and reassuring. It was almost dusk and the last night of their two-week honeymoon. Somehow, the scenery looked even more beautiful at that moment because they knew they would be leaving soon. The waves crashed in tune with the squawking of seagulls, creating a symphony of nautical sounds. A chill descended, which they both felt ripple through their bones. Soon, they would be back home, back to reality, and yet at the same time in a new terrain which they both had little experience in.

"Our flight is tomorrow," Marzia stated, matter-of-factly.

"It is," Elias affirmed.

"So, what happens next? What happens after the credits roll?"

"The rest of our lives," Elias replied.

CHAPTER THIRTY

❧

"Grief is the price we pay for love."

-Queen Elizabeth II

It all started when they got back from their honeymoon, you see. They had two whole weeks of bliss, exploring the cobblestone roads of Istanbul. But then, Elias started complaining about terrible headaches. He had been feeling that way for a while but only mentioned it when it got to be unbearable. At first, they assumed it was nothing to worry about. Elias was young. He could fight it, they told themselves. And for a while, he was. It seemed like things were looking up. He lost all his hair and a good portion of his strength and began looking like a shell of his former self. But they had hope that he could beat it. Marzia and Elias' mother took turns taking him to the hospital for his chemo treatment because he would usually be too tired to drive back by himself.

But things came crashing down when one day when the doctor took the two of them into a private room.

"The chemo has stopped working," he had told them grimly.

Marzia was shocked at the coldness. His voice sounded devoid of any emotion, completely detached. And for a moment, Marzia closed her eyes and pretended like this was all a bad dream. She kept her eyes tightly shut, hoping that she would magically be transported to their honeymoon when everything was alright, when Elias was still fine. Maybe this was all a bad dream, she thought. Maybe she would wake up, heart pounding, but then flooded with relief at the realization that none of it was real. But unfortunately, life doesn't work that way sometimes.

Throughout it all, however, the one thing Marzia gave herself credit for was that she never broke down in front of Elias. She always held it together because she knew that it must have been even harder on him than it was for her. A part of her was angry and jealous. Angry that they didn't have more time together and jealous that he wasn't the one that would inevitably be left behind. Towards the end, they brought Elias home to be around the people who loved him most. The day Marzia finally got the call from Elias' mother that it was time was one that she would replay in her mind years later. It was raining, which seemed appropriate.

"Marzia?" Elias called.

"How are you feeling?" she asked timidly, entering the room.

"Not great. I'm dying." Elias laughed weakly.

Marzia's lip quivered.

"Aww, c'mon, Peaches. From the look on your face, you'd think you were the terminal one," Elias said, wiping away a tear from her face.

"We could have had so much more time together..." Marzia said, her hands weaved tightly through his.

"No use thinking about what-ifs." Elias shook his head. "Here, I have something for you."

Elias struggled to his side and opened the drawer of his bedside table. Inside was a ring with a ruby stone. It was modest, but because it was from him, it meant the world to Marzia. She took the box from his frail hand and slipped the ring onto her finger.

"It's my birthstone," she said, blinking back tears. "I love it."

"Mara yaad, tura faramoosh," he said, letting out a warm smile.

This time, Marzia couldn't hold back the tears. She let out a strained laugh.

"I bought that after the time we all went to the fair," he said reminiscently. "It was the day I first realized I loved you."

"What am I going to do without you?" Marzia croaked.

"You're going to be happy, and you're going to get through this because you're strong," Elias said, holding Marzia in his arms.

"I'm not that strong." Marzia sobbed, burying her face in his chest. She didn't even care that her tears were falling onto his shirt.

"You are," he insisted, lifting her chin and giving her a soft kiss.

"Are you scared?" Marzia asked.

"A little, but not really. I know in my heart what I believe. I have no regrets," he replied pensively. "I just wish I could grow old with you, but it just looks like that's not in the cards, Peaches."

The two of them sat in silence for a few minutes, taking in what they both knew would be their final moments together.

"Hey," he said. "Tell me a story."

Marzia obliged, choking back tears.

"Well, there was this guy, and he thought he was all that. But when this girl comes along, she sees right through him."

Elias' ragged breaths morphed into a painful laugh.

"But she loved him anyway," he added.

"Though she didn't like to admit it, she loved him anyway," Marzia continued. She rested her head on his shoulder.

"Then they live a long and happy life together?"

"After many misunderstandings, they eventually get married. They have three children, and they live to be 98 years old. They die together, in their home, surrounded by the people they love," Marzia said.

Marzia felt Elias go still, and at that moment, she realized he was gone.

Now, I'm not going to sugar coat it. Marzia was hollow for a very long time afterwards. Sometimes it would come in waves. One minute she would be laughing about something he used to say, and the next, she wouldn't be able to breathe through the tears. One thing did give her solace, though, because Elias left a part of him with Marzia before he left. He would look like him, and at times would even sound like him. Especially when he laughed.

But if you asked Marzia if she would do it all again, the answer would be a resounding yes; a thousand times, yes.

She was the sun, and he was the moon, always destined to be apart. Separated by the changing light.

Until they meet again. InshAllah.

ABOUT THE AUTHOR

Lila Saqib is a second-generation Afghan Canadian from Toronto, Ontario. She lives just outside the city with her family and two cats. She loves trivia games and prides herself on her random knowledge of obscure facts. Her love of stories came from series like Harry Potter and The Lord of The Rings. At the time of finishing this book, she is in her final year of undergraduate honours degree in psychology and will be attending a teacher's education program in the fall, where she hopes to teach social studies and history.

www.ingramcontent.com/pod-product-compliance
Lightning Source LLC
Chambersburg PA
CBHW050918030726
47503CB00007BB/2357